Dear Readers,

As I write this, I'm sitting in my new office, surrounded by boxes. Actually, much of our house is in disarray, and probably will remain that way for the next year while we do some major renovations in our new home in Colorado.

A few hours ago, as I looked over the final version of *The Loyal One*, I had to smile. Though we did have our house on the market when I wrote the first draft of this book, my husband and I intended to buy a home in Colorado that was new, filled with bells and whistles, and about the same size as the home we were leaving in Ohio. I'm not sure what happened, but we ended up buying a house that was a little smaller, a whole lot older, and needed a lot of work. I can't believe that I wrote a novel about remodeling months before finding myself doing the very same thing!

Our recent move across the country encouraged me to think a lot about friends and family and the things that are important. I was reminded that so many "things" in our home were just "things." Saying good-bye to longtime friends and neighbors was both heart wrenching and affirming, too. I realized just how much I was going to miss the important people in my life . . . and how much I've been blessed to have them in the first place. I feel sure that God has been with me the entire time. Only He could remind me of all the blessings in my life—even when I was filled with doubt and worry.

I'm glad that the characters in *The Loyal One* realized the same thing. Our Lord doesn't waver, or turn His back on us, or declare us as unworthy. He really is a "loyal" God, and is with us through thick and thin, through good times and bad. I hope that you, too, have found this to be true.

This letter would not be complete without offering my thanks to you for giving this book and this series a try. Thank you, too, for joining me on Facebook chats, for your letters and encouraging notes, and for telling your local librarians, friends, and family about my novels. I'm so grateful for your support—and your loyalty!

Wishing you many blessings,
Shelley Shepard Gray

THE
PATIENT
ONE

Also available from
Shelley Shepard Gray and Gallery Books

THE WALNUT CREEK SERIES

*Friends to the End**
The Patient One
*A Precious Gift**
The Protective One

*ebook only

SHELLEY SHEPARD GRAY

THE

LOYAL

ONE

POCKET BOOKS

New York   London   Toronto   Sydney   New Delhi

Pocket Books
An Imprint of Simon & Schuster, Inc.
1230 Avenue of the Americas
New York, NY 10020

This book is a work of fiction. Any references to historical events, real people, or real places are used fictitiously. Other names, characters, places, and events are products of the author's imagination, and any resemblance to actual events or places or persons, living or dead, is entirely coincidental.

First Pocket Books paperback edition April 2020

POCKET and colophon are registered trademarks of Simon & Schuster, Inc.

For information about special discounts for bulk purchases, please contact Simon & Schuster Special Sales at 1-866-506-1949 or business@simonandschuster.com.

The Simon & Schuster Speakers Bureau can bring authors to your live event. For more information or to book an event contact the Simon & Schuster Speakers Bureau at 1-866-248-3049 or visit our website at www.simonspeakers.com.

Interior design by Erika Genova

Manufactured in the United States of America

10 9 8 7 6 5 4 3 2 1

ISBN 978-1-9821-2352-9
ISBN 978-1-9821-0090-2 (ebook)

To Heather, Hilda, and Cathy,
three of the most loyal and lovely women I know

Teach us to realize the brevity of life, so that we may grow in wisdom.

—Psalm 90:12

Things turn out the best for those who make the best of the way things turn out.

—Amish proverb

THE
LOYAL
ONE

PROLOGUE

*I*t was really too early in the season for a campfire near the Kurtzes' old cabin in the woods, but not a one of them had wanted to be anywhere else. The remainder of the Eight, along with a couple of new additions, had arrived just before sundown, each prepared to spend the night. An outsider would probably think they'd brought way too much.

Harley Lambright reckoned such a thing wasn't possible.

Though he was usually the first to arrive, Harley had gotten a late start. Therefore, he was still trying to shake off the stress of his workday. He remodeled homes and buildings around the area. It was a good job, and he often had more offers than he had time to do them—it wasn't always easy, attempting to make something old look new again.

Sometimes he just wanted to ask his customers to tear everything down and start from scratch. This had been one of those days. The house he was working on had been built in the 1930s and had already been through multiple remodels. Because of that, it was hard to make heads or tails of some of the plumbing and electrical work. His budget-conscious customers were having a difficult time understanding why he was insisting that everything needed to be brought up to code. After yet another contentious conversation, he'd actually considered walking off the worksite.

While the driver he'd hired slowly turned around on the narrow dirt road and headed back to town, Harley gave himself a moment to collect his thoughts and watch the activity around him.

Everyone was so busy, they would put a colony of bees to shame.

Will Kurtz was pulling out old folding chairs from a rickety storage shed just behind the cabin. Marie and John B. were carting over a cooler of soft drinks and a large straw basket filled with snacks. Logan Clark had his arms full with all the fixings for s'mores. Katie Steury was sitting on a rock, untwisting wire hangers.

The others? Well, the others did as they always did. They pitched in where they could and stacked wood. It was going to be a great night. A wonderful, *gut* one.

But then again, when had they not had a good time when they were all together?

With a bright smile on her face, Marie Hartman walked to his side. "So, what do you think, Harley? Are we ready?"

"I'd say so." Finally lifting the cooler he'd been carrying, he said, "I brought a mess of sandwiches."

She laughed. "While the rest of us brought soda, chips, and everything for s'mores, you are making sure we eat something healthy." Looping a hand through his arm, she tugged him forward. "What would we do without you?"

"I don't ever want to know." He smiled so she wouldn't realize how serious he was. This wasn't the night for that.

When they reached the fire pit, he spent the next ten minutes saying hello and finishing the final preparations.

And then, with a feeling of accomplishment, Harley pulled out a match, scraped it against one of the rocks surrounding the fire pit, and lit the kindling. Seconds later, a fire roared to life.

Logan clapped. "Look at that! We did it. And in spite of our jobs and family obligations, we all got here."

Elizabeth Anne raised her can of Sprite. "Amen to that."

"My boss asked me to stay late tonight, but I told him I had plans I couldn't miss," John B. said. "I've been looking forward to tonight for weeks."

"Me, too," Harley said. Looking around at all of his best friends, some Amish, some Mennonite, some English—most of whom he'd known for almost his entire life—he felt his body relax at last.

By the time the sun had completely slid down the sky and the first of the stars had begun to appear, the fire was crackling merrily and flavoring the air with the scents of fresh pine, old memories, and anticipation.

Looking at the flames, feeling the comfort and sense of contentment among all of them, Harley knew this was the perfect place to have a celebration. The evening was cool and crisp, the fire bright, the blankets surrounding them all were cozy . . . and the company even better.

But that was always how it had been. From the first summer the Eight had met, they'd felt an instant connection. Even though they all led very different lives, some firmly entrenched in the modern world, others steadfastly following the traditions and rules that so many generations had before, they'd stayed connected.

Over the years, they'd grown up together. They'd suffered hardships by one another's sides, and had commemorated everything from new kittens to first kisses to graduations in one another's company.

All that was why they'd come together to celebrate their group's first engagement. Logan had recently proposed to Tricia Warner, Andy's little sister, and few things had ever seemed like such a blessing.

But even though they all loved Logan and Tricia, it didn't mean that they couldn't resist doing a little bit of teasing and good-natured ribbing.

Or maybe even a lot of it.

"Come on, Logan!" Will Kurtz called out. "Kiss your bride-to-be one more time."

"All right. If I have to," Logan joked before pulling Tricia into his arms. Just as she placed her hands on his arms with a gasp, Logan gently kissed her cheek.

Groans abounded, along with someone tossing a paper cup at Logan.

"What kind of kiss is that?" John B. teased. "I kissed my first girl in the back of our barn with more enthusiasm than that."

"You probably kissed your aunt with more enthusiasm than that," Will quipped.

"Only on New Year's," John countered, quick as lightning.

Laughter filled the air as Tricia slapped a hand over her face in embarrassment. As for Logan? Well, he simply rested an arm around her shoulders and grinned. "It's the only kind of kiss you're gonna see, buddy. Now stop before you go and embarrass Trish."

"Too late!" Tricia called out, her face still covered.

As laughter erupted again, Kendra Troyer smiled at them all. "Isn't tonight perfectly perfect?"

Looking as contented as a cat at a dairy farm, E.A. nodded. "It's better than that."

Harley reckoned it was. Well, almost. Sometimes seeing Tricia Warner reminded him of the hole that

Andy's death had created in their lives. Even though it had been almost a year since Andy had taken his life, Harley still missed him tremendously. Andy had been brash, loud, and a little spoiled. He'd also been loyal, kind, and sensitive.

Andy had been everything Harley had never been. And, in his worst, most insecure moments, everything that Harley wished he could have been.

With force, he pushed the first tinges of depression he'd been battling away. He wasn't going to go there tonight. Not when there were so many other things to concentrate on.

As everyone around him started talking quietly, Harley allowed himself to glance at each one. Next to him were Logan and Tricia. On Tricia's other side was Will Kurtz. Will was Amish and worked at the trailer factory with John B., who was on Will's other side. Will's mother used to watch them all from time to time when they were young.

Sitting next to John B. was his sweetheart, Marie. John had grown up Amish but had recently jumped the fence for a variety of reasons, the main one being that he and Marie had fallen in love, and she was as English as a girl could be. Next in the circle sat Elizabeth Anne, all red hair, properness, and smiles. She was Mennonite and was best friends with Katie Steury, who was Amish like him.

Against his will, Harley let his gaze settle on Katie, thinking of how she looked so like the heroine in one of the more recent *Star Wars* movies. Back during his *rumspringa*, they'd all gone to the movies and thought Katie looked so much like a blond version of the actress Natalie Portman that they'd called her that for days.

Last but not least was Kendra Troyer, who was sitting on his left. Kendra was shy and a little awkward, and all of them were protective of her. He'd been glad that she'd become part of their extended group when they were teenagers.

"Harley?" Will called out. "You okay?"

"Hmm? Oh, *jah*. Just sitting here thinking."

"About what?" E.A. asked. "You look so serious."

Not wanting to admit that he'd been silently struggling with Andy's loss, Harley thought quickly. "Nothing much. I was only thinking about the night Marie and Andy graduated high school and we all went out together."

"Boy, I haven't thought about that night in ages," Marie said with a grin. "Hey, did any of your parents ever find out everything that we did?"

Will shuddered. "No way. *Mei daed* would have tanned my backside."

"You were lucky. My brothers found out," John B. said. "I had to do both James's and Anton's chores for a month in order for them to keep the secret."

Kendra waved a hand. "What actually did happen that night? I remember hearing that something had occurred, but I never heard the details."

"Believe me, you don't want to know," Marie said.

"I do," Tricia called out. "Come on, you Eight, don't be a tease. Andy never whispered a word to me about his graduation night."

"I ain't sure tonight's the best time to share it," Harley hedged. "I mean, it's a long story."

"Go ahead and tell it, Harley," Katie prodded. "It's Friday night, and none of us have anywhere else to be."

"All right. But don't say I didn't warn ya. It for sure doesn't show any of us in the best light."

"I'll try not to be too shocked," Kendra murmured, sarcasm thick in her voice.

Tricia reached for Logan's hand. "I am getting a little worried about what I'm about to find out."

"Don't get too worried," John B. said. "We didn't do anything that bad. I mean, we could have been a whole lot worse." Chuckling, he added, "As much as the story embarrasses me, I wouldn't change a bit of it."

"It ain't like we could ever change the past anyway," Will said.

Harley guffawed. "I do love it when you try to act all pious and perfect, William."

Looking sheepish, Will picked up his can of soda and sipped. "You're right. We were all once young and stupid. And for the record, I wouldn't have it any other way. Start talking, Harley. And don't leave anything out."

Feeling some of the pressure that had been weighing on him lighten at last, Harley stood up.

And, after mentally raising a toast to Andy, he began.

ONE

"I should start by saying that I always thought that everything would have gone a whole lot better if John had just let Andy or Marie drive us in one of their cars. Or, say, John and Logan hadn't suggested that we all go swimming in the lake on Mr. Schlabach's farm."

APRIL

*K*atie hadn't believed it was possible to both love and hate something at the same time. But that was how she felt about her house. Standing outside the front of it, attempting to look at the front door as a newcomer would, she supposed it didn't look much different from any of the other houses dotting Plum Lane.

A tourist leisurely driving down the narrow, winding roads of Walnut Creek might have even called the fifty-year-old house charming, with its shiny black door, wraparound porch, and carefully kept-up whitewashed siding. Many had told her that it looked like the perfect Amish farmhouse.

Unfortunately, every time Katie looked at the siding, all she saw was the long hours she'd spent scraping and sanding the old siding in the hot sun.

Boy, she'd hated scraping off old paint. For some reason, her older sister and brother had always gotten to be the painters.

Her sister, June, had said that Katie always had to sand and scrape because their parents didn't think she was a careful painter. Though the criticism had stung, Katie couldn't really disagree. She hated working on the outside of the house. It was hot, sticky, and bugs got in her face.

She'd always secretly suspected that the real reason she never got to paint was because she was younger than her siblings and therefore always got the jobs neither June nor Caleb had wanted to do.

As she slowly walked along the porch, glancing in one of the many windows facing the road, Katie knew there was a third reason.

It was because her parents had carefully worked on the outside of the old house but never on the inside. It perpetuated the illusion that everything was lovely and well cared for on the other side of the walls, too.

But that had never really been the case.

Hating the memories that were forming in her mind, matching the dark and cluttered interior she could spy from the windows, Katie turned away.

Just in time to see Harley Lambright park his bike against the black iron hitching post her great-grandparents had placed on the front walkway the week they'd moved into their new home.

Obviously seeing her watching him, he raised a hand. "Hiya, Katie. *Gut matin.*"

"Hello, Harley," she called out. "Good morning to you." She kept the smile on her face even though she was starting to wonder if they were ever going to become completely at ease around each other again. "Thanks for coming over."

"Thanks for talking to me about the job." After grabbing a pencil and notepad out of the backpack he'd just pulled off his shoulders, he paused. "So, how do you want to do this?"

Though she knew he was referring to the remodeling job, Katie couldn't help but think of the other thing that they needed to work on—their awkward, stilted relationship.

While it might not be evident to the rest of the Eight, whenever she was around Harley for any length of time, the terrible tension between them buzzed loud and clear. Their relationship did encompass many *wonderful-gut* memories of the Eight. But it also included their argument about his old sweetheart Melody. Katie had never liked the girl, and once had even made the mistake of sharing her opinion with E.A.

Which had been within the hearing of Harley.

Who had not been pleased. Not at all.

If they were going to work together on this house then they were going to have to clear the air. No, if she was going to be able to trust him with the secrets behind the walls, they were going to need to get in a better place. Ignoring their past problems wasn't an option.

"Harley, I think we should sit down on the front porch and talk about everything before we go inside."

His hands, which had been flipping pages in his notebook, froze. "Say again?"

She was kind of irritated that he was going to play opossum. Hardening her voice, she said, "I've thought a lot about it and I think the only way we are going to be able to work well together is for us to talk about things once and for all."

His expression darkened. "I have no idea what you are talking about."

She felt like rolling her eyes. "Of course you do. I'm talking about what happened three years ago."

"With Melody."

"*Jah.*" Who else would she have been talking about? Three years ago, he and Melody had been together constantly. Harley had even looked smitten, which she'd always thought was entertaining, given the fact that Harley was never one to show much emotion about anything.

But then, just when they'd all been expecting

Harley and Melody to announce a wedding date, he'd instead shared that they'd broken up. Harley had never given a reason, but she'd always thought it had something to do with her big mouth.

He sighed. "Are you playing a game with me? I thought you needed your house remodeled. I thought that was why you asked me over here. I know that was the reason I came."

In other words, he wouldn't have come for any other reason. "Harley, of course I really need your help. This *haus* is . . ." It was a mess. It was an albatross around her neck. It was her only inheritance and everything she'd yearned to walk away from. Finding her voice again, she said, "I mean, it needs to be remodeled in order for me to make it into a bed-and-breakfast."

His gaze softened. "You are finally going to make that dream real?"

He'd remembered. He'd remembered the time the eight of them had been lying on their backs on the grass in the Warners' yard and they'd each shared their dreams for the future. Marie had wanted to be a movie star, Will had something about being bigger than his brothers, and Harley had admitted he'd wanted to raise goats. She'd gathered her courage and whispered that one day she wanted to own a bed-and-breakfast. "I really am. *Mei mamm* gave the house to me."

"Truly? That's wonderful."

She nodded. "Mamm said she'd only been biding

her time until my brother, Caleb, built his *haus* down in Kentucky. Caleb didn't want to live here."

"What about June?"

"You know she jumped the fence as soon as she could." Even now, almost eleven years later, Katie felt her sister's absence. "We see her at Christmas." Sometimes. If June didn't have anything else going on and felt she could handle coming back.

"So you got the house."

"*Jah.* I got the house." The gift had truly been a double-edged sword. She'd gotten to keep her dreams, but in order to have that dream, she was going to have to deal with everything that her mother and siblings were running away from.

Harley's posture relaxed. "I'm happy for ya."

"*Danke.*" She tried to smile, hoping to cover up her unease. "So, may we talk for a moment? I really do think we need to finally discuss what happened with you and me and Melody."

The warmth that had momentarily filled his dark green eyes vanished as his expression became hard again. "I don't agree. As far as I'm concerned, what happened between me and Melody ain't none of your concern. Ever."

Maybe Katie should have backed off or even apologized for bringing up his old sweetheart in the first place. It was obvious Melody was still a sore subject. But . . . so much had happened between them all lately. Logan and Tricia had recently gotten engaged. John B. and Marie had finally admitted their love for each other and were now a real couple.

And just as important, they'd all been learning to live with the loss of Andy Warner.

That, at the very least, had shown her that holding on to old hurts and imagined slights did no one any good. Surely he felt the same way? "Harley, I don't want to argue, but—"

"I don't want to argue, either. But just because I don't want to argue, it doesn't mean I want to rehash all of our problems." Sounding like his father, he said, "I do not."

All of their problems? They had more than one? "All right, Harley. I hear you loud and clear."

"Now, do you want me to work on this house or not?"

Did she want to finally make this place into something she was proud of? Have it help her become someone she could be proud of?

Katie turned and looked at it. So almost good on the outside. So completely wrecked on the inside. Much of how she felt about herself these days.

"*Jah*, Harley, I want your help. I want to hire you to remodel this house."

"*Gut.* Then let's go inside. I want to see what it looks like."

"All right." After taking three steps, she paused

with her hand on the door. "Um, I feel that I should warn you that it's not pretty inside."

Instead of replying in a patient way that she knew he would've done with Marie, Harley clenched his jaw. "It doesn't need to be pretty, Katie. All I care about is that it's a job. You do have money to pay me, don't you?"

"Yes. I do have that."

"Then stop stalling."

"Fine." Opening the front door, she led him inside.

Harley might only need time and money to get this job done. She, on the other hand, was going to need every bit of patience and forbearance she possessed. It was going to be a long couple of weeks.

TWO

"I didn't think Mr. Schlabach allowed kids on his property," Tricia said. "Did he used to?"

"*Nee*. He hated anyone coming on his land uninvited, which was why walking all the way over to the farm was our first really bad idea."

$\mathcal{T}$he muscles that were forming tight knots at the top of his shoulders were fitting symbols of how Harley felt around Katie: she was a pain in his neck.

What was sad was that he knew better, too. She wasn't a painful person. Most people he knew liked her a lot. And how could they not? Katie, with her light blond hair, blue eyes, and tiny frame reminded him often of a sprite, an opinionated, bright, tiny fairy in a children's storybook.

He'd always been drawn to her brightness but then had gotten stung by her sharp tongue. He'd learned to keep his distance. All that was why agreeing to consider this remodeling job had been a bad idea.

No matter how he wished it was different, he was uncomfortable around Katie. Had been for years— even before her mouth had gotten him into trouble with Melody. She was forthright and honest and even blunt at times. She didn't hold back and didn't be-lieve in secrets. And because of that, there was simply something about her that made him doubt just about everything he said or did.

Harley didn't appreciate that.

So, out of a need for self-preservation, he'd begun to try avoiding her. It wasn't a blatant thing, or even that he didn't think she was a good person. It was more like their personalities didn't mesh well.

When they were with the rest of their friends, they got along fine. They kept their conversations light and didn't spend too much time one-on-one.

But when it was just the two of them? Well, it was like it had been today. They bickered and fussed at each other. Every conversation was exhausting.

Then, too, he couldn't pretend that she hadn't embarrassed him in front of Melody. While Katie didn't know that he and Melody had already been having problems, her announcement that none of the Eight liked the girl had ended things lightning fast.

All of that should have been enough of a reason for him to have refused the job.

Now, as he followed her inside her home, Harley

realized that there were about a hundred other reasons he should have said no.

This house was a crowded, dark, mismatched
mess.

The musty smell caught him off guard, as well. So
had the darkness. There was so much junk and debris
in the hallway that it blocked several of the windows.
"What happened in here?"

"My mother."

Taken aback, he glanced at her, but she wasn't
looking at him. Instead, she was studiously watching
a beetle march up the side of a cardboard box. He
waited for her to kill it, but she didn't move.

Unable to take it anymore, he grabbed what
looked to be an old magazine clipping, slipped it under the creature, and tossed both the paper and the
bug out the door. Turning back to her again, he waved
a hand around the room. "How?"

Walking around a pair of chairs and an old table, all
three piled high with papers and magazines, she glared
at him. "You're gonna have to be more specific, Harley.
Are you wondering how it got so bad, how is it that I
live here, or how come I have beetles in my home?"

"All of it." Realizing he was sounding disgusted
(which he was) and judgmental (which he couldn't
help but be), Harley attempted to temper his reaction. "I don't mean to be cruel, Katie, but the inside
of your house is a surprise."

Her blue eyes sparkled like she'd found his comment amusing. "I bet. Um, let's go into the kitchen, have some tea, and sit down." Putting a hand on one hip, she murmured, "And before you ask, *jah*, the kitchen is safe and *nee*, it ain't infested."

"Lead the way and I'll follow."

Jaw tight, she turned and walked into the living room.

He followed close behind. There was considerably more space in this room, but it still was claustrophobic. Stacks and stacks of clothes, books, quilts, and old blankets littered the floor and every available space. In the midst of it was a well-worn crooked path through it all. It reminded him of some mice he'd seen once at a science fair. The mice had had to make their way through the maze as quickly as possible. When he'd watched them perform, he hadn't been all that impressed with either of the rodents. Now, he was starting to think he'd done those little guys a terrible disservice.

The living room opened up into a small kitchen. It was surprisingly clean and orderly. From the looks of the shiny countertops and polished table, it was also where Katie spent much of her time. "This is nice."

Her laugh sounded like it was filled with hurt. "It's not nice in here, but it's a far cry better." Filling up a kettle with water, she gestured to the two chairs next to the table. "Go sit down, Harley. I'll be right there."

He sat and watched her work. He'd now remodeled six homes. In each of his previous jobs, he could hardly contain his excitement for the project and usually had so many ideas filling his head, he would constantly write them down.

Not this time, however.

All he could think was that Katie Steury, who was always so blunt and honest, had been carrying around her fair share of secrets.

When she handed him a cup of tea, she sat down across from him. "I guess you're shocked by how bad it all looks."

He considered being kinder but decided glossing over his thoughts wouldn't do either of them any favors. "I am shocked. I had no idea your house was in this condition."

"It wasn't anything I wanted to brag about."

Walking on eggshells, he asked, "Has it been this way for a long time?"

She shrugged. "My mother always fought the idea of getting rid of anything. She has the hardest time even throwing out old newspapers. But when my father was alive, he helped her with that." She smiled grimly. "On her worst days, my father would encourage her to take a nap, and while she did, Caleb, June, and I would have to run around and discard things. When she woke up, she'd immediately search the house, looking for changes. It used to be a game for me, to get rid of things in such a way that she wouldn't notice."

"It sounds difficult." Which was a giant understatement.

"It was. When I was little, all I would understand was that our father was in a panic and that I was supposed to take things and hide them away and pretend I didn't." She shrugged. "As you can imagine, it was all so confusing. Caleb would always worry that we'd either pick up too much or too little or put things in the wrong container. Then, when my *mamm* would come downstairs, she'd act like she was fine, but there was always a sense of panic on her face. Even when I was just five or six, I knew that she didn't like our father getting rid of anything." She grimaced. "If she had to deal with everything when he wasn't around, she would get really angry at us." After a pause, she murmured, "Especially June."

"I'm sorry, Katie."

Looking embarrassed, she stopped to take a sip of tea. "I grew up never knowing what to do with anything. One parent would tell me that the pile of books on the floor needed to be dusted and shelved or donated and then the other parent would yell if I moved them an inch."

"I can't imagine all of that. Katie, I knew your parents. They were nice people."

"They were, and my mother still is. She's always

been kind and loving. This wasn't a house of horrors or anything. My mother just had a bad problem. An illness, really. When my father passed away, her condition kind of steamrolled into something much worse. All of us kids realized that our *mamm* had been leaning on our father to keep her functioning. After he died, we didn't know who to lean on."

"I'm guessing June, since she was the oldest."

"We tried to. But then June left almost two years after Daed died," Katie said with a sigh. "June was eighteen then. Caleb was sixteen, and I had just turned thirteen."

"I'm sorry she left you."

Looking vulnerable, Katie said, "Me, too." After a second, she seemed to pull herself together. "June's leaving was difficult, but I knew even back then that Mamm's problem wasn't the only reason she took off. She never really got along with either of our parents—it was almost like she couldn't help but question everything they did. Because of that, they questioned everything she did right back. One day June'd had enough."

"That had to be hard." He remembered when her sister had left, but had he ever actually worried about how Katie had been dealing with the loss? He didn't think so.

What did that say about him? Had he really been that selfish?

Oblivious to his self-recriminations, Katie continued. "It was hard to see her go, but I've tried to come to terms with it. She just wanted something different from living in a run-down *haus* in the country, you know?"

Not knowing what to say, Harley nodded. "And Caleb?"

"He got married to Vanessa and bought some good farmland in central Kentucky. Now they have two babies and need help. For some reason, being around the *bopplis* helps our mother. She loves fussing over them. They built a little two-room house on their property for her and she just moved out there. So far, it's working."

"Which means you got to have your dream."

Katie smiled, suddenly brightening up the conversation. "I did. At first, I felt guilty about getting the house, but Caleb convinced me that turning this house into something beautiful would be good for all of us. I sold off some of our land to pay for the remodeling, and now I'm ready to start up the business."

"I *canna* believe they left this all for you to deal with." That was an understatement. Though his father had never been especially open or affectionate, Harley had never gotten the feeling that the man wouldn't have dropped everything if he'd been in trouble. And his *mamm*? Well, she'd been strict but had often gone out of her way to do something sweet for him, like surprise him with peach ice cream on his birthday.

"Don't fret, Harley," Katie said, bringing his mind back to the present. "*Jah*, this *haus* is in poor shape, but I told Caleb I could handle it."

"And so he let you." Harley had always thought her brother was a bit spoiled and lazy. It seemed he'd been right.

"*Nee*, don't be like that." Leaning back in her chair, she gestured around the room. "All in all, the mess is a small price to pay for having the means to dream. Ain't so?"

Having the means to dream. The words struck a chord with him, reminding him of the sacrifices he had made when he'd first begun his remodeling and construction business. They also signified that maybe he and Katie weren't so different after all.

Or, at the very least, they had something in common. "*Jah*," he said as he stood up. "Well, let's see the rest of this house. It's looking like you and I are going to have a lot to do."

Her eyes lit up. "You're going to do it? You're going to accept the job?"

He leaned down a few inches so he could look directly into her eyes. "Of course I will. I would never refuse to help out one of the Eight. You know that."

For a second, she paused, maybe wishing that he

had told her something else? But then she stood up as well. "Let's get started with the tour then. But watch your step, okay? The halls and stairs are narrow and crowded."

"I'll make sure to follow wherever you go, Katie."

She smiled before turning and leading him out of the kitchen. As he followed her slim frame clad in a bright purple dress, Harley paid little attention to where he was going and more on her. Katie Steury. So tiny and slim, but with the temperament of a stubborn, braying goat. Bleating loudly to be heard, getting into trouble more often than not . . . and as loyal and steadfast as anyone he'd ever met.

Over the last couple of years he'd seemed to have forgotten that. Thinking about so much in his life that he took for granted, it occurred to him that he'd forgotten a lot of things of late.

"Careful of the fourth step," Katie called out as they climbed the stairs to the second floor. "It squeaks something awful."

The stairs had worn carpet that looked like it should have been replaced back in 1982. Curious about the squeak, he stepped on the stair and heard an answering groan. And, if he wasn't mistaken, a faint crack.

"Katie, this step doesn't just squeak. It's about to break."

But instead of acting alarmed, she just laughed.

"Wait until you see June's old room. Her floorboards are even worse!"

Once again, he realized he was charmed and intrigued. Both by the house in need of care and by Katie, who was so alone but still knew how to laugh.

Drawn to the sound, he followed her down the hall and wondered what she was going to show him next.

THREE

"Um, actually, I think the first really bad idea was telling my parents I didn't want a graduation party because I was going out with all of you," Marie said. "If I had told them yes, I would have gotten a lot of great gifts and wouldn't have told so many lies."

Once, when Katie was eleven or twelve, June had gotten so mad at her that she'd said Katie was missing the important part of her brain that prevented a person from blurting every little thing that appeared in one's mind.

That one had stung.

And, because she was who she was, Katie had replied by telling her beautiful sister that she had a pimple on her forehead and that all the boys had been talking about it during church. June had blushed furiously, covered her face with her hands, and run to her room.

Katie had watched her go, pleased to have gotten the last word for once. However, to her surprise, no sense of triumph had flooded through her. Instead, she'd felt guilty.

Though she hadn't been lying—June had had a blemish and one of the boys had indeed remarked on it—it hadn't been all that noticeable. Tears had filled her eyes when she'd realized she'd been mighty cruel for little to no reason. June had been right, she really did have a tendency to blurt out whatever was on her mind. Katie swore to herself right then and there that she would one day learn to mind her tongue.

Unfortunately, that resolve hadn't lasted long. Maybe twenty-four hours. But the realization that she had a problem with saying too much too quickly had stayed with her. Pounded her psyche and poured salt on her feelings of guilt for the rest of her life.

She'd tried to do better. Attempted to listen more and talk less. Unfortunately, it seemed whenever she was around Harley, such a thing wasn't possible. There was something about him that set her on edge and made her every vulnerability raise its head and take notice.

Around Harley, she could count on the fact that he was going to be manly and handsome, quiet and capable . . . and that she would talk too much, reveal too much, and never be at her best by his side. But maybe today she would be different.

"Is this Caleb's old room?" Harley asked, interrupting her thoughts.

Katie walked into the small bedroom and ran a hand along the basket weave quilt one of their aunts had made when Caleb graduated eighth grade. "*Jah.*"

"It looks all right."

"*Jah.* This room isn't in too bad of shape." She turned and led the way to June's room. Bracing herself, she opened the door as much as she could. "This used to be my sister's."

Harley took two steps in and then with a quick intake of breath, retreated.

Quickly, she closed the door again, wishing she could lock it off forever.

It took a moment for Harley to collect himself. "Ah, Katie, it smells like . . . " His voice drifted off. Even now, Harley measured each word carefully.

"I know." For once her ability to say all kinds of harsh things was helpful. "It smells like an animal died in there."

"You don't sound surprised."

"Well, unlike you, I'm used to it. And, like I've told you before, there wasn't anything I could do. Soon after June left, my mother started storing snacks and wrappers in here. I'm sure they attracted a variety of mice and bugs. After three years, that happened." She pointed to the closed door like it wasn't obvious enough.

"Has June seen her old room?"

"*Nee.*" Because she'd hardly seen June since her older sister jumped the fence and reinvented herself. Lifting her chin, she said, "Shall we continue?"

He gestured with a hand for her to go forward. There were two more rooms left on this floor, hers and her mother's. She wasn't especially eager for him to see either.

Opening up her mother's door, she said, "As you can see, this is my mother's room." Stacks of boxes, clothes, newspapers, and old fabric littered every available surface, including the majority of the bed.

"Is that a bathroom?" he asked, pointing to a door in the back-left corner.

"*Jah.*"

"Is it in working order?"

"I'm sorry to tell ya that I haven't had the nerve to check for some time."

He slowly turned his head to stare at her. "Truly? But she's been gone a couple of months now, right?"

"Three months." She knew he was shocked, and if she hadn't lived in this situation, she proba-bly would've been shocked, too. But lately she'd been all about self-preservation, and inspecting and cleaning her mother's bathroom had seemed too big a task and far too painful to contemplate. If she entered, she would be forced to acknowledge that her mother's problems had reached new heights—and she'd never gotten her help. "You are welcome to look, if you'd like."

"I'd better." Looking as if he were entering a crowded classroom or a noisy chicken coop, Harley took a deep breath and stepped forward.

Katie didn't follow. There wasn't much room, and she wasn't eager to see the mess her mother had left behind or the expression on Harley's face when he realized that she'd let it simply stay that way.

Instead, she leaned against the doorframe and watched him pick his way around stacks of newspapers, piles of bits and pieces of broken toys and plates and plastic containers. All the many things Mamm had collected and sorted, rescued from the trash, or found on the streets. Useless items that she'd bought or, in some cases, filched from the crowded aisles of the dollar store.

At last he got to the bathroom door. He turned to her, then stopped. "You don't want to come in as well?"

"*Nee.*"

After treating her to an annoyed look, Harley entered the bathroom, then exited almost as quickly as he had June's room.

"Well?" she asked as she watched him carefully make his way back to the hallway. "Is it usable?"

"I don't know. Your mother used both the shower and bathtub as storage facilities. And then there were . . . there were a lot of papers and such piled high."

There was no reason to comment on that. Instead, she walked to the last door that was closed. "This is my room."

He opened the door and stepped inside. She followed, but was no less eager to see his expression. Because her room was almost bare. She reckoned it looked something like a prison cell, not that she'd ever seen one, but she'd read about them once.

She had a twin bed with two blankets, a wall of pegs with three dresses hanging from them, and a small chest of drawers holding her tights, undergarments, and nightgowns. There was a plain metal table with a flashlight and a candle on it. And her glasses. That was all. It was plain and serviceable. It also was the only room in the house where she didn't feel that she had to fight for oxygen.

He turned back to her. "You sleep here?"

"Obviously."

"Of course." Walking back out, he pointed to the last room. "Is that the bathroom?"

"*Jah.*" She walked to the pink-tiled bath. It was sparkling clean with a big tub that was also the shower, one small sink, a toilet, and a little table that held towels and soap.

"Pink."

"We might want to change that."

He smiled. "Maybe so, or maybe not. It's pretty."

Momentarily relieved by the break in the tension, she said, "You've got one more floor to see."

Looking at the stairs like they were going to lead him up to an uncertain future, he murmured, "What does the attic look like?"

"It's not as bad as the rest of the house. There are two bedrooms up there and a small water closet."

"I better go look. I'll be right back."

With some embarrassment, she realized that he was now trying to spare her. Didn't want to make her see more of this run-down place through his eyes.

What was worse was that she was letting him.

When he appeared again, she started walking down the stairs to the main floor. Harley walked behind her, each step slow and sure.

Katie walked him back to the kitchen. "I made a pound cake last night. Would you like a slice?"

"*Danke*, but *nee*. I'm *gut*."

"All right. Harley, if you've changed your mind, all you have to do is tell me. I would understand." Of course, she'd be devastated and embarrassed, but she would understand.

"I haven't. But, well, Katie, we are going to have

to clear this place out before I can do anything. You're going to need at least one more bathroom on the second floor and the one upstairs expanded. But I *canna* bring in plumbers until . . ."

She didn't blame him for hesitating. "Until a plumber can work without being afraid he's going to either run into a wall of boxes or get bitten by a stray varmint."

Looking even more sympathetic, he sighed. "*Jah.* But don't worry, Katie. We'll find a way to get through this."

We? Did that mean he was still going to take the job? "I know I should've already gotten to work clearing the rooms. I don't know why I haven't."

"I do. Some of these spaces are going to take days to sort."

"I know. But most of it just needs to be thrown out. I can do that." She started walking to the front door. "How about this? I'll call you when I have it cleaned out."

"Katie, *nee.*"

Nee? Ah. Harley had changed his mind after all.

Feeling like she'd torn herself open and he'd seen the ugly, Katie walked faster. Harley was never going to forget what he'd seen. It was going to be imprinted on his brain.

Always there. Always coloring the way he thought about her.

Loathing ate at her. Why in the world hadn't she contacted a stranger to help her with this remodel? She wouldn't have cared what he would have thought, and he probably wouldn't have cared, either, as long as she'd paid him enough.

"Katie, wait for me, wouldja?"

She ignored him. Didn't stop until she threw open the front door and was standing on the front porch. There was space here. Cool, fresh air. She breathed it in deep.

"Hey. What's going on?" His voice was impatient now.

She turned to him. Winced when she saw how annoyed he looked. After taking a deep breath of air, she forced herself to say, "Harley, I'm sorry I asked you over. I should've known that this wasn't something you wanted to do."

His brows snapped together. "I have no idea what you're talking about. I told you I would take the job."

She shook her head. "But you changed your mind, *jah?*"

He rubbed the back of his neck. "I did not."

"*Nee,* you said *nee* when I said I'd contact you when the house was empty."

"Of course I said no. I wasn't going to let you do that alone." Studying her closer, a new understanding crossed his features. "Hey. Wait a minute. You didn't think I was going to back out just now, did ya?"

"I guess I did." Though it would've hurt, she wouldn't have blamed him, either.

He looked affronted. "What kind of person do you think I am?"

A loyal one. A good man. Someone stronger. Embarrassed now, she muttered, "You know what I think of you, Harley."

"Well, I thought I did. Now? I ain't so sure." He looked down at his polished boots before meeting her gaze again. "Honestly, Katie, sometimes, I just don't know what to think. I mean, I've known you since we both lost our front teeth the same summer." His voice was still liberally laced with impatience. "Now, what I was trying to say was that we need to get the rest of the Eight involved. Many hands and all that. I'll put the word out and then we'll get started on—"

"*Nee.*" The reply was so automatic, she was hardly aware the response had left her mouth.

"Why not?"

"I don't want them to see."

His voice gentled. "They're our best friends in the world. Are you really worried about what they will think?"

"Of course. Please, Harley. I don't want everyone else to see the *haus* like this." She didn't want her best friends in the world to see how she'd been living.

"You really mean that, don't you?"

"Please. Let's try to do this first without their help. You know, just the two of us."

He stared at her. Closed his striking green eyes.

"I'm sorry, but we're going to need help. You're so small. We need to move furniture. All those books . . ." After a pause, he said, "What about my brother Kyle?"

"Your younger brother?"

"He's eighteen. Strong as an ox." When she still hesitated, he added, "Katie, we have to get more help. You and I can't do this alone. You're going to have to accept that. Now, do you want to run a bed-and-breakfast or not?"

He had a point. She was going to have to swallow her pride. "All right. Fine. Ask him if he'd help me. But . . . ask if he could keep my mother's sickness a secret."

Harley's expression tightened again. "Get some rest, Katie. Kyle and I will be here tomorrow morning. Expect us at seven."

"*Danke*. Thank you so much, Harley. I really appreciate you taking on this job."

"You don't need to say that. Of course—"

Realizing that she'd forgotten the most important thing, she grabbed his arm. "Oh, hold on and I'll get you some money."

The muscles under her fingers contracted. "You don't need to pay me yet."

She dropped her hand. "Of course I do. I mean, it's a down payment, *jah*?" Didn't he have to go buy wood and such?

"Katie Steury, I swear you would try the patience

of a saint. Keep your money and I'll see you in the morning."

Feeling like she'd just lost a battle she hadn't even known she was fighting, Katie stood like a fool and watched him walk away, never once looking back at her.

When he was out of sight, she sat down on the front porch and tried to concentrate on her dreams instead of on all the feelings churning inside of her.

She almost succeeded.

FOUR

> Harley rolled his eyes. "Anyway, there we were, crossing through Mr. Schlabach's farm, just as bold as you please, when his herd of goats found us."

*H*arley knew he could have handled things better. No, he could have handled it all—the house, the job, the clutter, his reaction, and Katie—much better. Especially Katie.

Jah, he could have used a bit more patience and a whole lot more finesse.

Instead, he'd acted like a dolt and had inadvertently made one of his best friends feel even more uneasy about her own home.

He was ashamed of himself.

Walking home, he attempted to ignore the wind that had picked up and seemed set on seeping through his clothes and chilling his skin. He stuffed his hands in his pockets and picked up the pace.

In spite of himself, he smoothed his expression,

adopting his father's blank stare. The last thing he would ever want was for his father to see him acting chilled from a little bit of wind. Daed would see that as a sign of weakness and gruffly talk to him about being tougher.

As the oldest of five children, three of whom were boys, Harley had had more than his fair share of lectures and warnings about being responsible and tough. He'd been brought up with high expectations and little positive reinforcement. Neither of his parents had ever believed in giving praise for things one was expected to do.

When his family's farm came into view, he breathed a sigh of relief. His father wasn't in the fields, which meant he wouldn't be expected to go out to the fields, either.

Fifteen minutes later, he was washing his hands in the stationary tub in the mudroom and removing his boots.

"Harley, is that you?" his youngest sister, Betty, called out from the kitchen.

"*Jah*," he said as he entered the kitchen and sniffed appreciatively. "You're making soup?"

Betty, all green eyes, dark brown hair, and confidence smiled at him fondly. "Italian meatball. Are you ready for a bowl? I made some breadsticks, too."

"I am ready. *Danke*."

As he moved to grab a bowl from one of the shelves that lined the far wall, she shooed him away. "Sit down. I've got this."

Knowing she had as many rules drilled into her as he had, he didn't argue. "Where is everyone?" It was only noon. Usually several of his family members would be having dinner right about now.

"Well, let's see. Mamm and Jimmy went to visit Sarah and her mother."

His twenty-two-year-old brother had just become engaged to his longtime girlfriend. Unfortunately, less than a month after they'd announced their engagement, Sarah's mother had been diagnosed with breast cancer. That meant the engagement and wedding were up in the air.

"Any news?"

"I guess we'll find out when Jimmy gets back," Betty said as she set a bowl in front of him, then returned with a plate of breadsticks and a dish of freshly grated cheese.

"This looks *wunderbaar*."

"*Danke*. Now eat," she said while she poured him a glass of water.

Harley bowed his head and gave thanks for the meal and for his sister's way in the kitchen. Everyone said she could work in a restaurant if she chose to. She was that good.

After taking that first sip of his soup, he grinned. "You could sell this soup, it's so tasty."

She laughed. "I'd like to see Daed's expression about that."

"You are almost old enough to do what you want."

She sat down next to him. "Almost, but not yet."

That was Betty. Always so impatient to grow up. "Tell me about everyone else," he said as he broke a breadstick in half and dipped it into the rich broth.

"Daed went to the Bylers' to help with a foal who's sickly, Kyle's been working in the barn all morning and should be coming in any minute."

"And Beth? Is she at work?"

"She is. I doubt she'll be back until dark."

It took some effort, but he didn't smile at the wistful tone in his little sister's voice. Beth was a nanny for an English family in town. She worked long hours and usually spent the night at the family's home one or two nights a week, on account of both parents traveling a lot.

But even though it was a demanding job, she was paid well and lived a very English life when she cared for the two children under her watch. All of them knew that Betty constantly yearned to leave the house and do new things.

After releasing a little sigh, Betty said, "Let's talk about you, Harley."

"Not much to talk about."

"Maybe. Maybe not." Eyeing him closely, she said, "I didn't expect you home so early."

"I wasn't doing construction today. I was just checking out a house to see if I wanted to do the remodel." And why he was making his visit to Katie's house sound like a formal meeting with strangers, he didn't know.

Betty stared at him curiously. "But I thought you were going to Katie Steury's *haus*? Was I wrong?"

"*Nee*, that's where I went."

"Then there was no question of you taking the job, right?"

His little sister was way too smart for her own good. She also had a cadence in her voice that echoed their father's.

Because of that, he could never seem to evade his answers to her. "Right," he replied slowly. "But still, I needed to talk things over with Katie."

Betty's eyes lit up with humor. "How did that go?"

"What do you mean?"

"Oh, only that she's always rubbed you the wrong way."

Had that really been so obvious? "That ain't true."

"Sure it is. You two argue more than the five of us ever have," she said as they heard the door open and shut. "Kyle?"

"*Jah.* Mamm and Jimmy are in the barn, putting up the buggy. They'll be in shortly." After a pause, Kyle said, "Harley, you're back from Katie's already?"

He took a spoonful of soup instead of stating the obvious.

When Kyle entered the kitchen, he was grinning. "Ha! I was right!"

"About what?"

"I told Jimmy that you'd be home by dinner. Good of you to help me out."

"You better not have bet on me." From the time Jimmy and Harley were nine or ten they'd had a habit of betting on all sorts of things. Never for money, and the bet was never even about anything serious. No, it was all for bragging rights, and the loser had to do the winner's chores for the day. As soon as Beth and the others got of age, Harley and Jimmy had let them in.

There were only a few rules. The loser had to do the winner's chores without complaint, and they could *never* tell their parents what they were up to. Of course, their *mamm* found out pretty quickly that something was going on when Beth was mucking out stalls or Jimmy was washing supper dishes. But other than a shake of her head, Harley was fairly certain she'd never told Daed about their game.

It went without saying that he wouldn't find either betting or shirking duties to be anything other than a bad idea.

Harley figured that they were entitled to a small

break from time to time. Their father kept them busy and expected them to do all of their tasks well. Each of them had learned the hard way what would happen if they attempted to cut corners—they'd be forced to do the job all over again, this time under their father's watchful eye. Few things were worse than that.

All that said, none of them appreciated being the object of a bet.

When Kyle merely looked amused, Harley sighed and secretly vowed to get him back.

Looking almost angelic, Kyle turned to their sister. "May I have some soup, Betty?"

"Sure. Sit down."

While their sister readied the bowl, Harley leaned close. "What did you bet?"

"Nothing that concerns you. Don't worry about it."

"Kyle, for the record, me and Katie ain't none of your concern."

"Sure it is," he quipped with a bright smile just as they heard the door open again.

"Betty, your soup smells like Heaven," Mamm called out as she entered. "Oh. Harley. You're home for dinner."

"*Jah*." He didn't miss the look of triumph Kyle sent Jimmy as he entered.

As Betty brought over a bowl to Kyle, she glanced at Jimmy. "You want some soup, Jimmy? Mamm?"

Their mother shook her head. "None for me.

Sarah served us chicken salad sandwiches. I'm stuffed."

"I'm not," Jimmy said. "I'll have some, Betty."

Back she went to the stove.

Jimmy, all freckles and dark red hair, closed his eyes to pray then grabbed one of the breadsticks. "How's Katie's *haus*?"

"It was all right, I reckon."

All four members of his family stared at him. Obviously waiting for him to continue.

Though he ached to share that it was crowded and uncomfortable and seemed to have more sore spots for Katie than a bad case of measles, he said, "It's going to need a lot of work in order to be a bed-and-breakfast."

"Does that surprise you, her wanting to run a place like that?" Mamm asked.

"Not really. Should it?"

"It surprises me," Betty said. "She can't cook."

"Maybe not as well as you, sister, but I know she cooks. I think she bakes well."

"Not well enough to entice guests, I bet."

"I've never stayed at a bed-and-breakfast. I don't know what is needed. And neither do you, Betty."

"Ouch," Kyle said. "You're touchy about Katie. I guess some things never change, do they?" He looked around the table, obviously expecting an answer. "Ain't so?"

"Watch it, Kyle," Harley muttered.

"*Jah*, you know our big brother don't take kindly to us teasing him about any of the Eight," Jimmy said before slurping another spoonful of soup.

"Kyle, as always, you are incorrigible," Mamm chided.

And so it continued. Another meal shared around a well-worn table, with several conversations going on at once, some out loud, and others whispered or silently shared between one or two of them.

It was familiar, and yet, now that he had a better understanding of how Katie's family really had been, he realized that he'd probably never truly appreciated it. Despite the way they'd all had a mighty strict upbringing, there was love here.

He finished the soup just as the door opened again. Little by little all of them stopped the bantering and teasing. Postures straightened and expressions tightened just in time for Daed to enter the room.

He stopped, looking a bit surprised to see all of them sitting together in the middle of the day.

"Is there a holiday I don't know about?" he asked gruffly as he took the empty chair at the end of the rectangular table.

"*Nee*," Jimmy replied as he stood up and brought his dish to the counter. "We were all just enjoying Betty's soup. It's mighty *gut*."

Betty beamed. "*Danke*, Jimmy."

Looking at their little sister with an almost fond

expression, Daed said, "And what did you make today, Betty?"

"Italian meatball soup, Father," she said primly. "Would you care for any?"

"I would."

She served their father while Harley got up, washed his bowl, and set it on the drying rack. After they'd all stayed silent while Daed prayed, Harley turned to Kyle. "I need to speak to you about the job over at Katie's."

"I can talk with you now." Not wasting a minute, Kyle stood up, also washed his dish.

His father looked up from his soup. "You decided to take on that job at the Steury *haus*, Harley?"

"*Jah*." If they'd had a different relationship, he might have gone into more details. Oh, not about Mrs. Steury's hoarding, but about how Katie's longtime dreams of having a bed-and-breakfast were going to be finally realized.

But that was not how Harley ever spoke to his father.

After taking another spoonful of soup and then carefully wiping his lips and dabbing at his beard with the paper napkin, Daed nodded. "That's *gut*. Your Katie needs you. Ain't so?"

A new, amused silence slid into the room as Harley struggled to answer. Katie was not "his." But he had twenty-five years of never correcting his father.

Finally he took the road of least resistance. "*Jah*," he said at last. "Kyle, I'll be waiting upstairs."

"Sure. I'll be there in five minutes."

"Take your time." He turned and started walking before any of the other occupants in the room could tease him about anything else.

FIVE

When Logan groaned, Tricia giggled. "Oh, come on. You all aren't going to try to tell me that you were afraid of a bunch of goats. They're as cute as can be."

"Not those goats," Logan said.

*K*yle was beginning to feel like his head was about to explode. He had too many thoughts and emotions spinning around in it and not enough guts to share his feelings or worries with anyone who could help.

After thanking Betty for the meal, he walked upstairs, needing to take his time getting to Harley's room. Harley would be all-business, a younger carbon copy of their father, and there was only so much of that he could take without a break.

He wandered into the bathroom, did his business, and then took his time washing his hands and splashing warm water on his face and neck. Working in the barn all morning was a dirty job. If he'd been alone in the house, he would've taken a shower to get the rest of the dust and dirt off.

But his parents didn't believe in taking unnecessary showers during the day.

It was one of many rules that he'd learned long ago to never question, but it had always chafed at him something awful. He figured at eighteen, he was far too old to have to explain to his parents why he didn't want to smell like barns and manure all the time.

Realizing that he couldn't put it off any longer, he walked down the hall and up another flight of stairs to Harley's room. He and Jimmy shared the attic. Because of that, Kyle had his own room on the second floor. The privacy was nice, but he'd always been jealous of his two older brothers' close relationship.

After knocking twice, he turned the knob and looked at his brother's desk, which was in the far corner of the wide-open space, under one of the three windows. He opened his mouth, ready to pull out a made-up reason why he hadn't gotten there more quickly. But his brother wasn't there.

"Harley?" he murmured as he turned his head.

"I'm here."

Harley was lying on his bed, his sock-covered feet crossed at the ankles and his hands folded on his stomach. Kyle couldn't recall if he'd ever seen his brother relaxing like that in the middle of the day.

It shocked him.

"Are you all right?"

"Hmm?" He raised up on his elbows. "Yeah. Why?"

After debating about two seconds, he said, "Uh, don't know if you noticed but you are sprawled out on your bed in the middle of the day."

"I was hardly sprawled." He got to his feet. "And I'm not sprawled any longer." To his surprise, Harley looked irritated that Kyle had even asked him about what he'd been doing.

"You can lie down up here, if you want. I won't tell."

"Are you giving me permission, *glay broodah?*"

Little brother. Harley loved to call him that, even though Kyle wasn't a kid any longer. "You don't need to sound so sarcastic. I'm trying to help you. That's all."

"Well, I do need your help, but not for anything here." The defensive look on his face turned to something slightly more guarded as he continued. "I am going to need your help for a while. Katie's *haus* is gonna be a far bigger job than I'd realized."

"What are you going to need done?" As far as Kyle was concerned, it was a fair question. He wasn't a builder and didn't have a lot of experience in doing the intricate jobs that Harley usually hired professional trade workers to do.

"I'll pay you," came his reply.

Becoming even more confused, Kyle tried again. "Harley, what is the job you need me to do?"

"Honestly, can't you ever just agree? Why do you have to be difficult?"

Kyle stared at his eldest brother in shock. Who was this man who'd taken his steady, closed-off brother's place? Kyle could count the number of times on one hand that Harley had lost his composure. "I'm not arguing. All I'm doing is trying to figure out what kind of job exactly you need me to do. We both know I ain't all that skilled."

"Sorry." He leaned back in his chair with a sigh. "All right, fine. I guess I need to take some of my own advice. Ain't so?"

Kyle didn't answer. Simply stared.

"Katie's mother was a hoarder."

"Sorry?" He wasn't trying to be difficult, but he wasn't exactly sure what that was.

"She kept things." He waved a hand. "Lots of things."

"Okay."

"*Nee*, it ain't okay. It's awful inside. I'm fairly sure that something died in one of the rooms. That's how bad it was."

"Something died and Katie Steury couldn't clean it up?"

With a jerk, Harley leaned forward. "Don't talk about her like that. It would have been impossible for her to clean out that house by herself."

"She is one of the Eight, right? Why don't you get all of them to help?" It was a fair question and he was sure that this time his voice was so even it didn't betray his usual jealousy whenever he mentioned his older brother's tight group of friends.

"She is embarrassed about it." He waved a hand. "I couldn't believe it, but she acted like she didn't want even me to see the house." His voice rose. "What do you think about that?"

Well, he thought that their father had been exactly right. Katie really was Harley's Katie. That's what he thought, but he would rather be poked with a stick instead of being subjected to another one of his older brother's lengthy lectures. "I don't know," he murmured instead.

After staring at him a long moment, Harley grunted. "I didn't know how to respond, either. I was shocked, I'll tell you that. I thought she would've trusted me more. Why do you think she doesn't?"

"I couldn't say."

"Me, neither." Harley turned and looked out the window for almost a full minute before looking back at him. "So, will you do it?"

"Will I help you clean Katie's *haus?*"

"*Jah.* Will you help me empty the house of all the trash, help her organize the items that she wants to keep, and then get the whole place ready for remodeling?"

Harley was talking lots and lots of hours, which meant he'd have lots more spending money than he did at the moment. "*Jah.* Sure," Kyle said eagerly. "When do you want to get started?"

"I'd like to start this afternoon, but I guess tomorrow morning would be better. Katie acted like she needed some time before I got started."

"All right. Do you want to tell Daed about the job or shall I?"

Looking lost in thought again, Harley blinked. "Huh? Oh, you can, if you want."

"What, exactly, should I tell him?" Their father wasn't a man to accept vague explanations.

Harley started to shrug, then groaned. "You're right. He's going to ask questions about Katie's *haus.* I'll talk to him. Just . . . just be ready tomorrow at six thirty."

Kyle had been more concerned about their father getting upset that Kyle wasn't going to be able to do most of his chores. That was going to be a problem. But if Katie was who Harley wanted to protect, so be it. At least now he wasn't going to have to have that conversation.

His brother looked lost in thought again. "Hey, Harley?"

"Hmm?"

"Are you okay?"

His expression sharpened. "Of course. Why do you ask?"

Because his older brother didn't usually lie on his

bed, stare off into the distance, or act so distracted. "No reason. I'll see you later."

He walked downstairs. Paused on the second floor and considered sneaking into his room for another fifteen minutes. But there were still chores to be done and he wasn't going to be around tomorrow to do them. So he kept walking.

Besides, if he got through with his chores early enough, he could head down the road and maybe see Gabby.

Gabrielle, but always Gabby to him. Even though she was everything wrong for him, he couldn't help but wonder if the Lord had also thought maybe she was everything right.

No woman who was so perfect could ever be anyone's idea of wrong.

Well, no one would ever think that, unless they were a part of his family. Then all they would see was that she was English.

And because she was, Gabrielle Allison Ferrara was everything that was wrong.

Now all he needed to think about was if he cared enough about that to stay away from her.

SIX

"Logan ain't lying," Harley said. "That herd of goats was huge. There had to be at least thirty of them, and they were worse than ornery. They also didn't take too kindly to us trespassing through their property."

Elizabeth Anne grunted. "That's for sure. They were downright mad."

*T*hey'd been working hard for two hours. Katie, Harley, and Harley's youngest brother, Kyle. She knew Kyle, of course. All of the Eight knew one another's families. And, since they were both in the same church district, she'd had the chance to talk to all of Harley's siblings on more than one occasion. But while so many of the members were more open, Harley's family was not.

That was why she'd been pleasantly surprised to get to know Harley's brother, who seemed to be far more open and outgoing than Harley had ever been.

Kyle had entered her house with a bright smile and an amount of chattiness that comforted her frayed nerves like few things could.

She'd been grateful he was there from practically the first moment he'd said hello. Nothing seemed to faze him, not the stacks of books and newsprint and debris. Not the smell.

Not her nervousness. And, it seemed, not the strange new tension that bloomed between her and his brother.

Around his brother, Harley seemed quieter than usual with her but more patient with the chatty eighteen-year-old than Katie would have thought possible.

Such as now, when they'd begun carting trash downstairs to the Dumpster that Harley had ordered to be delivered early that morning.

"*Nee*, Kyle. Take less. You'll hurt yourself."

"I'm eighteen, not eight. I can carry my fair share."

"You are strong, to be sure," Harley responded quietly. "But we must remember that this is the first of many loads to carry, *jah*? Slow and steady is best for both our backs, I think."

As Katie watched Kyle set half of the items in his arms down before descending the stairs, she couldn't help but smile at the way Harley had managed to both help his brother but still give him his dignity. Growing up, she would've loved for either June or Caleb to have treated her with such care.

"Uh-oh, I know that amused look," Harley said. "What did I do?"

Katie had just sat back down on the floor to sort through another pile for the men to cart away. Looking up as he approached, she attempted to look innocent. "You didn't do a thing, Harley. I was just thinking about something."

"Would you like to share what that was? I haven't seen you smile like that in months."

Had she really been that glum of late? She supposed so, what with Andy's death and her mother moving away and leaving her with this whole mess to sort out.

And . . . had he been watching her that closely? She wasn't sure what to think about that. "It wasn't anything, Harley. My mind had drifted. That's all."

"Oh." He turned away, pulled out another stack of old clothes that had mildewed. He wrinkled his nose before obviously trying to change his expression into something more neutral. "Katie, ah, do you want to sort through these clothes before I take them outside?"

Though she appreciated his kind tone and the careful way he was treating her, it wasn't necessary. She knew what those items smelled like. "*Nee.* You can take them right out." It might have been a waste, but she'd long since given up the idea of either cleaning, repurposing the fabric, or donating the items. She needed them out of her life.

"I'm going to set them on the porch."

"That sounds *gut. Danke.*" As she continued to sort through an old laundry basket filled with scraps of quilting fabrics and notions, Katie heard him speak to Kyle. Another five minutes passed.

When he walked back inside, he said, "I hope that I didn't ruin everything between us yesterday."

"How could you do that?"

He looked down at his boots. "By being too blunt, maybe?"

"*Nee*, you were only being honest, Harley. I appreciated that, too. We definitely needed help. Your brother has been a godsend."

Harley didn't look as if he completely believed her. "Kyle has been helpful. That is true." He took a deep breath. "But I know that this is probably mighty difficult—"

"I heard you say I was helpful!" Kyle called out as he walked up the last few steps of the front stairs. "You can't take that back, Harley."

Katie giggled. She thought Kyle's exuberance was infectious. But, perhaps Harley didn't feel the same way.

"I *wasna* going to take anything back," Harley grumbled. "But you shouldn't have been listening to a private conversation."

"Overhearing a conversation exchanged in a front hallway ain't exactly eavesdropping," Kyle retorted. "All I did was acknowledge that I heard what you said. About me."

Harley folded his hands over his chest. "Oh, brother."

Looking her way, Kyle grinned. "Come on. Am I right, Katie?"

"I don't think I should answer," she teased. "I need both of your help. I can't risk making either of you mad at me."

Kyle whistled low. "Now, there's a woman who knows how to speak diplomatically."

"There's no need, at least not on my account. It takes more than that to make me upset with you, Katie," Harley murmured.

"Does anyone ever get that angry at you?" Kyle asked.

Recalling just how upset Harley had been when he'd blamed her for his breakup with Melody, Katie swallowed. The pain sliced through her, almost like it had happened a few weeks ago instead of years earlier. "Believe it or not, it does happen. It seems I make just as many mistakes as everyone else." She smiled to take the sting out of her words.

Harley grunted as he turned around.

Kyle's eyebrows rose as he looked at both of them. Then, he did what he seemed to do so well—defuse the situation. "Well, lucky you, Katie. I, on the other hand, seem to annoy people constantly."

"He doesn't lie." Harley's green eyes were shining with mirth.

Kyle shrugged. "It's a gift, you see."

Katie giggled. "I was just thinking to myself how glad I am that you came here today, Kyle. You're making a difficult day so much easier."

Kyle's expression stilled. "You're welcome. I . . . well, I bet it is a mighty hard day."

"I need to toughen up, don't you think?"

"I reckon you're tough enough, Katie," Harley murmured. "Now, we better get more loads taken to the Dumpster or all of this is going to take even more time than it already will."

"I'll go take those clothes over there now," Kyle said.

Harley followed on his heels, leaving Katie alone again.

She took the time to take stock of the guest bedroom. After four hours of sorting and clearing, they'd barely made a dent in the room.

Though it was painful, she allowed herself to recall the many days her mother used to walk into this room after supper, carefully close the door behind her, and not walk out until late into the night.

Katie and Caleb, and for a time, June, had often cleaned the kitchen and dining room on their own.

When Katie had been in school, Caleb or June would sit by her side and try to help her with her homework.

Then, later, they'd all go to bed. Katie would stare at the light shining from under the door and wonder what her mother did during all that time.

No, she'd wondered what was so much more important than Katie, June, and Caleb.

She couldn't count the number of times she'd almost gotten the nerve to ask. But she never did. She doubted Caleb had, either.

And June? Well, her older sister had just left.

It might be too late for Mamm to mend things with her older sister, but Katie hoped it was still possible for her to mend their relationship.

She supposed she really could still ask Mamm what had been driving her all this time to need so many things and to worry so much about it being there that the rest of her life suffered.

Hearing Kyle's voice again, chatting eagerly as he and Harley walked up the stairs, Katie got to her feet.

"You know, I was just thinking we should take a break," she called out as she walked to the door. "I could make us some ham sandwiches."

"Is that offer for all of us?" a new voice called out.

She knew that voice.

Dismay engulfed her. Harley had brought some of their friends to her house, even though she'd specifically asked him not to. Was he really about to escort them inside, like he had that right?

Looking around the entryway, seeing all the piles of discarded clothes, the bins of mildewed fabric, the garbage bags . . . she panicked. Thinking of the things they would see and maybe judge her for, she darted out and grabbed the door handle, only to be stopped by two strong hands gripping her shoulders. "*Nee*, Katie, don't do that. It's all right," Harley murmured.

"*Nee*, it's not. You *promised*, Harley. You promised that you wouldn't ask everyone over here. How could you lie about that?"

His grip on her shoulders eased up but it didn't leave entirely. Still looking directly into her eyes, he murmured, "I didn't tell anyone about the state of your house except for Kyle."

"Then why are they here?"

"I don't know." He was still speaking gently, almost like he was trying to calm a skittish foal. "Maybe they only wanted to say hello."

Still in a panic, she shook her head. "That can't be right."

"You need to trust me, Katie." Squeezing her shoulders gently once more, he stared intently at her with his dark green eyes. "I would never hurt you on purpose. I would never betray you."

She shuddered as she finally came to her senses. He was right. They might snipe at each other from time to time, but they did have a bond. And besides, Harley was Harley. Few men were more calm and dependable. "I want to believe that . . ."

"*Nee*, you should. Katie, on my honor, I—"

Logan tromped inside. "Hey, Katie? Harley? What's going on? Where are you? Didn't you hear us? Oh!"

And the already tense moment had just gotten worse.

Harley turned, but not before everyone had seen the two of them standing the way they had been. Very close. Harley's hands on her shoulders. Staring intently at each other.

If one didn't know better, they would've thought that the two of them were having a private moment.

An intimate, *romantic* one.

She was sure her face was beet red.

Harley turned on his heel to face the newcomers. "Hey, everyone."

"Hiya," John B. said, his voice strained. "I'm sorry if we were interrupting something."

"You weren't," Harley said.

Katie could practically feel the tension in the air tighten.

Feeling awkward, Katie felt other eyes on her and turned around to face whoever was there.

It was worse than she imagined. There stood Marie and John B. and Tricia Warner and Logan. All standing in stunned silence at the open doorway.

Harley was behind her and Kyle was behind their friends, looking as worried and horrified as she felt.

For the first time, she couldn't summon a single thing to say. There was no way Harley hadn't told some of the Eight about her house, given who was here. And he'd clearly invited them over, all without informing her. He'd gone against her wishes and lied to her.

So because of that, there was nothing to make things all right. Nothing at all.

SEVEN

"After the head goat gave a couple of warning bleats . . . well, they all came running," Harley continued, his voice ringing with amusement. "It was surely a sight to see."

"It was something, all right," Marie muttered.

The moment Harley got a good look at Katie's expression, he realized he'd made a huge mistake in judgment.

Katie wasn't just a little irritated. Nee, she was real upset. And angry. With him.

But even though he might have deserved her wrath, he was still determined to make things right between them as best he could. Something—something he couldn't quite put his finger on—was pulling him toward her. The thought of her being furious with him was physically painful.

Ignoring all of their friends who were still standing nearby, he said, "Katie, I didn't—"

Glaring at him, she stood up straighter, which on most days would be mighty amusing, given that she was barely an inch or two above five feet. But now? Well, now it simply broke his heart.

"Everyone, it's *gut* to see you, but I'd like you to leave," she said. "Harley brought you here without my permission."

John B. raised his eyebrows. "What are you talking about?"

"And since when do we need permission from Harley to do anything?" Logan asked. "Katie, you look so glum. What's wrong?"

"*Jah*, did something happen?" Tricia asked.

Katie was looking panicked. Hoping to ease the situation, Harley cleared this throat. "Well, now. Maybe we could . . ."

"*Nee*, I can speak for myself," Katie said. Facing their friends again, she said, "What's wrong is that I didn't ask you all over. I need you to leave."

Everyone looked at each other. "Is she serious?" Logan asked John B.

John shrugged. "It seems so."

Marie stepped forward and reached for Katie's hands. "Does that mean you don't want to have dinner together?"

Harley shook his head. "Marie, now ain't the time to joke."

She stiffened. "I'm not joking, Harley. Sheesh."

This was such a mess. "I was only trying to help," he said.

"And I already said that I don't need you to speak for me, Harley, " Katie said.

Marie frowned. "Katie, this isn't like you. What happened? What is wrong?"

Tears formed in Katie's eyes. "Please, I really do need you to leave." Looking at Harley, she added, "All of you."

"You're serious," Logan said. He continued to stare at Katie, obviously trying to read her mind.

But Harley didn't need to be a mind reader for this. Katie was about to crack, she was holding herself so stiff. "I'll walk you all out. Now ain't the best time for a visit."

"But it's okay that you're here?" Tricia asked Harley.

"I'm working here. I mean, I was . . ." His voice tapered off as he realized that Katie wasn't going to change her mind. "We should go."

Holding Marie's hand now, John hesitated. "Katie, are you sure about this?"

"I've never been more sure of anything," she murmured before turning back into the house and closing the front door on all of them. It clicked shut with a resounding slap.

Beside him, Marie made a little pained noise.

Harley exhaled. "I'm sorry about this."

"Me, too." She exhaled, too, her breath coming out in a ragged sigh.

"Come on, Marie," John said as he reached for her hand. "Let's get you out of here."

Marie didn't budge. "Do you think that's the best thing to do? Maybe we should wait a bit?"

"No," John said, giving her a little tug again. "We've known Katie for most of our lives. You know how she gets when she's in a dither. We need to let her calm down."

"He's right, I think," Logan said as he started walking down the cement walkway toward the large driveway.

After a pause, Tricia followed, and then Marie and John did, too, their fingers intertwined.

Unsure of what to do, Harley stared at the front door. Even though Katie had closed it tight against them, he didn't want to leave her. He wanted to make sure that she knew that he was there for her. No matter what their past entailed, it felt like she was hurting so badly now.

"You coming?" Logan asked from the drive.

"I think you should, Harley," Kyle said. "In a few minutes, I'll go inside and clean up a little bit. That way she won't be alone."

"You don't mind?"

"Not at all."

He realized then that his brother wasn't just

growing up, he *had* grown up. In this case, he was right, too. Katie wouldn't want to see him. He needed to give her some space. "I'm coming," he finally said.

"I'll walk with you to the end of the drive," Kyle said. "I don't want to just stand here."

As they all started walking down the drive, Harley could practically feel their friends' questions floating in the air. He was going to have to tell them something, but what? If he told the truth, he would betray Katie's trust in him even more.

But if he said nothing, they'd all think the worst of her, which wasn't fair, either.

"You need to tell us what's going on," John B. said after another few minutes passed. "Nothing that Katie just did is like her. Something must be really wrong."

Harley knew their friends could help her. Knew it as surely as he knew his *daed* expected him to get up at five every morning and tend to their animals. However, he also knew that no matter how much all of them wanted to help her, going behind her back wasn't the way. "I can't share this."

"Can't or won't?" John pushed.

"Obviously, it's a won't. It ain't my story to tell."

While Logan looked resigned, Marie just looked irritated. "Harley, come on," she snapped, her voice thick with impatience. "I get that you need to keep her secrets, but you and she owe us something."

"Marie, stop."

John frowned at Harley.

"*Nee*. You can absolutely tell us why Katie Steury just slammed that door on us," Marie said. "And don't tell us that you were as surprised as we were because you didn't look shocked, only disappointed."

"You aren't making this easier, Marie." He looked over at John and sent him a plaintive look. John and Marie were a couple now. Couldn't John intervene at least a little here?

After a pause, John did chime in. "Harley, I'm all for keeping private business private, but I think you're taking things a bit too far. We've all been friends for decades. We've mourned Andy together. We've all cried together. Whatever she has going on is safe with us."

Marie nodded. "You know we all only want the best for Katie."

Harley knew that to be true. But he wasn't going to be the reason Katie was further upset. Though he hated doing it, he kept his silence.

However, just as he folded his arms over his chest, Kyle blurted, "*Mei broodah* and I are cleaning out the *haus* because it's in a real bad way."

Feeling betrayed, Harley shook his head at him. "Kyle, you'd best keep your mouth shut."

"I'm only helping you keep your promise, Harley. Now you won't betray her and your friends will know what's going on."

He was splitting hairs. "You know this isn't right."

Unfortunately, not a one of them seemed interested in taking his side. Ignoring his protests, Logan faced Kyle. "What's the rest of the story?"

"The rest of the story is Katie didn't want you to see the inside of her home," Kyle finished.

"Because it was in such disarray?" Trish asked. "Really? Does she really think we all keep spotless houses?"

"It's not in disarray, it's a lot worse than that," Kyle said.

Before his little brother could say another word, Harley said, "This isn't just a case of her being embarrassed about a mess. She feels that way because of several reasons—none of which are my place, or my brother's, to share."

Marie looked back at the front door. "What do you think she's doing now?"

Before he could answer, she continued. "You know, sometimes when things have been really bad in my life, I didn't realize what I needed until someone else pointed it out. Other people had to intervene. She's essentially alone now, right?"

Realizing that he hated the idea of her possibly crying alone, Harley changed his plans. Even if she ignored him the rest of the day, he couldn't leave her care to Kyle. "As soon as you all get on your way, I'll go in and talk to her."

"Why you? It isn't like you are any closer to her

than the rest of us," Logan said. "I mean, come on, Harley. We all know you carried a grudge about her interfering with Melody for years."

"I *canna* believe you are bringing up Melody right now."

"Why shouldn't I?" Logan countered. "She's history. Isn't she?"

"Of course," he answered immediately. But even to his own ears, he didn't sound convincing.

"Uh-oh," Tricia murmured.

"Have you really blamed Katie all this time for your breakup, Harley?" Kyle asked. "You should've been thanking her. Melody was awful."

"She wasn't awful, Kyle. That is unkind."

"*Nee, she* was unkind. Maybe not to you but to everyone else," Kyle said. "Betty would hide in her room every time you brought Melody by the house."

He felt his ears turn bright red, and it had been ages since that had happened. "Melody—"

"Was difficult at best, Harley. And you know it," John B. said with a slight smile. "She wasn't the woman for you."

"Melody and my relationship ain't anyone's business." And he was really starting to hate how John and Logan thought they had all the answers now that they had fallen in love.

Marie waved a hand in frustration. "Oh my word,

but you are so closed off. Getting information from you is like getting water out of a . . . a . . . beet."

"I believe that would be turnip," Tricia corrected.

"Whatever it is, it's true. You hold a lot inside," Marie said. "Too much."

Beyond frustrated now, Harley turned to John. "Are you really going to let her say all this?"

John closed his eyes. "Harley, that was a stupid thing to ask."

"Are you thinking that John is now supposed to make me keep my mouth shut?" Marie asked. Her hands were on her hips and her voice had risen. She was fuming.

And rightly so. Swallowing hard, he realized that for a moment he actually had expected John to tell Marie what to do. Just like how his overbearing father acted with his *mamm* from time to time.

Just like he'd always hated.

"I'm sorry. You are right. I shouldn't have said such a thing. I don't know why I did."

"I do. It's because you keep too much inside and it all comes rushing out when you're upset. Like now, when we're all worried about Katie," John supplied.

Harley couldn't even believe that this was where the conversation had gone. "All I'm trying to say is that you need to give Katie some space."

"If that's what she wants, then I'll do that, though it sure doesn't feel right." Marie flipped a lock of her hair over her shoulder. "Katie came to my house several times after my car accident in the fall." Her voice softened. "Boy, I had such a tough time recovering from both the accident and the fact that that Amish boy had died."

"It wasn't your fault, Marie," John said.

"I know that, but it was still traumatic." She reached for John's hand and squeezed. "But my point is that when I was having a really hard time, Katie was there. She put up with my anger and pain and tears. How can I repay her help by leaving her now?"

"I'll tell her that Harley made you leave," Kyle said.

"She also asked for us to leave," Tricia reminded Marie. "We need to respect her feelings."

"I guess that's all we can hope for. Let's go on," John said, wrapping an arm around Marie's shoulders. "We'll stop by later this week."

Marie nodded but said nothing.

Logan clapped him on the shoulder. "You may not want to hear this, Har, but all of us are still grieving Andy. Don't be afraid to admit that you need your friends as much as we've needed you."

Before Harley could comment on that, Logan turned and walked away.

When they got out of earshot, Harley glared at Kyle. "What were you thinking? These are my friends, not yours."

"Someone had to say something."

"I don't agree. Instead of helping, you only made things worse. Go on home."

Kyle's eyes widened. "No."

"*Nee?*"

"There is way too much stuff to dispose of and you cannot do it by yourself. All of your so-called great friends would have chipped in and made things a whole lot easier, but you were too stubborn to let them in."

"This is Katie's house."

"Pretend that's the reason if you want, but I'm still going to take trash out to the Dumpster. You promised me a job this week and I'm going to do it. I'm counting on that money."

"For what?"

"Like I would tell you anything right now," he said as he turned back toward the house.

And with that, he left Harley essentially in no-man's-land. His friends were gone, his brother was angry with him, and the one person he'd tried to help was no doubt crying inside her home because she thought he'd betrayed her.

How could something that was supposed to go so right suddenly become so very wrong?

EIGHT

"Warning bleats? Head goat?" Kendra shook her head. "I'm having a hard time believing this all happened. Surely those goats weren't that bad."

"Oh, they were. They were practically feral," John said.

"Those goats could run like the wind," E.A. said. "When they started chasing us, I've never run that fast in my life."

*K*yle heard Katie crying on the other side of her sister Jane's old bedroom door. They were loud and noisy tears that he had a feeling stemmed from so much more than a simple argument with his brother.

Panic set in. He didn't have a lot of experience with situations like this. His family kept everything locked tight inside. They were near experts at it. So while his sisters had cried from time to time, he couldn't recall either of them ever getting this upset with such abandon.

It was enough to make a grown man's palms sweat. Uncomfortable with that, and the fact that he was sorely out of his depth, he almost walked right back downstairs.

But Harley was waiting there, and Kyle sure didn't want to see him anytime soon. No matter how many times he told his brother that he didn't need another father, Harley seemed determined to prove him wrong.

Because of that—and because Kyle truly felt sorry for Katie—the moment she grew quieter, he knocked twice and tried the knob. To his surprise, it turned easily.

She was sitting on the floor cross-legged, surrounded by all of the items her mother had been so fiercely protective of . . . but had still left without a backward glance. It seemed only grandchildren and the idea of a completely fresh start could encourage such a change.

As he expected, her face was blotchy and her eyes were red rimmed. She also looked exhausted.

"Hey," he said.

She swiped her cheeks with the side of her fist. "Kyle, I didn't know you were still here."

"I've been outside but I came back in." He elected not to mention that Harley was downstairs in the kitchen.

"You came back? Why?" She swiped at her face again. "Did you . . . uh, did you need something?"

If they'd known each other better, he would've smiled. Really, if they were even a little closer in age, he probably would've teased her, too. But given the circumstances, he didn't really know where to begin.

"Not really." While she gaped at him, he walked in and sat down on the narrow open space beside her.

She swallowed. "Where's your brother?"

"When I left him, he was still outside. But I think he's pacing in your kitchen now."

"Pacing."

"*Jah.* He does that from time to time. Don't worry. He'll settle down soon and get back to work."

"Why didn't you both leave?"

"We ain't got no time for that. There's a lot to do around here." That was almost the truth, too. But somehow he knew she wasn't going to take the idea of being watched over well.

"Ah," she murmured, not telling him anything but maybe signifying the same thing that he was thinking . . . that he was currently lying through his teeth.

Wrapping his arms around his knees, he said, "I heard you crying when I first came upstairs."

"I'm not surprised. I wasn't very quiet."

"No reason to be, I don't guess," he said easily. "If you decide to go cry, you might as well cry all you want, and as loudly as you want."

She raised her eyebrows. "Are you always like this?"

No. No, he was not. He didn't go around sitting in women's rooms. He didn't offer comfort or ever go against his brother's wishes.

But here he was.

"Not usually."

Her lips tipped up. "I'm special?"

"Maybe." He smiled, ready to tease her a little. "Or maybe I'm not usually this bored."

"Ouch!" She pressed a hand to her chest. "Boy, I'm glad I wasn't depending on you to help me feel better."

"My sisters say that *mei broodah* Jimmy is the most comforting of their brothers. I imagine they aren't wrong."

"I don't know Jimmy well." She frowned. "Isn't that something? I've known Harley so well for most of my life, yet I never got real close to Jimmy, and he's only three years younger."

He didn't think it was all that odd. Everyone in his family gravitated toward Jimmy when they needed sympathy . . . and Harley when they needed something done. "Well, Harley and Jimmy are way different."

"And you are still different from them."

She'd said that as a statement. "I reckon so. I'm younger."

"No, there's still something more. Maybe it's that you seem a lot more outgoing."

"Well, a rock might be more outgoing than Harley."

A reluctant smile appeared. "That's hardly nice. But . . ."

"But it's still true, *jah?*"

She shrugged. "Perhaps." After a few long seconds, she shook her head and made a motion to stand up. "Well, I had better go see if I can repair things with Harley. I was awfully rude to him."

"There ain't anything to repair, Katie. You can't help how you were feeling."

"That's kind of you to say, but I overreacted."

"Harley didn't know your friends were coming over here," he said boldly. "They just showed up."

"You're telling the truth, aren't you?"

"*Jah.*" He shrugged. "I don't know why you think that's surprising, anyway. All of you Eight often visit each other without notice. Everyone knows that."

"You're right. I'm sure they just wanted to see what was going on." Frowning, she got to her feet. "Now I really need to fix things."

Climbing to his feet as well, he shrugged. "He didn't seem that upset with you." No, Harley was more upset with himself. And with him.

"If he's not mad at me, I'd be surprised. Any ideas of how to make my behavior up to him?"

"Nah. He can be prickly, but he'll figure it out. I mean, it's not like when . . ."

"When I put down his girlfriend?"

"Melody was a pain, and you weren't the only person who wasn't real fond of her. But yeah. Today's actions ain't anything to worry about."

She smiled sweetly. "Thanks for coming in here and talking to me. I feel better already."

Embarrassed, he looked down at his feet. "It weren't nothing."

Just as she was about to open the door, she said, "Are you seeing anyone, Kyle? I was just thinking that you are going to be a catch for a special girl one day."

This time, he felt like he was in the hot spot. "I like a girl, but we aren't together or anything."

"Why not?" She held up a hand. "No, wait. You don't have to tell me. It's none of my business."

"If I confide something, will you keep it to yourself?"

"Sure."

"The girl I like . . . well, she's English."

"Wow. Does she know you're Amish?"

He gestured to his clothes. "It's a little obvious that I am."

"You know what I meant. Do you dress Amish around her? Some teenagers dress English when they're about your age. I didn't, and neither did Harley, but lots of kids we knew did." She was talking about Amish kids experimenting with English things during their *rumspringa*.

"I've always dressed Amish. But no matter what, I would tell her. It's too hard to pretend otherwise."

"Well, if she knows you're Amish, then what's the problem?"

"Uh, everything?"

Katie didn't look offended by his sarcastic comment in the slightest. "I don't follow."

"She's English, Katie. And my family? Well, we aren't the most open-minded people when it comes to outsiders."

"I kind of feel like that isn't so. Harley is open-minded and accepting of others. You seem that way, too."

"We are, but my parents aren't."

"But you're already eighteen. A grown man, right? What does that mean to you?"

The question caught him off guard. He realized suddenly that while he'd been going around acting like he was so grown up, he really wasn't. He was still used to following his parents' directions—and used to depending on Harley or his other older siblings to help him fix things when he made a mistake. But liking Gabby wasn't a mistake, and it had nothing to do with his siblings. For the first time, he was having to stand on his own two feet and face the consequences. "If I continue things with Gabby, then I'll risk making my parents upset."

Her expression softened. "That's her name? Gabby?"

"*Jah*. It's Gabrielle Allison Ferrara."

"Wow. That's a fancy name, for sure."

He chuckled. "I told her the same thing when I first heard it. But she ain't exactly fancy. She's real down-to-earth."

"You really do like her, Kyle."

"I told you that."

"*Nee*. I mean, you *really* like her a lot. She isn't just a dream, is she?"

Feeling struck a little dumb, he nodded. "You are right," he said slowly. "She is more than that."

"I'm not one to talk, but if I were, I would encourage you to see where things go with her."

"Even if it risks the relationship I have with my family?"

"It sounds to me like your lying and secrets have already changed your relationship with them." When he gaped at her, she waved a hand. "Look, maybe everything I'm saying doesn't make much sense."

"I didn't say that," he said quickly. Because, well, he was beginning to think that maybe it all did make a lot of sense.

Looking reassured, she continued. "What I'm trying to say—pretty poorly—is that maybe this Gabby isn't the girl for you. She might not be. But if she is, then there has to be something about her that God thought you needed. And something about you that God thought she needed. I mean, He wouldn't have put you two in each other's path without a reason, would He?"

"I never thought of it like that."

"If that's the case, then the two of you ought to figure that out."

"Maybe I will."

She smiled at him brightly. And to be honest, for the first time Kyle thought that maybe there was something more to her than just being a petite woman who was often a burr in his brother's side.

Suddenly, Katie Steury was pretty. No, it was more than that. She had a shine about her that was hard to shy away from.

And that, combined with her recent words of advice, made him realize that maybe she and Harley were a little bit like him and Gabby.

There was more to the two of them than there seemed to be at first glance.

NINE

"Even though those goats were horrible, we probably would've been all right if Mr. Schlabach hadn't come out with his shotgun."

$\mathcal{G}$abby knew she was being rude, but she couldn't help herself. She was that surprised. "Kyle, what are you doing here?"

"Huh?" His blue eyes looked completely confused for a second before he caught himself. "Oh. Well, I was working today and I just happened to be walking by on my way home. I decided to say hey since I was here."

She loved that he'd thought of her. His excuse for being on her street didn't fly, though. "You were working near here? Where?" The duplex that she shared with her mother and sixteen-year-old brother wasn't anywhere near where Kyle lived, which was at least two miles away. He lived on a big farm that her bus used to pass on the way to school.

Every morning and afternoon, back when she was in seventh and eighth grade, she would take a peek at it. His farm was so big and pretty, everyone said it looked like it should be on the cover of one of those magazines at the checkout counter in the grocery store. Or on one of those remodeling shows on cable. She'd always thought the same thing.

But then she would go one step further and would daydream about the family who lived there. She used to imagine that they were happy and comfortable. And rich, of course. So rich that they didn't eat tons of leftovers or only bought meat when it was on sale.

She couldn't believe it when she'd learned that Kyle lived there.

Where she lived, on the other hand, was in the middle of a row of six duplexes, each in need of paint and maybe a good scrubbing, too. Each building was also surrounded by a yard that couldn't seem to hold on to a single blade of grass. It was the complete opposite of his home.

Kyle looked down at his feet. "To tell you the truth, I wasn't actually all that close to here. I was working, but I really just came over here to see you."

"Oh." It was a struggle to even think about what to say next, so many thoughts were running through her head.

He winced. "Yeah. Can you come out and talk?"

She looked at the two chairs her mother had

placed out on the porch six months ago, saying that they would brighten up the place. They might have, too, if sitting on the front porch were relaxing.

It was not.

"How about you come inside instead?" Even though her mother was going to have a fit if she ever found out Gabby had brought a boy inside, Gabby knew it was the only real option. There were some scary boys in the next building over and they usually hung out on the street, watching everyone and everything nearby. Though they didn't really bother her, she didn't want to give them the opportunity. Plus, Lane would be home soon.

"Um, well, all right." Looking as awkward and ill at ease as she felt, he stepped across the threshold and into the small living room.

She locked and bolted the door behind him.

He turned to face her. "Do you always do that?"

"Do what?"

"Turn the dead bolt as soon as you walk in the door?"

"Yeah. This street—well, it's not the safest place."

"Do all the locks keep you safe?" He looked skeptical.

She was safe enough. So was her younger brother, Lane, and that was what really mattered.

But did she really want to talk about that with him? Ah, no she did not.

Hoping to make a joke of it, she raised her eyebrows. "Am I safe with you? Gosh, I hope so." Gesturing to the pair of worn beige love seats, she said, "Want to sit down?"

He sat. But his eyes were darting around the room. At their TV that worked great but wasn't anything fancy. At the stack of library books on the coffee table. At the shelves filled with books and picture frames.

"I guess it all looks pretty weird to you, huh?" Still feeling awkward, she fired off another question. "Have you ever been in a regular house before?"

One brown eyebrow rose. "Regular, like English?"

She shrugged. "Well, yeah."

"I've been in English houses before, Gabby," he said, sounding offended.

"I'm sorry. Was that rude to ask?"

After a couple of seconds, his expression lifted and he shook his head. "Nah. It's just—well, I'm around so many of my older brothers' *Englisch* friends that I forget not all *Englischers* aren't used to being around the Amish. Your question surprised me." His lips curved up a bit. "I don't think you could be rude if you tried, Gabby."

That was one of the things she really liked about Kyle Lambright. He was completely different from any other guy she knew. He always answered her honestly and never tried to make her feel dumb.

Gabby was pretty sure she could be rude to a lot of people. Growing up the way she had—with a single mom who meant well but didn't always put her and Lane first—had taught her to keep her guard up.

Except with Kyle.

That was why she hated that she might have offended him. "I guess I have a lot to learn about the Amish. If we're going to continue to hang out, I might need to ask you a ton of questions."

Instead of looking amused, Kyle looked pleased. "I don't mind that none. Nothing wrong with needing to learn something."

She smiled weakly.

He looked around. "So, is your mother home?"

"No, she's still at work. Or, she might be running some errands after, I'm not sure. Why, do you need your hair cut?" Her mother was a hairdresser.

"Nee. I just realized that we were alone." His hands were braced on either side of him now, like he was ready to push off the couch and put even more distance between them.

"Yeah. I . . . well, I'm usually alone this time of day. Unless I have something else to do." And . . . that sounded even more stupid. Chewing on her bottom lip, Gabby told herself to stay quiet. If she did, he would be able to finally get a word in edgewise and then she'd know what he'd come over for.

He folded his hands in his lap and gazed at her.

But stayed quiet. Each second felt like an hour. And each "hour" that passed made her revisit every stupid comment she'd made since he'd knocked on her door. Boy, she'd give a lot to be able to start all over again.

After another half a minute passed, she felt like she was on pins and needles. It was all becoming awkward. Really awkward. "Kyle—"

But, of course, he'd started talking at the same time. "Gabby—"

"Oh! You go first."

"Thanks." Looking like he was gathering himself together, he said, "Listen, the reason I stopped over was because I'd like to see more of you."

She looked down at her shirt, wondering how he could want that when she looked like she'd just rolled out of bed and was acting so stinkin' stupid. "You do?"

His eyes widened. "I don't mean more of your skin. I mean more of you, like visits."

As soon as she realized what he said, she started laughing. After a pause, he chuckled, too.

"Boy, I really put my foot in my mouth there, huh?"

She smiled at him. "I'm just glad you don't need me to take my clothes off. Then, I would have really wished my mother would have been here."

He closed his eyes and tilted his chin up. "Do me

a favor and never remind me about this conversation again."

"Kyle, did you mean that? About wanting us to see each other more?"

"I did." He looked at her warily. "Are you appalled? Do I sound like a boy of thirteen instead of all the guys you are used to seeing?"

All the guys? "I don't know who you think I usually see . . . I haven't dated a lot."

"Really?"

He sounded so incredulous, she stood up. "Look, I know I don't live in a great place and my, um, reputation isn't great. But that doesn't mean I'm easy." Was that why he'd come over?

Kyle got to his feet, too, and stuck his hat back on his head. "Gabby, I think I'm going to go. I've really messed this up."

Just as she was about to agree, the door opened and her mother rushed in with a rustle of paper sacks. "Gabby, come help me with these bags!"

Gabby ran over and grabbed a bag that looked like it was seconds away from sliding to the ground. "I've got this one."

"I'll get it, Gabby. The others, too," Kyle offered as he lifted another tote from her mother's arm.

Her mother let him, but she stared at Kyle like he was a new creature that she'd never encountered before. "Who are you?"

"I'm Kyle Lambright."

After blatantly looking him over, her mom turned to her. "What is he doing here, Gabby?"

"Kyle and I are friends," she replied as she led the way into their small kitchen. "He only came over to say hi."

"Is that right?" Her mother kept staring at him like he carried a disease. "How did you meet?"

"We first met at the fall fest, and then saw each other every now and then. This is the first time he's come by."

"I just happened to be nearby," Kyle said. "I knocked on the door to say hello."

"And you invited him in, Gabby." Her voice was flat, and she was still talking to Gabby like Kyle wasn't in the room.

Oh, this was bad.

After another second or two, Kyle cleared his throat. "Mrs. Ferrara, it was nice to meet you."

"It's not Mrs."

Looking even more wary, Kyle took a step backward. "I'm going to leave now, Gabby," he said quietly. "Could you walk me out?"

She nodded and walked him to the door and then practically shoved him out to the stoop. The minute the door shut behind her, she said, "I'm really sorry about my mother. I bet you don't even know what to think."

"I think that coming over here without notice was a bad idea. I'm sure your mother thinks I have no manners."

As far as Gabby was concerned, it was her mother who didn't have any manners. "I don't think my mom's upset with you."

No, her mother was definitely upset with *her*. The moment Gabby walked in the door, her mom was going to have a lot to say about her actions.

"Gabby, what is keeping you?"

Her mother's voice sounded harsh even through the door. "I'd better go in."

"Wait, Gabby."

"Yes?"

"Um, would you like to stop by my *haus* one day soon? Like maybe on Sunday afternoon around two o'clock?"

She couldn't believe that he wanted to see her again. "Are you sure?"

"Of course I'm sure. You could join us for a meal, or just come over for a spell." He smiled suddenly. "You could meet the goats."

Instead of telling him no, she blurted, "You have goats?"

He grinned. "Oh, *jah*. They're small, too. And black and white. And not mean. They'll follow you around like puppies if you have carrots."

"They sound so cute."

"They are. My sister Beth is right fond of them. Do you like goats?"

"I think I do, but I don't know. I've never gotten too close to one."

He grinned. "Well, it's time you did then. Come over to meet the goats."

It sounded so nice. And she could finally see the farm she'd been longing to visit for what seemed like forever. "Are you sure your parents won't mind?"

"Nah." He rocked back on his heels. "I'm one of five kids. We always have big gatherings. I promise, one more in the mix won't make a difference."

"Even if I'm English?"

"I have lots of English friends, Gabby. It will be fine." He paused. "So, will you?"

"Well, all right. I mean, I will. Thank you."

"Gut." He looked pleased. "Do you know where I live? It's the white house with the black metal roof up on the hill near—"

"I know which one it is," she interrupted.

"Okay. Two o'clock?"

"I'll be there."

"Thank you, Gabby. I promise, I'll be better." He stared at her for a long moment, then turned away and started walking.

She watched him for a moment, half afraid that the kids on the corner would give him a hard time, but beyond looking at him for a minute, they didn't say a thing.

She wondered why.

Walking inside, her mother was almost done putting away the groceries. "Want to tell me what is going on with you and that Amish boy?"

"Not especially. There's nothing to say."

"You two were alone in here. The lights weren't even on."

"Mom, I'm eighteen. Don't start acting like I'm about to get caught making out on the couch. And you know why we were inside. We can't hang out on the stoop."

"I suppose you're right." She nibbled her bottom lip.

"And as far as the lights go, I didn't think about it. Kyle's used to dark houses, you know?"

"No. I don't know about what the Amish are used to. But I'm interested in finding out how you know so much."

"I'll make dinner and tell you what I know."

Immediately her mother brightened. "You'll cook tonight? That sounds great. I was on my feet for eight hours today. I'll go shower."

Once her mother left the room, Gabby opened the refrigerator and cabinets and took stock, then decided to make plain old macaroni and cheese. It was easy, they had all the ingredients, and she'd be able to do some thinking while she put everything together.

She was going to need to figure out what to tell her mother about Kyle, and figure out why she'd told him that she'd go over to his house on Sunday when everything inside her was telling her to stay away.

The door opened again. "Gabby? Mom?"

"I'm in here, Lane," she called back, thinking that somehow, over the years, she had become the person whom her brother looked for first when he got home.

"What's going on?"

"Mom's in the shower and I'm getting ready to start cooking dinner."

Tossing his gym bag on the ground, he walked to the sink. "Awesome. What are we having?"

"Mac and cheese and hamburger patties. Sound okay?"

"Yeah. Sounds great," he said as he opened the refrigerator door and grabbed a pair of apples.

Watching him, Gabby wondered again when she and her mother had switched places. She was the one who made sure he got up, had clean laundry, and cooked dinner nine times out of ten.

She was the one who tried to help him with his homework, listened to him gripe about his teachers and his coach, and helped him make a sign when he'd asked Janice somebody to the homecoming dance his freshman year.

Their mom? Well, she'd been around, but not

completely. It had always been like she had one foot with them and the other foot with all the other places she'd rather be.

Feeling guilty, Gabby reminded herself that their mother worked hard and always had. She always paid their bills and even tried to give them a little extra spending money from time to time. That counted for a lot.

After Lane tossed two apple cores in the trash, he watched her form hamburger patties and place them on a plate. "Do you want some help?"

"I've got it. You might as well start your homework."

He shrugged. "Maybe later."

"Don't you have a government test tomorrow?"

"Yeah."

"Then pull out the study guide and we'll work on it together."

He grinned at her. "You never give up, Gabby. You never take a break."

"Sure I do." But even to her own ears, her protest sounded pretty weak. "I mean, I'm going to start taking more breaks soon," she added, thinking that was yet another reason why she'd said yes to Kyle.

Sure, she wanted to spend time with him. Why wouldn't she? He was really cute and really nice. And then there was his house and the goats. She wanted to see them. Absolutely.

But she also wanted, no needed, something for herself. Something that didn't have anything to do with their house, their neighbors, her mother's absence, or her brother's needs. She wanted to be just Gabby for a couple of hours.

Maybe on Sunday afternoon, when she drove up to that big, glistening farm, ate a meal that someone else cooked, and walked around inside a barn filled with black-and-white friendly goats, she could have a little vacation from her life.

If that happened?

Well, it would be amazing.

TEN

"Andy told me that the old farmer would never actually use that thing," Logan said. "Unfortunately, he was wrong."

Dear Katie,

I hope this letter finds you well. I've gotten settled in Caleb's house and have been trying to be as useful as I can. Vanessa has said she appreciates my help with the babies and the laundry. I'm hoping that is really the case and not just words. Sometimes I catch her looking at Caleb like they'd rather be alone.

Maybe he agrees? I don't know.

How goes your plans for the bed-and-breakfast? I received a letter from my friend Esther. She said you have hired Harley Lambright to work on the house. That ain't a surprise. You two always were close.

The letter continued, meandering about Kentucky, the heat, the babies, and her feelings of confusion about living with Caleb and Vanessa.

Katie had only been able to read it in sections. Otherwise, she felt herself get too muddled up. She wasn't sure what she was supposed to do with her mother's information.

Or how to respond.

Should she remind her mother that Caleb always had worked behind the scenes best? He wasn't a confrontational sort. Far from it! Even back when they were little, he'd be the one whispering the plans in June's ear and encouraging her to share them with their parents. Oh, but that used to drive June up the wall.

But yet, even though they'd never gotten along all that well, she'd still done what he'd asked.

Now Katie had a feeling that he was doing the same thing with Vanessa. Here it seemed that their mother was yet again playing along, like she didn't know who was the instigator.

For some reason that really bugged Katie. Wasn't it time for everyone to finally be honest with each other?

She supposed she wasn't one to judge. Here she was, doing the same thing she'd always done. Pretend to herself that nothing was all that different from how it used to be.

But so much was.

Especially the way she and Harley weren't getting along. Again.

This was her fault, however. While she'd been

talking with Kyle about his feelings for Gabby, Harley had dragged out more debris from her house. Then he'd called for his brother, and they'd left. All without a word to her.

She'd been stunned. Then hurt. Then angry. Then accepting. Because he'd been right to leave without another word to her. She'd blamed him for things that weren't his fault and then had pouted in the room they'd been working in, forcing him to work in another section of the house. Then she'd talked with Kyle for way too long. Even though she felt the conversation was important, Kyle was there to work, not converse with her.

Now she was staring at the day's mail and dwelling on too many ghosts and insecurities.

Once again she started feeling that same tight feeling in her chest. The one that used to make her fear she was having a heart attack. This house, all her plans, and all the work that had to be done was threatening to suffocate her. She needed a break from her life, if only for a little while.

Slipping on her favorite pair of tennis shoes, she grabbed her purse and started walking. Fifteen minutes later, she was standing outside her girlfriend Kendra Troyer's tiny apartment. Kendra had never been an official part of the Eight, but Katie had always been close to her. Kendra, like her, hadn't always had the easiest childhood. Though neither of them shared much, there was something about knowing that she wasn't the only one not to have wonderful memories that made everything seem easier.

Before she talked herself out of it, she knocked on the door. While she waited, a puppy stared at her through a narrow pane of glass situated on the side of the door's frame. It had matted white fur, lopsided ears, and a pair of wary eyes. It was barking at her so shrilly, Katie took a step back.

"*Nee*, Blue!" Kendra called out. "Hush, now. You mustn't bark so much."

When she opened the door, Kendra was leaning down and holding the dog's collar. "Hey, Katie. Come on in, she don't bite."

Hoping that was really the case, Katie hesitantly stepped in, one eye on the barking dog. "I didn't know you got a *hund*."

"She's new. I've had her only three days. Since then, all I've been doing is trying not to regret my decision."

Katie noticed that Kendra's voice was far sweeter than her words. She didn't regret a thing. "Where did you get her?" Noticing that the dog was now slowly wagging her tail, Katie knelt down and held out her hand for the dog to smell. When Blue sniffed her curiously then stepped closer, she breathed a sigh of relief.

"Where else? The pound. I was volunteering at the shelter when I was asked to clean her cage. She fell asleep in my lap. It was the sweetest thing. After that, I surely couldn't let her go. Of course, as soon as I got her home, she turned into a barking menace."

Blue chose that moment to look up at Kendra with a look of adoration. Katie chuckled. "Maybe not so menacing?"

Kendra smiled. "Maybe not." She let go of Blue's collar and ran a hand down her fur.

The dog wagged its tail once then trotted off.

"Maybe Blue just needs some time to adjust?" Katie mused. "Moving to someplace new is always stressful."

"I hope so." She pointed to the coffee table, where the dog had just crawled under and lain down. "If she doesn't settle down soon, I fear we are going to have a very long life together."

"Couldn't you just give her back?"

"Oh, no. I could never do that. She's mine now, you know?"

Katie smiled at her. "That's what I love about you, Kendra. You are so loyal."

"We're all loyal to each other, don't you think? I mean, why else would we have stayed friends for so long otherwise?"

"I suppose." Kendra's words made a lot of sense. But what didn't was how eight friends could have so much loyalty for each other, but her own family could remain so disjointed and full of secrets.

Kendra stared at her for a long moment, then

guided her to the back porch. "Let's go sit outside. I want to show you something."

Katie followed her out onto the tiny patio, which was really little more than a five-by-five-foot cement slab with two folding chairs on it. The moment she sat down, though, she realized that she hadn't been very fair. The small area was shaded and had some privacy, too. In addition, Kendra had some colorful clay pots in two of the corners and a black charcoal grill set up.

And since it was only Kendra living there, she probably didn't need anything else.

But though Katie would have usually loved nothing but relaxing in the cozy spot, at the moment, all it was doing was serving as a reminder of just how far she was from having her own dreams realized. She currently didn't have anything even remotely comfortable at her own home for herself, let alone for future guests staying at the bed-and-breakfast.

And that realization made her feel less relaxed and even more uncomfortable. "Kendra, what did you want to show me?"

"Oh." She slowly edged up the skirt of her dress over her right leg. First her calf was bared, then her knee, lastly, the bottom half of her thigh. "This," she said at last.

Curious, Katie leaned forward, then froze when she saw what Kendra was displaying. It was a scar. A bad one. The skin was raised and red, and its width was almost a quarter inch wide. And its length? At least two inches.

It had obviously happened some time ago. Years.

"Oh, Kendra. Are you all right?"

"I'm fine. I mean, this happened a very long time ago."

It was a reminder of just how bad Kendra's life had been with her father. Though, of course, Katie felt sorry for her past, she was confused why Kendra was picking this time to show the scar to her. Her friend had never been one to either talk about her past or to do something to induce sympathy.

Looking down at her thigh, Kendra ran a finger along the raised skin. "When I was seven, I got in very bad trouble and my father locked me in the shed out behind our house," she said quietly. "It was in the winter and so very cold."

Katie didn't want to hear about that. It was bad of her, but sometimes she didn't even like to think about how bad Kendra's life had been. It always made her feel sick inside. Kendra had grown up New Order Amish and away from all of them. How could God have given Katie the Eight while making a girl like Kendra feel so all alone?

Forcing herself to concentrate on Kendra and not her own feelings, she said gently, "You were seven, you said?"

"*Jah.*" Still looking at the scar, she said, "The

shed was dark, and there were tools and such in there. Nails, old traps, all sorts of things. I was scared."

"Of course you were."

"After the first hour, I tried to sit down, but there wasn't much room and I couldn't see much anyway. I was little, too. Not very strong." She frowned. "And so, I tried to push a rake out of the way. But while I was doing that, I tripped and fell and cut my leg here."

Tears were in her eyes now. "Oh, Kendra. That's awful. I'm so sorry."

Her girlfriend shrugged. "It hurt and it bled a lot. It finally stopped, of course, but because I'd been in that dirty shed, it got infected before I finally was allowed to leave."

Finally? "How long were you in there?"

"I think two days."

"You don't know?"

"It was dark and I was young." Frowning, she gazed at the scar again before sliding the fabric back down her leg. "I guess you are probably wondering why I decided to share this with you."

Yes. Yes, she was.

Looking at her intently, she said, "I've known you for years. We've been friends for a very long time."

Was Kendra thinking that she didn't realize that, or that she didn't appreciate her? "We're *gut* friends, Kendra. I've always been grateful for your friendship."

"I feel the same way." Her brown eyes warmed

before they flicked away. "But even though we've been such good friends and I love you like a sister, I've never wanted you to see this. I never wanted to talk about it."

"Of course not. I'm sure it was painful to recall."

"To be honest, that memory wasn't all that painful to recall. It's, well, it's pretty vivid in my head. Lots of things that happened back then are." She paused, then said, "Katie, I never told you because I was embarrassed."

"You were a little girl. You had nothing to be embarrassed about."

"You're right. No matter what I did, I didn't deserve to be locked in a garden shed in the middle of winter for two days. I didn't deserve a lot of the things that happened to me. But even though my mind knew this, my heart, and maybe my pride, too, didn't want all of the Eight to know."

"Why?"

"Because I didn't want all of you to think less of me. When Elizabeth Anne first introduced me to all of you, I knew your group was something special. Then, later, when she and Logan asked me to join y'all for one of your campfires, I was so excited, I knew I didn't want to do anything to make you all regret the invitation."

Katie was surprised and maybe even a little embarrassed that they'd made Kendra feel like she couldn't be herself. But she also understood the feeling. "So you kept much of your past a secret so you could keep joining us."

"I did." She shifted. "I guess I should ask you if you still want to be my friend. Now that you know."

Katie rubbed Kendra's arm. "Don't be silly. Nothing has changed between us. Of course I want to be your friend. Kendra, I'm sorry I didn't know you back then, but I know and love you now. I'm always here if you want to talk. There doesn't have to be a special time or place to share what is on your mind."

Kendra lifted her chin. "Marie told me about visiting your house."

"She did?"

"Um hum," Kendra replied, as if the fact that Marie gossiping about Katie wasn't a big deal. "Why did you think the state of your house would change how all of us felt about you?"

Katie was so taken aback and embarrassed, she lashed out. "Kendra, *that's* why you told me about your scar? In order to teach me a lesson?"

"I shared that to let you know that I might have a nasty scar on my leg, but I'm not the only one who has something to hide. Every one of us has something that we don't want the others to know about."

"I know that." Yes, Kendra had a point, but had she really thought that their two situations were the same?

But maybe they were.

"Think of Andy, Katie," Kendra said, her voice pleading. "He had something going on that upset him so much he didn't want to live. What it was, we'll never know. Maybe it was big. Or maybe it was little. Or, maybe it doesn't matter. He didn't feel he could share it."

"This isn't the same."

"I hope not. If it was the same, you'd be contemplating ending your life. All I'm trying to tell you, is that you've got to decide who and what you are going to be loyal to. Either to yourself and your pain and your past, or your friends and the future."

"You are making too much of this."

Kendra stood up. "No, you are making too little of all you have. You might have a past, Katie, but there is really so much more to you than that. All of us are so much more than just our pasts—or our families."

Everything Kendra had said had been hard to hear, and difficult to think about. But it was also time for Katie to stop worrying so much about her insecurities. "I'll try to be better."

Kendra smiled softly. "Katie, if nothing I said made sense, then maybe seeing Blue here helped. I mean, if Blue, looking like she does—all scraggly and unkempt—can expect to be loved in spite of her flaws and past, any of us can. Even you."

As Kendra sat back down, Katie chuckled. "Thanks, Kendra. I guess I really did need this talk after all."

Looking really pleased, Kendra leaned back in her chair. "I'm glad I could help."

ELEVEN

> Will held up his right leg. "*Jah*, he was wrong. I still have the scar from his buck-shot."

"*P*ass the carrots, Harley," Jimmy said from across the table. "If you please."

"Huh? Oh, here," Harley said as he picked up the stoneware serving dish that had been a fixture of their supper table since he'd been a small boy.

When he noticed that Jimmy took the dish with a look of annoyance and that the rest of the family was staring at him curiously, he asked, "Does someone want anything else?"

"Maybe you could share the mashed potatoes, too?" Beth asked with a bit of amusement in her tone.

As he did as she asked, he raised his eyebrows. "All of you are looking at me like I've done something wrong. What did I do?"

"Not much," Betty muttered under her breath.

"You haven't been doing anything at all," Jimmy

said much more loudly. "Well, besides staring off into nothing and hoard all the food."

With a start, Harley realized that he did, indeed, have quite a collection of serving dishes arranged in front of him. There was the platter of roast beef sitting right next to the bowl of gravy, a dish of broccoli salad, and a basket of fresh rolls. And that was after he'd given up the potatoes and carrots.

"Sorry. Do any of you need any more food?"

"I'll take the roast and gravy if you can spare it," Kyle said around a cheeky grin.

Betty pressed a napkin to her mouth, half-heartedly stifling a giggle.

Becoming more embarrassed by the second, Harley glanced at his parents. His mother was simply drinking water. Daed, on the other hand, looked like he was trying mighty hard to not yell at him. "I'm sorry, Daed. I don't know where my head is."

"Is that right?" One eyebrow arched. "Hmm. I would think that answer would be obvious."

Harley didn't know how to respond to his father's cryptic statement, so he kept his head down and ate another bite of broccoli salad.

"I don't blame you for thinking about Katie Steury so much," Beth said. "There's always been something brewing between the two of you."

Betty giggled again.

"I'm not thinking about Katie," Harley protested,

116   *Shelley Shepard Gray*

though it was a lie and everyone knew it. For the last several hours, he hadn't been able to do much without thinking about her.

"Of course you are," Jimmy said. "And who could blame ya? She's been holding on to quite a secret. I knew her mother kept to herself, but I didn't know she had so many problems. It's going to be a miracle if you two ever get that place clean."

Fury ignited inside him so quickly, it was only because their father was there that Harley was able to keep from yelling at his little brother. "Kyle, what have you been saying?"

"Only the truth," he protested. Lifting his chin, he added, "You *canna* deny that Katie's *haus* is a real mess and she's embarrassed about it."

"You have no right to talk about her. I told you to not gossip about her."

"I'm not. I only told Jimmy and Beth."

"And I overheard," Betty said. "So it's kind of like he told me, too."

This family! "Kyle, I *canna* believe you."

"Talking about Katie being sad and her mother having hoarding issues ain't gossiping," Jimmy said. "No one here is going to talk about her to anyone else. We're family."

Just as he was about to tell Jimmy exactly what he thought about that statement, Harley glanced at his father again.

Daed, as usual, was sitting silently, watching all of his grown children say too much. No doubt he was mentally preparing another lecture for Harley on the virtues of not bringing one's personal problems to their mother's supper table.

It would be no less than what he deserved, too. He knew he should have given Kyle more instructions— and maybe threatened him a bit, too. His brother might have listened better if he'd thought Harley would fire him if he didn't follow his directions.

"Daed—"

"No need to speak of this right now, son. Eat your supper." Then, to Harley's surprise, he murmured, "And perhaps you could pass the rolls now?"

Bold as brass, Beth grinned across the table at Jimmy.

Feeling his face burn, Harley passed the bread basket. Had any meal ever been this awkward? He doubted it. He couldn't wait for it to be over so he could retreat to the peace and quiet of his bedroom.

Just as he was about to ask Beth how her day at the *Englischer's* house was, they heard a knock at the kitchen door.

Almost as one, they all looked at the door.

"Hmm, I'm not expecting anyone. Are any of you?" Mamm asked as she stood up.

"*Nee*, Mamm," Kyle replied sweetly. "All of my friends know we eat right now."

Harley felt like throwing one of the four extra rolls at him.

The knock came again.

"Emma, you sit down. You've done enough for this meal. I'll get it," Daed said, already walking through the kitchen. He opened the door just as another knock sounded. And then, his whole posture and voice gentled. "Why, Katie Steury. Now, isn't this a mighty nice surprise? It's *gut* to see you." He stepped back. "Come in, come in."

"*Danke*, Mr. Lambright," Katie replied as she stepped into the kitchen. She looked like she was about to say something when her eyes darted to the filled table.

And yes, all of them were staring back at her.

Her blue eyes widened. "Ack! I'm so sorry. I didn't think about what time it was."

"Stuff and nonsense. Come in," he said. "Have you eaten supper?"

Beth turned her head to Harley and Jimmy. *Stuff and nonsense?* she mouthed.

Looking just as mystified, Jimmy shrugged.

His siblings had a point. Harley had never heard that phrase come out of their father's mouth. Ever.

"Harley, come help Katie get a plate," Mamm called out as she moved the rest of their spots around the table. "Betty and Kyle, fetch a chair and silverware for our guest."

Still standing awkwardly in front of all of them, Katie shook her head. "There's no need to go to so much trouble, Mrs. Lambright." She glanced at Harley in a silent plea for help.

Usually, he would have rushed to her side to help her, but he knew she rarely had meals like this anymore. A filling, hot supper would do her good.

His *mamm* brushed off Katie's weak protest. "I'm Emma, and don't be silly. This isn't any trouble at all. Please do join us. We have more than enough for one more person."

"All right then. *Danke*."

Harley walked over to Katie as his siblings went to do their mother's bidding.

Katie had changed her dress. Now she had a dark yellow dress on, the color of the first marigolds of the season. Over it was a light black cardigan. She looked like a tiny bumblebee, or would have if she weren't so slim.

Or wasn't so pretty.

"Let me take your sweater, Katie."

She was holding the edges of the knit like it was a suit of armor. "That's kind of you, but I'll keep it on. It got a little chilly when the sun went down."

"Did you walk here, child?" Daed asked.

"*Jah*."

"That's a long way." Hardening his voice, he turned to Harley. "You'll need to take her home in the buggy."

"Of course."

Katie's expression turned even more pained. "There's no need for that. I know you must be so tired."

"It's no trouble. Now come eat. We have plenty."

"We sure do," Kyle said with a bright smile. "Thanks to Harley trying to keep all the food to himself."

Usually Harley would have "accidentally" knocked into his side, just to get him to shut up, but now he was glad for Kyle's exuberance. His brother's teasing had made Katie relax, and for that he was grateful.

Five minutes later, Katie was sitting to his father's right and was looking at the amount of food in front of her like she'd never seen the like.

"Is this a special occasion?"

"You being here?" Jimmy teased with a bright smile. "For sure it is."

Beth coughed, obviously trying hard not to laugh.

Katie was still eyeing her plate in wonder. "*Nee.* I mean, all this food. Is it a special day?"

"It's a Tuesday," Betty said. "That's the only thing special about it."

"Not that our Tuesdays have ever been very special," Beth said.

"Until now," Kyle whispered with a wink at his sisters.

Their mother looked at each of them like she

wasn't sure where they'd come from. "Don't mind them, Katie. William and I have tried our best, but they can still be incorrigible. They have no company manners."

"*Nee*, it's my fault. I think my company manners are lacking as well. I shouldn't have asked such a thing. I don't know why I did."

"Don't worry about manners none. Yours are fine. And to answer your question, *jah*, we are blessed with a large family, so Emma makes large meals." Glancing at the lot of them, Daed's voice deepened. "It's good of you to remind us of this bounty. Now, start eating, child, don't be shy."

After quietly praying, Katie dutifully popped a slice of carrot in her mouth.

While she chewed and speared another carrot, Kyle said, "Katie, as a matter of fact, you came at a perfect time."

"Oh?"

"*Jah*. We were all just sitting here teasing Harley."

She glanced Harley's way. "About what?"

"Nothing out of the ordinary," Harley said quickly.

Jimmy leaned back and stretched his arms out in front of him. "Actually, we were quizzing him about the Eight."

Katie immediately relaxed. "What about the Eight?"

"Nothing special. We just like hearing the stories," Beth added quickly.

Katie smiled at Harley. "There are plenty of stories, for sure."

Harley cast Jimmy a grateful look. The Eight was as good a topic as any to use as a distraction, and it was a topic Katie could easily contribute to, as well. "We've known each other for a long time, for sure," he said.

She smiled at him. "You all have been blessed with a big family. I've been blessed with a good group of friends. The Eight have helped me through a great many things over the years."

"What about Harley, then?" Betty asked.

"Harley? Oh, he has more blessings than he's known what to do with," Katie said. "It's always been that way."

Harley kept his mouth shut because he realized, seeing his life through her eyes, Katie was right.

TWELVE

"Well, the noise convinced the goats to run in the other direction. That was a blessing. Having all of Mr. Schlabach's attention on us was definitely not."

"*I* feel bad that your father is making you drive me home," Katie told Harley as he guided his horse out of the barn.

"Don't be. If he hadn't suggested it, I would've done it anyway. It's dark out and not safe for a girl to be out walking alone. Anything can happen, you know."

He was right. The back roads where they lived were windy, full of hills, and barren of streetlights. Then, of course, there was always the worry of being a woman walking alone. Walnut Creek was a safe place, but bad things could happen anywhere. Her parents had always reminded her that it was better to be safe than sorry. Not that she always heeded their advice.

"Well, I appreciate the ride. And supper." Thinking of how they'd all sat there chatting and teasing each other while she ate, she said, "Harley, I didn't come over for a free meal."

After giving his horse a reassuring pat, he walked to Katie's side and lifted her into the courting buggy. "Don't worry so much. It was nothing."

She was tingling from his assistance. She couldn't remember another time when he'd lifted her into a buggy. Had he ever and she'd simply forgotten that?

No. She wouldn't have forgotten.

Studying him while he walked to the other side and got settled next to her, she took another look at him.

And suddenly, it was almost as if she were sitting next to a stranger. Even though the air had turned chilly, his sleeves were still rolled up. She noticed the muscles of his forearms. When he scooted closer to her, she noticed how tall he was. The way his body had filled out. The way his brown hair curled around his collar.

The way he spoke softly to his horse and guided her carefully down the drive and at last onto the street.

He glanced at her. "You sure are quiet."

"I know. I bet you hardly know what to do about my sudden silence."

"It's a little disconcerting, that's a fact." Clicking the reins softly, he motioned the horse into a gentle canter. The mare seemed pleased, and the buggy charged forward.

She laughed at the horse's exuberance. "She's a *gut* buggy horse. Young."

"Her name's Peanut, and *jah*. She's a good one." He kept his eyes on the road and the horse.

"To be honest, I didn't even know you had a courting buggy." As Peanut clip-clopped along, Katie felt the light breeze on her face. The first batch of wildflowers was growing alongside the road and the air smelled faintly of horse and freshly plowed dirt. She couldn't resist smiling. Somehow, traveling in the little open-air buggy made everything just seem better.

"I haven't used this buggy much over the last couple of years. Jimmy takes it out when he calls on Sarah."

She'd seen Jimmy and Sarah together many times. "They are a cute couple."

He chuckled. "I reckon Jimmy never thought about them as being 'cute,' but I daresay you are right. They do go well together. Like peas and carrots."

Fingering the black leather of the bench seat, she smiled at him. "And what about Kyle?"

"Kyle? What about him?"

"Come now, Harley. He's eighteen and mighty handsome. Surely he is courting some lucky girl."

"Boy, I don't know." A line formed in the middle

of his forehead. "Come to think of it, he never acts too eager to sit with any of the girls after church dinner or go to any of the Sunday night singings. I guess that is something of a surprise. He's always been fairly social."

"Why do you think that is?" Even though she and Harley had always been best friends with the rest of the Eight, the two of them had still attended the singings, which was actually just a reason to spend time with other Amish teenagers in the area.

"I'm not sure. But sometimes I have to think that Kyle has as many secrets as the rest of us."

"I'm surprised. He seems so open."

Harley grinned, his white teeth fairly gleaming in the waning sunlight. "He is open and often says what's on his mind. One could say that he was even the opposite of me. Ain't so?"

"I'm not going to answer that."

"Well, actually . . . I'm fairly sure that my little brother is interested in an English girl."

She was tempted to tell him that she already knew but didn't want to betray Kyle. "What do you think about that?"

"I don't rightly know. Part of me isn't all that shocked."

"And the other part?"

He looked even more uncomfortable. "I guess I'd have to say I wish he wouldn't be."

"Really?" The moment she blurted that, she wished she could take it back. "I'm sorry. This isn't any of my business. I shouldn't have said anything."

"You can say whatever you want, Katie." He glanced at her. "Especially since we both know that you hit the nail on the head. Though I know a lot of Amish parents are of the mind that getting baptized is a grown man and woman's choice, mine haven't really adopted that mind-set. Courting an *Englischer* isn't going to go over well." Looking like he was worried about that, he frowned. "Not at all."

"What are you going to do?"

"Me?" He looked surprised about the question. "Ah, nothing. It don't concern me, right?"

"You're not going to warn Kyle that he could upset your parents?"

He chuckled. "Kyle don't need to be warned, Katie. He's been living in the same house as I have for eighteen years."

"But you're older and he looks up to you."

"I'm also just his brother and he hasn't even confided in me. I think it's best that things pan out the way they are supposed to. Kyle knows what he's going to be coming up against, and what the consequences will be. Either he is going to put our parents' wishes first . . . or this mystery girl."

"If he chooses her, what are you going to do?" She held her breath, for some reason needing him to reassure her that he was still the man she thought he was.

After a couple of seconds passed, Harley shrugged. "Love him, I guess."

Pleased, she released a sigh.

He didn't look at her and she didn't turn her head, either. But that was okay, because answers like these were what made her heart feel so full. This was why Harley Lambright was so special. He was closed off and solemn, but he was also as loyal as the day was long. "Kyle thinks the world of you, Harley." She did, too, she realized. Even when they argued or didn't exactly see eye to eye, she thought he was special.

His voice was soft when he replied. "You think so?"

"I know so."

He glanced her way again, just as they approached her house. "How do you know? I mean, how can you be sure?"

"I can just tell. He wants to be like you."

"I don't know about that. My siblings enjoy reminding me that I am a lot like our father." He frowned. "That ain't a compliment."

"Maybe, maybe not. I happen to see a lot of similarities."

"I know. I'm trying to be better . . ."

He sounded really frustrated with himself, which was such a surprise. "Don't sound so upset. Your father is a *gut* man, Harley. He's stalwart and sure.

And he's always treated me with kindness. Especially tonight."

"To be sure, he was mighty kind to you tonight, Katie."

She chuckled. "I even saw Jimmy and Beth exchange confused glances."

"If they did, it wasn't because of anything you did." He hesitated, then said, "It's just that our father has never been one to coddle us much. Not even our Betty, and she's his favorite."

"Maybe your father thought I needed a free meal," she said dryly. After all, she was too skinny.

"*Nee*, that ain't it. I think . . ." He paused, seemed to consider his words. "I think he must know that you are a nice woman and could use some kindness. I wouldn't disagree. You are due, for sure and for certain."

While Katie dwelled on Harley's surprising statement, he guided Peanut up her drive and set the brake on the buggy. "Stay there and I'll come around and help you down."

Maybe another time she would have reminded him that she was perfectly capable of climbing out of a buggy. But this time, she did as he asked and then even pressed her palms to his shoulders when he leaned close and gripped her by the waist.

Next thing she knew, she was getting swung out and carefully placed on the ground.

Still leaning close, he met her gaze. "You good?"

Her mouth felt like cotton. "*Jah. Danke.*"

He straightened but still seemed intent on studying her face. "I'm glad you came over tonight," he murmured as Peanut pawed the ground beside them and the crickets in the yard chirped in protest. "It . . . it was a nice surprise."

It had been nice. But not a surprise. Feeling foolish, she blurted, "I actually came by because, Harley, I wanted to apologize to you. I realize now that you hadn't invited anyone over, and even if you had, it shouldn't have mattered. I need the help and I need to stop being ashamed of my mother's sickness."

"What do you want to do now?"

"I want to accept everyone's help. I mean, if they still want to offer it."

He nodded. "I'll pass the word on, then. Now, I had better walk you inside."

She followed him to the door, then pulled her keys out and placed them in his awaiting palm. When he opened the door, she was besieged by the same musty scents and overwhelming clutter. "I can't wait until this feels the way I need it to."

"I know." He frowned. "It's mighty dark in there. Where are your flashlights?"

"I keep one in the kitchen drawer."

"Care to take my hand?"

Would she care? Swept away by his phrasing, she

slipped hers in his and let him guide her inside and through the maze of debris, which she knew far better than he did. When they got to the kitchen, she opened the first drawer and pulled out two flashlights. Luckily both turned on easily and offered bright beams of light.

She handed him one. "This is better now."

"*Jah*." Still looking worried about leaving her, he said, "Would you like me to walk through the *haus* and make sure everything is quiet?"

"There's no need. I'm used to being here alone. I'll walk you out."

Now guided by twin beams and missing his hand, she walked back through the maze.

At the door, he turned back to her. "I'll be here in the morning with Kyle."

"All right, Harley. *Danke* for taking me home. Be careful on your way back."

"Me and Peanut will be fine. We always are."

Just as she was about to step back and bid him good night, he leaned toward her and brushed his lips on her cheek. "Sleep well, Katie Steury. Tomorrow will be a better day."

She watched him turn away before closing the door.

Then took a moment to give a little prayer of thanks. Today had actually been pretty good.

Maybe even better than that.

THIRTEEN

"As you might imagine, he wanted to know exactly what we were doing in his field," Harley said. "Since we had no good answer, I figured it would be best to say nothing. So did everyone else. Well, everyone except for one of us."

"*I* invited the English girl I've been seeing over to the *haus* on Sunday afternoon," Kyle said after they'd walked about half of the way to Katie's house a couple days later.

Glad that he had a to-go cup of coffee in his hand, Harley took a fortifying sip. As he swallowed, he reminded himself of Katie's comment the other evening. Kyle looked up to him. He needed to tread carefully. "Oh? I'm sorry, I don't recall her name. Who is she?"

Kyle drummed his fingers against his leg for a few feet. Then he blurted, "Her name is Gabby."

It looked like he'd been right. There was a reason

Kyle hadn't been too interested in Sunday singings. "And you've been seeing her in secret."

Looking a little green, Kyle bobbed his head. "*Jah.*"

It was worse than he had imagined. "And now you plan to simply invite her over to the house?" Their parents were going to freak out—one of Andy's favorite expressions—and that was only a minor exaggeration.

"You know why I didn't tell Mamm and Daed earlier."

Harley sighed. What to do? He had no real experience in love and romance. "I know, but . . ."

"But I really like her, Harley," Kyle said immediately. "Plus, she is so alone. I also think Gabby needs us."

This was a whole new revelation, and maybe it put a new spin on things, as well? His parents might be rigid and strict, but they'd always had a soft spot for someone in trouble or in need of a helping hand. "Why is she so alone?"

"Because she just is."

The boy sounded impatient. Thinking things through, Harley realized that he needed to stop asking questions and let his little brother say what he needed to. "Okay . . ."

"Then, there's the fact that I don't want Gabby to ever think that I would be ashamed to be seen with her."

Harley studied Kyle as they continued to walk.

He was walking purposefully, looking straight ahead, and his jaw was set in a firm line. Kyle was not hoping to gain his approval.

And though he was a little surprised by that, it also, for some reason, made him feel a little better. He didn't know what the right advice was to give and he didn't want to make a mistake.

He also wasn't sure what Kyle was expecting him to say.

After they'd taken a few more steps, passing an old sign directing the way to Berlin, Harley decided it was finally time to speak about the inevitable. "When are you planning to tell Mamm and Daed about this big event?"

"Tonight. After supper."

"So soon? Are you sure that you want to have Gabby on everyone's minds for so long?" Even though his brother had already made his decision, he couldn't resist offering some unsolicited advice. "You know how it goes, everyone is going to have something to say about it—and you really won't have a choice about listening."

"I don't see how it's going to matter one way or the other. They aren't going to be happy with me." He grunted. "But I figure at least this way they might have settled down enough by Sunday to not yell at Gabby."

"No matter how unhappy they might be, no one's

going to yell at her." No, his parents were far more likely to stare at her silently.

Which might be almost just as bad.

As if Kyle was thinking the same thing, he said, "Harley, I need you to be there. Could you be in the house on Sunday when Gabby gets there?"

He'd already planned on it. Someone had to be the buffer between Kyle and their parents. But he'd been planning to just happen to be there so Kyle wouldn't feel like he was on display.

"Why do you want me? I'm sure Jimmy or Beth will be around." In some ways, he was closer to them as well.

"You know why. Because you have lots of English friends. Because of the Eight. You'll know what to say to Gabby and make her feel okay." He waved a hand. "I keep telling her that all of us have English friends, but she's going to be nervous."

Kyle's words were sweet and unexpected. But they also amused him a little. Here, hidden in all of Kyle's self-assurances, was a good amount of plain and simple puppy love. His brother wanted Gabby to like him as much as he liked her.

"You know, if she agreed to come over, it was because she wants to be near you. She's not going to care about anything I have to say."

Kyle darted a glance his way. "But still . . . it might be easier on her. So, would you?"

"Of course. If you want me there, I will be."

Kyle exhaled an almost comical sigh of relief. "*Danke*."

"You're welcome, Kyle."

"I feel better already."

"Um, if you are so worried about having Gabby over, why did you invite her in the first place? There's got to be other places you two could have met."

"I stopped by her place the other day. She lives with her mother and brother." He frowned. "It's not in a safe place. And any other place we meet is going to be kind of awkward because we won't have any privacy. I mean, it's not like I could drive up on her street in a courting buggy."

A courting buggy? Boy, things between Kyle and this girl had really progressed, especially if he was looking for privacy. "Tell me about her."

"I already told you that she's English."

"That tells me nothing, since the majority of the population is English. How about something else?" he coaxed.

"Well . . ."

"Come now. Just talk. I'm interested, not giving you a quiz. Kyle, what do you like about her?"

"I like that she's honest."

Honest? That was the special thing about Gabby that Kyle wanted to tell him about? "Honesty's *gut*." He smiled encouragingly. "What else?"

"And, though this might make me sound bad, I like that she needs me. No one else really does, you know?"

"I'm not sure why you'd think that. You're a pretty important part of our household."

Kyle scoffed. "I'm the youngest boy and I also happen to have the biggest mouth. Neither of those are points in my favor, you know? All my life, I've felt like you and Jimmy wished I was more mature."

"We all have our own loads to bear, Kyle." Of course, the moment he said the words, Harley wished he could take them back. He'd sounded sanctimonious.

Kyle fisted his hands. "I hear what you're saying, Harley. And I have a pretty good idea about your burdens in the household. I know it ain't been easy, being the oldest son."

It was on the tip of Harley's tongue to tell his brother that he didn't know the half of it. That he and Jimmy had been working in the fields before school by the time they were ten. He'd certainly never had much free time, not with four younger siblings underfoot. But he forced himself to take a deep breath and remember that this conversation wasn't about him, it was about Kyle.

"It wasn't," he said slowly. "But that doesn't matter. Each of us has had to carry our own burdens."

"My workload has never been as heavy as yours,

Harley. But even though that's the case, I can promise you that the expectations for me have been just as high."

"I'm sure that is true." And, to his shame, he didn't know if he and Jimmy or even Beth had tried to think of things from Kyle's or Betty's perspective. Their parents were fond of using him as his siblings' good example. Harley had always resented it, feeling like he'd been put on an awkward pedestal instead of standing on even ground with his brothers and sisters.

But it seemed it had been just as difficult for Kyle to be forced to look up at him.

Kyle waved a hand. "As much as I enjoy talking about my place in the Lambright household, we aren't talking about me, remember?"

"I remember. And, just to let you know, I'm still waiting to hear about Gabby."

"She has dark brown hair. Almost black. Dark brown eyes, too." Kyle paused. "She has kind of olive skin, too. I guess her mother's side is Italian."

"She sounds pretty."

"Oh, she is. She's really pretty." His voice lowered. "You should see her smile. It sounds corny, but it can light up a room."

That description sounded sweet to him. "What does she do?"

"She's a senior in high school."

So, she was Kyle's age. That was good news. "She's going to graduate soon."

Kyle nodded. "*Jah.*"

"And then, what are her plans? College?"

"I don't know."

"Really? Most graduating seniors are full of plans. Marie, Elizabeth Anne, and Andy sure were."

Looking troubled, Kyle said, "I think she's still deciding what she wants to do."

"Have you talked to her about your plans? Maybe she's waiting for you to share, too."

Looking embarrassed, he shook his head. "*Nee.*"

"I'm thinking there's a reason you haven't done that, Kyle." He took a breath and then said, "What are her interests?"

"She likes to help her mother around the house and take care of her brother, Lane, though I guess he doesn't need all that much help because he's sixteen." Barely taking a breath, he continued. "Gabby also babysits a lot. And she loves to do crossword puzzles."

Harley smiled to himself. As *Englisch* teenaged girls went, this Gabby sounded fairly meek and mild. That would be in her favor when their parents met her.

That is, if they would give her a chance.

Seeing Katie's house looming ahead, he clapped Kyle on the shoulder. "I'm glad we talked."

Kyle looked panicked. "That's it?"

"We talked a lot, don't you think?"

"But we didn't decide anything!" he retorted.

"And, you didn't even tell me what I should say to Mamm and Daed so they don't start lecturing me."

"If you can tell me about Gabby, you can tell our parents about her, too."

"Do you really think it's that easy?" Blatant skepticism colored every word.

No, he did not. But he was also starting to realize that he shouldn't try to manage his siblings. He wasn't good at it, and he didn't want to be their substitute father, only their older brother. If he tried, he was fairly certain he could be good at that. "I'm not sure how your talk with them is going to go. I'll hope and pray it goes well."

Kyle's expression fell. "So, you think it's going to go as badly as I fear."

"I didn't say that. Lately, they've surprised me. Maybe they'll surprise you, too." He wanted to stop right then, but something inside him kept encouraging him to speak. "Just, well, do some thinking and prepare yourself, all right?"

"About what?"

"I'm not saying this is going to happen . . . but prepare yourself for how you are going to handle things if Mamm and Daed try to talk you out of seeing her again."

When Kyle turned away, looking even more uncomfortable and crestfallen, Harley placed his hand on Kyle's shoulder. "Hey, what I'm trying to say is if you aren't prepared to pick this girl over Mamm and Daed, then don't bring her by before you know you are. If they convince you to never see her again, she'll wonder what happened. You'll hurt Gabby's feelings."

"You're speaking to me like I have a choice."

Harley knew what Kyle really meant. He was talking to his brother like he was an adult and making adult decisions about a woman he really liked, and might even grow to love. "*Jah,* I am."

Kyle stared at him hard, then shook his head, as if he was trying to come to terms with the fact that things were changing between the two of them, too. "*Danke.*"

"No reason to thank me. You . . . you grew up some time ago, Kyle. I just hadn't wanted to recognize that. I do now."

As they approached Katie's house, with the Dumpster in the front yard and so many secrets fairly bursting out of its seams, Harley realized he needed to take some of his own advice.

Katie was a part of his life. In her own way, she needed him as much as Gabby needed Kyle.

He already knew that he would never put his parents' wishes over her needs. But what he wasn't sure about was why he felt that way.

Was it simply because she was one of the Eight and he was loyal to their friendship?

Or was it more that he was loyal to her?

"Hey . . . hey, Harley?"

"Mmm?"

"Do you really think I'm ready for this?"

Harley stopped and looked directly at his brother, noticing that Kyle was almost as tall as he was, maybe weighed only twenty pounds less.

But no longer did Harley see a boy who had inches and pounds to go until he was a grown man. Instead, he simply saw Kyle. He was outgoing. Smiled easily, never met a stranger he didn't like. He had a way with people, an ease that Harley never would. He was scrappy, more impulsive, and cared deeply about people who mattered to him.

In short, he'd turned into a very fine man—a man their father would be proud to call his son.

"*Jah*," he said finally. "I think you are ready for anything, Kyle. Of that, I have no doubt."

FOURTEEN

"Who talked?" Tricia called out.

"Oh, Tricia. Do you really not have an idea?" Logan asked. "Who among us can never seem to keep her mouth shut?"

*F*our hours after he and Kyle had arrived, greeted Katie, put on work gloves, and got to work, Harley heard something that made him go completely still.

It was Katie, and she was laughing.

About an hour after he and Kyle had arrived, E.A., Marie, and Kendra had shown up. By their sides were Will and Logan, and all of them were wearing work clothes and carrying gloves. They'd also brought with them continual rounds of joking and steady chatter.

Eager for the help, Kyle had been thrilled to see them. Harley had felt that way, too, but he had been far more tentative, more worried about Katie's reaction than looking forward to their help.

As he'd feared, when Katie had first greeted

them, she'd smiled and been polite, but there had been a look of resignation in her eyes, as well. Harley had almost feared that she'd break in half, her nerves seemed so brittle and on edge.

But the others didn't allow her to be self-conscious even for a minute. The girls had pulled her into a storage room next to the kitchen and started sorting piles, like they'd done it a million times before.

Harley had taken the men up to June's old room. With Kyle supervising, the four of them had continued to empty and clean the room. Now it was almost empty, and the girls' laughter was floating through the house.

Unable to help himself, he stepped into the upstairs hallway and just listened. And after a low murmur from Kendra, he was rewarded. Katie burst into gales of laughter.

Just like she used to.

Shaking his head, he grinned. Katie Steury laughed like she spoke her mind—with force. No, her laughter was surely no delicate giggle or feminine snicker. Instead, it was loud, infectious, and completely without restraint. At the moment, he fancied he'd never heard anything so sweet.

After listening for another few seconds, he walked back into June's old room. Kyle looked up at him from his spot on the floor.

"The girls were good medicine. Ain't so?"

"*Jah*. Good friends—and all of our progress."

"It sure looks much different from when we started."

"Like night and day," Harley agreed. Maybe throwing out all the unwanted debris had also helped Katie to unburden herself as well. He felt that they were over the worst of the cleanup now.

Once Logan and Kyle returned to the room after lugging an old bureau downstairs, Will spoke. "How about we all take a break and go out to eat?"

Harley looked down at himself. He was sweaty, covered with a fine layer of dust and maybe even a spiderweb or two. "Lunch sounds *gut*, but I'm not fit for a restaurant."

"You sure ain't. None of us are," Will said with a grin. "But we could wash up a little, grab some sandwiches, and have ourselves a picnic with the girls."

"That sounds perfect," Logan said. "We could run into Walnut Creek Cheese and have them make a mess of sandwiches to go and a bag of chips."

"And a couple of cookies, while we're at it," Will said. "I'm starving."

Kyle's eyes were bright with anticipation. "What do you think, Harley?"

Harley drew in a breath, about to remind him that this was a workday in the middle of the week, not a Saturday afternoon, and that this was his job, not just a project to help Katie.

But then he remembered how Kyle was depending on him to be someone different from their father. And how Katie might have given him a job, but she was more important to him than any paycheck. He reckoned she could use a break as much as they could.

Plus, these were his friends, no, his best friends. They'd taken time off work to help both her and him. Was he really going to say he didn't want to spend the time to have lunch with them? "That sounds great," he replied at last, liking how the words felt on his tongue. "Let's go see if the girls are good with this plan, too."

When he checked in on Katie, he found her sitting on the floor, giggling at something E.A. had said. A few wisps of her blond hair had escaped from her *kapp* and had curled around her forehead and temples. Her eyes were sparkling, and her cheeks were pink. She was such a pretty sight, he couldn't help but simply stand and gaze at her.

All too soon, Marie noticed he was lurking in the doorway. "Ah, did you need something, Harley?"

He spoke before thinking. "*Nee.*"

"No?" She raised her eyebrows. "You just came down here to stare at Katie?"

Katie looked in his direction, then looked down at her folded hands.

He was almost sure she was blushing.

"Harley?" E.A. prodded.

"Um, what I really meant is that I only came downstairs to see if you girls wanted to take a break and go get some lunch." When he saw the same expressions on their faces that he'd at first been wearing, he rushed to explain. "Not eat in a restaurant. Will suggested we get sandwiches and stuff from Walnut Creek Cheese and have a picnic."

Katie raised her eyebrows. "*You* want to stop to have a picnic?"

"I know. This ain't like my usual way, but it sure sounds like a good idea. Ain't so?"

"I think it really does," Marie said.

"It might even be the best idea of the day," E.A. murmured as she got to her feet. "Give us ten minutes, Harley. We'll wash up and be ready soon."

He noticed Katie got up slower. Still watching her intently, he couldn't help but frown. Was she okay?

Or, maybe Katie hadn't wanted to leave after all?

Worry and a burst of surprise flitted through him as he realized he was now wanting to make her life easier. As if her problems were now his.

"Ah, Harley?" Katie asked.

"*Jah?*" He gazed at her expectantly. Glad to be of some help. "Did you need something?"

While the other girls grinned at each other, her eyes lit up. "*Jah.* I need you to move."

"Move?"

She nodded, as if he'd turned simple. "You're blocking the door, you see."

"I am?" That's when he realized that she wasn't wrong. He was standing in the middle of the doorway like a stuck pig, except it hadn't been his body that had been stuck there, it had been his attention.

He was never going to live this down. "Sorry."

Feeling like his face was bright red, he turned away and hurried back upstairs before he did anything else stupid.

The girls' laughter drifted up behind him. He knew he should be mighty embarrassed, but recognizing Katie's happiness in the midst of it, he couldn't honestly say he regretted his foolishness after all.

He was coming to realize that he'd do most anything for Katie Steury. Almost anything at all.

FIFTEEN

"Fine. It was me," Katie said with a sigh. "And for the record, I realize I should've known better."

"Oh my stars, Katie!" E.A. whispered in a voice that really could have been a whole lot quieter, "Harley really likes you."

Katie turned off the bathroom faucet and grabbed hold of the pink towel on the rack. "Elizabeth Anne, you know that isn't true. I mean, we're all friends."

"No, you know I'm right," E.A. countered. "I've known Harley since I was seven years old and I've never seen him act like this. Something new has happened between the two of you."

"She has a point, Katie," Marie said as she took her turn washing her hands. "Harley was standing there staring at you like he'd never seen you before."

She'd noticed that as well. But did she want to admit it? Um, not really. "He was looking at all of us."

Marie flipped her ponytail over one shoulder.

"No, he wasn't. And before you start arguing, listen. First of all, John and I are together, so he wouldn't be looking at me even if he wasn't looking at you."

"Which he was," E.A. said, sounding triumphant.

"Stop," Katie said as forcefully as she dared. "The men are going to hear you."

But E.A. only shrugged, like that concern wasn't important. And Marie? Well, Marie just kept talking like she was a lawyer proving her case.

"Secondly, he was staring at you like you were the most fascinating thing he's ever seen. You couldn't have missed that, so stop pretending otherwise. What has been going on between the two of you?"

"Nothing." Fearing she was going to say something that she might later regret, she rubbed some lotion on her hands and walked toward the door. "Come on, let's go. The men are waiting."

"Oh, they can wait another minute or two," E.A. said. "Look, you don't have to tell us everything."

"That's right," Kendra said with a nod. "Just the important things."

"What happened in this house that made everything between you two change?" Marie finished up.

It was becoming obvious that she was no match against three curious women. She also didn't want to lie . . . and maybe sharing a bit would help her get a handle on things? "We started talking more, I think."

"You two weren't talking before?"

"Not like this. I mean, first there was the whole Melody thing. Once I told Harley I was sorry that I talked bad about her and he admitted that they would've broken up anyway, we started talking about things that mattered."

E.A. wrinkled her nose. "That's all that took?"

"The Melody issue was a pretty big obstacle, Elizabeth," Katie said.

"So, you two just needed to iron things out," Kendra murmured.

Katie shrugged. Honestly, she didn't know what had happened. Only that one day she wanted to avoid him . . . and on the next she couldn't wait to see him again.

Marie smiled. "I get it now. Thanks, Katie."

"Um, I don't," E.A. blurted. "What is there to get?"

"I'll tell you later. Let's go meet the boys," Marie said softly as Will called up to them.

"Fine," E.A. said in a huff.

Marie linked her arm through Katie's as they followed E.A. and Kendra down the stairs. "You okay?"

"I'm just not used to being the focus of speculation."

"We all love both you and Harley. You can't fault us for being curious, Katie. We're loyal but we're also human."

"Point taken." After all, she'd kind of done the same thing to Marie when she and John B. were first dating.

When they got downstairs at last, Will was staring up at them with a scowl on his face. "It took you ladies long enough."

"We had to wash our hands," Marie retorted. "I hope you washed yours, too."

"We did. Let's go, *jah?*"

Logan waved a hand. "Lead on, ladies. We'll follow right behind."

"Oh, brother."

As they started walking down her driveway, Katie caught Kyle's eye and smiled. He smiled back before walking to his brother's side.

Fifteen minutes later, they were all in Walnut Creek Cheese Shop and started ordering sandwiches, chips, and the last cups of iced tea and lemonade.

Right when they were headed out, the door opened again. A pretty brunette English girl with chocolate-colored eyes entered. She had on short blue jean shorts and a snug-fitting striped T-shirt. She smiled at all of them, then stilled. "Oh my goodness. Kyle?"

Kyle turned and gaped at her. After visibly collecting himself, he walked over to her. "Hey, Gabby."

Looking over at Harley, Katie raised her eyebrows. She'd been thinking that his interest in an *Englischer* girl was probably just a passing phase, but both the woman's looks and Kyle's reaction told a different story.

He was hooked. Line and sinker. And she was fairly sure his parents were going to have plenty to say about that.

SIXTEEN

Pretending to be aggrieved, Harley closed
his eyes and shook his head. "Katie Steury,
just as bold as you please, chirped, 'We
were going to go swimming in your lake.'"

$\mathscr{B}$oth she and Kyle Lambright were in the middle
of Walnut Creek Cheese Shop at the same time, and
Gabby Ferrara had never felt so awkward in her life.
That was saying a lot, given the way things had gone
for most of her life.

She'd just stepped out for a minute after turning
in her application and being told that the manager
could go ahead and interview her if she didn't mind
waiting. She hadn't minded waiting. Not one bit. If
the interview went well, she could start really making
some money, which meant that she could finally start
having some choices in her life. She really needed to
start having some choices.

But now her decision to apply for a job at the
famous establishment felt pretty dumb. Lots of Amish

shopped here, which meant she would see Kyle pretty often.

Which was going to be pretty hard, since she liked him a lot while he was probably thinking that she was just a reason to let off a little steam before he was baptized and found a suitable Amish girl.

Standing there, with all of Kyle's friends looking at her like she was an unusual sight at the zoo, Gabby didn't know where to look. She felt her skin flush and her palms get a little damp—both telltale signs of just how awkward she was finding the situation. This was the first time that her world and Kyle's had intersected.

Why had she even called out his name, anyway? He was with a bunch of his friends. He probably would've never looked twice at her if she hadn't called attention to herself.

Maybe Kyle knew that, because he solved the problem right away.

"It's sure a surprise to see ya here," Kyle said with a soft smile.

"I thought the same thing about you."

He held up a paper sack. "We've been working at a house today and decided to take a dinner break. What about you?"

"Me?" A sudden thought occurred to her. She glanced at the phone in her hand. "You eat dinner at eleven in the morning?"

"I mean lunch. We're breaking for lunch." Smiling in that cute way of his, he lowered his voice. "My family calls lunch 'dinner' and dinner 'supper.'"

"It sounds confusing."

He chuckled. "I guess it sometimes is. Anyway, what brings you here? Are you getting lunch/dinner, too?"

"No. I only ran in here to pick up a job application and fill it out. But the manager said if I waited, I could get an interview right now, too."

"You want to work here?"

Maybe she only imagined that he was staring at her bare legs and T-shirt like it was the world's worst outfit to wear to apply for jobs.

"Maybe, though I would've worn something else if I'd thought I was going to have an interview."

"*Nee*, that wasn't what I meant. I was just surprised that you wanted to work here, that's all. I thought it might be boring for you."

Feeling more comfortable, she teased him. "Not so much . . . I mean, look what already happened. We ran into each other."

"That we did."

Tearing her gaze from him, she noticed all the people with him were watching their conversation intently. "So, you're here with a lot of people," she whispered. There had to be seven people with him, men and women. All about the same age. Some were Amish, some English. One of the girls looked to be Mennonite.

After darting a glance behind him, he smirked. "*Jah.* We decided to take a break from work."

"But I thought you worked construction."

"I do. I mean, that's my brother's job."

"Are all of you working construction today? The women, too?"

He looked around, like he was surprised his friends were still there. "Ah. We've been doing some cleaning today. No real construction."

"Oh."

"Kyle?" a man called out, sounding impatient. "You coming?"

"What?" Whatever he saw must have made him nod. "Oh, sure. I'll be right there."

Gabby backed up. "I'm sorry. I'll let you go."

"*Nee.*" He rolled his eyes. "I mean, no. You don't need to do that."

"Are you sure?" She lowered her voice. "That man looked like he wasn't happy with you standing here."

"Him? He don't matter. I mean, it's just my brother."

She took another peek at him. When she saw he noticed her looking at him, she averted her eyes. Boy, he probably thought she was so rude.

Kyle was still waiting for her to agree, but something was holding her back.

No, it wasn't something, it was because she was afraid his brother was going to find another reason to warn Kyle away from her after they talked.

As the seconds of awkward silence passed between them, she knew it was time to move him along. "So, I better go stand over by the manager's office before they forget that they asked me to stay." She pasted a smile on her face. "I'll be seeing you."

Kyle reached out and pressed his fingers against her bare arm. "Gabby, wait."

When she looked down at his hand, trying hard not to notice how even that one simple touch could affect her, she looked back into his eyes.

They looked hesitant. "I mean, I want to introduce you to my brother." Before she could say a word, he called out, "Harley, come here, wouldja? I want you to meet a friend of mine."

"Kyle, do you want to introduce the rest of us, too?" a handsome blond man asked, amusement thick in his tone.

"Ah, *nee*. I do not."

While the others laughed and walked out the door, the man who had called out to him earlier approached. He looked much like Kyle, except he had green eyes and a thicker build. He also was wearing a far more serious expression. She didn't see any of the warmth and humor that was always lurking around the edges of Kyle's eyes.

Feeling nervous, she smiled tentatively.

Kyle stepped closer to her. "Harley, this here is Gabrielle. Gabby to most everyone. Gabby, this is my oldest brother, Harley."

She held out her hand. When he only looked at it, she let it drop. "Hi. It's nice to meet you."

"Hello." He drew in a breath. "I'm glad to know you, as well."

Kyle's eyes widened as an Amish woman approached. She was slim and couldn't have been much over five feet. Gabby felt gargantuan next to her at five foot seven.

"Kyle, I know you didn't invite me over, but I couldn't stay away. May I get introduced, too?" Before Kyle could even take a breath, she smiled brightly at her. "Hi. I'm Katie."

"I'm Gabby. It's nice to meet you."

She held out her hand and clasped Gabby's between both of hers. "I'm really happy to meet you."

Katie seemed nice enough, but she was looking at her and Kyle like they were about to profess their love for each other right in the middle of the store.

Sorry, Kyle mouthed, looking really embarrassed.

"You know what? We should probably leave. Come on, Harley, let's go join the others outside."

Kyle's brother looked like he might argue for a second before murmuring, "Good day," and walking outside.

When they were alone, Kyle shook his head. "Sorry about that. I promise, I haven't been talking about you. Katie is . . . well, she says what's on her mind."

She wasn't sure if Kyle was upset with Katie or still embarrassed that Gabby had called out to him. "I didn't mind. I'm glad to meet your brother." Which was kind of a lie, because he hadn't been very friendly.

"He's not so bad. I promise. Now, I've gotta go, but why are you here? I mean, besides applying for a job. I thought you had school today."

"I do. I'm running late." She'd also had to take care of her brother, who'd woken up with a fever, headache, and a bad sore throat. After their mom told her that there was no way she could take any time off work to run him to the clinic at the pharmacy, Gabby had known it was going to be up to her.

Lane, of course, had complained, saying that he was fine and far too old for his sister to take him to the doctor, but Gabby had been pretty sure he had strep throat again. The doctor there had taken one peek down Lane's throat, grimaced, and written out a prescription for penicillin. She was at the deli getting him a sandwich to drop off before she finally headed into school.

So, the majority of her day had been like it always was. She'd done the best she could for Lane all while trying not to care that their mother couldn't step in and be, well, a mother.

But there was no way she was going to share all that.

But as if they'd known each other for years, Kyle scanned her face, his expression filled with doubt. "Is everything all right? Do you need anything?"

"Of course not. I mean, everything is fine."

"Fine?" He raised his eyebrows, showing that she wasn't fooling him for a minute.

"I really do have to go, Kyle," she said. "I'm not positive I want to work here, but I don't want the manager to have to come looking for me. Plus, I need to drop off this sandwich for Lane."

His look of concern deepened, but he only nodded. "Will you still come over on Sunday afternoon?"

"You still want me to come over?"

"I really do. We're all planning on it."

"Really?"

"Really." He smiled at her. "So? Will you?"

She shouldn't. She was going to be a nervous wreck. And what if the rest of his family was as stern-looking as his older brother? What if his parents asked questions about her parents? Was she going to be able to lie to them?

"Please?" he murmured.

Please? Please, would she come over and be his guest for his family's Sunday supper? "Okay," she said at last. Because where Kyle was concerned, she couldn't say no. The idea of him was too good.

Thirty minutes later, after a very brief inter-view with the manager, Gabby got back in her car and started home. Just before she pulled out onto the highway, she whispered, "Thanks, God. I was wonder-ing why all this had happened today but now maybe it was so I would have another chance to see Kyle. If so, thanks. I needed that."

She suddenly found herself smiling. Even as she ran inside, gave Lane two pain relievers with a fresh glass of ice water, then told him to eat at least half the sandwich before he went back to sleep.

Smiling when she texted her mother about Lane, the antibiotics, and his lunch, and only got a "thnx" in reply.

Smiling as she drove back to school, got the lecture from the office receptionist about how disappointed they all were that she didn't take her responsibilities at school more seriously.

Even smiling as she took her seat in biology and took notes on gene pools.

Kyle Lambright had said he was looking forward to seeing her on Sunday, and she had promised him that she'd go. Now, no matter what happened, she couldn't back out of it.

She'd never been so glad to make a promise.

SEVENTEEN

"I don't know why I didn't lie," Katie said
with a chuckle. "I honestly meant to."

$\mathcal{K}$yle was still reliving their conversation when he
finally joined his brother and the rest of the group at
the picnic tables by the side of the store.

As he should have expected, all conversation
stopped as he sat down.

Then, looking like he could hardly stand to
wait another moment longer, Logan blurted, "Is
Gabby your girlfriend, Kyle?"

After glancing at Harley, and seeing that he was
back to his old tricks of remaining quiet and closed
off, Kyle shook his head. "*Nee*. She's just a friend."

Logan looked surprised. "Really?"

"What's wrong with that?"

"Nothing," Will said easily. "It's only that the
two of you seemed pretty close." Before Kyle could
say that they actually weren't all that close yet, Will

continued. "Not that I would blame you for wanting to know her. She's pretty and she seems sweet, too."

"She is sweet. Shy as well." And as for her looks? As much as he wanted to say that he hadn't noticed, he certainly had. But Will had it all wrong. Gabby wasn't pretty. She was beautiful.

But her sweet, shy personality and beauty didn't mean that they had a future.

There was still a lot keeping the two of them apart.

As every word of their stilted conversation floated back to him in waves, Kyle wished he could go follow her and make things better. He had been distant and awkward. Poor Gabby hadn't known how to act.

He took a bite of his roast beef sandwich, hoping everyone would take the hint and stop asking him questions.

But this was the Eight, not a group of polite strangers.

"What do your parents say?" Marie asked. "Do they like her?"

"They haven't met her," he said before taking another large bite. Maybe if he kept his mouth full they would get bored with their questions?

That was not the case. They all looked at each other again, then stared at Harley, who was still eating his Trail bologna sandwich like it was a special treat.

Marie cleared her throat. "Kyle, no offense, but are they going to be okay with you courting her?"

Surprisingly, Katie rushed to his defense. "I think he just said they were only friends."

"It sure seemed like there might be something more between ya," Logan said. "Take it from someone who has recently been in your shoes."

Logan didn't lie. Just a few months back he had begun courting Andy's younger sister, who was English. He'd had to go through many of the same things that Kyle could possibly face . . . if Gabby would ever learn to relax around him.

Before Kyle could stop himself, he asked, "Did you really see something between Gabby and me?"

Logan slapped him on the back. "Absolutely." Will and Marie nodded, too.

A strange feeling of happiness hit him because he had *felt* something between them. From the first moment he'd gotten the chance to speak with her. "I hope you're right. I don't know what is going to happen between the two of us, but I've been telling myself that maybe it's one-sided."

Logan grinned. "Trust me, brother. It ain't."

Feeling almost optimistic, Kyle took another bite of his sandwich, already imagining ways to tell his parents about Gabby's upcoming visit.

"So . . . when are you planning to see her again?" Will asked.

"Well . . ."

"Stop, everyone," Harley interjected. "My brother's business ain't no concern of yours."

Kyle couldn't believe it. Harley had just defended him.

"I'm not trying to be rude, I just was thinking about your parents," Will said. "I mean, they ain't like John B.'s." As if he had just realized how rude that sounded, he murmured, "No offense."

"Our parents will be fine," Harley said, his voice as cold as their father's when all five of his siblings had forgotten to do their chores. "Just because they don't talk to everyone nonstop, they're not as evil as you make them sound."

"We all know they ain't evil," Logan said. "Of course they aren't. Nobody thinks that."

Looking contrite, Logan added, "I only meant that they really like you all doing what is expected. And they expect all of you to get baptized and join the church. They really like you being Amish."

"Logan and Will, you really are being rude," Marie said. "You know Kyle doesn't want to talk about this with all of us. We may be close, but he is Harley's little brother. Not a part of the Eight."

Logan put the last fourth of his sandwich down. "I'm sorry, Kyle. Marie is right. I guess I've been so used to everyone asking questions about me and Tricia that I forget that it's not appropriate." Looking over at Harley, he added, "I wasn't trying to be rude."

Before Harley could say anything, Kyle spoke. "Don't worry about it. I'm not a kid." After glancing at his brother, he said, "Actually, I'm kind of glad you asked me all those questions. It's made me think about a lot of things I've been avoiding. I should have already been thinking about the future or what could happen."

"There's no timetable or right way to navigate friendships," Harley said, darting a glance at Kyle. "And you know that Mamm and Daed would never be rude to Gabby to her face. Don't worry."

"I'm not worried." Which was almost a lie. After all, Harley hadn't given him any reassurance about what their parents might say to him when they were alone.

"For what it's worth, I think she seems like a real nice girl," Katie said. "Once, Caleb and I ran into a bunch of his friends at a horse auction. I felt completely intimidated. It doesn't matter how nice or friendly an older sibling's friends are. They are still older, and sometimes that makes all the difference."

Katie was exactly right. Though he would've never asked his older brother's friends for advice, he sure appreciated it now. "*Danke* for saying that about Gabby," Kyle murmured.

Ten minutes later, when they were walking back

to Katie's house, his brother walked to his side. "I'm sorry about earlier. Logan shouldn't have put you on the spot." He sighed. "In his defense, I think since he fell in love with Tricia, being younger and an *Englischer*, he was trying to be supportive. It just didn't come off that way."

"It wasn't your fault, and I really meant what I said. I've been telling myself that all the differences between me and Gabby don't matter. Or that they weren't something I had to worry about yet. But I should.

"The older I get, the more I realize that relationships and friendships are hard. There isn't only one right way to do things."

EIGHTEEN

"Well, as you can imagine, Mr. Schlabach's eyes bugged out like Katie had begun stripping right in front of him. Then, Andy went and groaned like he'd just been kicked in the ribs." Harley chuckled. "It was a nightmare, I tell ya."

Katie rolled her eyes. "It wasn't just Andy who acted like I'd spoiled all the fun. As if the feral goats and old Mr. Schlabach's rifle didn't have anything to do with it."

$\mathscr{H}$arley hoped he wouldn't have another day like this anytime soon. First had come the stress of helping Katie continue to clear her house without hurting her feelings or making her even more self-conscious. The whole time, he'd been torn between keeping silent and saying anything to put her more at ease. Unfortunately, more often than not, he'd felt like he'd made the wrong decision. He wasn't good at small talk, and his silences only seemed to make her more uptight.

Then, there had been Kyle's conversation with

Gabby. Kyle had been such a bundle of nerves that Harley had once again walked a tightrope. He hadn't known whether it was better to keep his distance and let Kyle have his privacy or invite Gabby to join them.

One would have thought he would have been far better at navigating social situations by the time he was in his midtwenties.

He'd settled on standing back and out of the way. But that only made him seem more like their *daed*, which, of course, had put Kyle on edge.

But all of that would have been okay if Logan and Will hadn't decided to play twenty questions while they were eating.

The confusion and hurt in his little brother's eyes had been hard to take. He'd wanted to leap to Kyle's defense and intervene completely, but when he'd glanced at Katie, she shook her head.

Which had been one of the strangest things ever. Katie was never the voice of reason, rarely the cautious one. And he? Well, he couldn't remember the last time he'd looked to another person for advice. It had been the right thing to do, however. He'd followed Katie's signals and had navigated the lunch without any new crisis.

The rest of the afternoon had been quieter. By one o'clock, Kendra and E.A. had left. By two, all the others had, also.

Seeing how exhausted Katie looked, he'd sent

Kyle home. And now, here they were, just the two of them, standing in June's old room. It was now completely empty and spotlessly clean. He'd felt more than a little pride about that. Clearing the room hadn't been easy, but he'd been very aware that it had no doubt been even harder for Katie to say good-bye to everything.

"I'm going to sure sleep well tonight," she said, stretching her arms out in front of her.

"I am, too. We worked hard in here. Ain't so?" There. That was the ticket. He should concentrate on the work.

She smiled. "That we did. It's now ready to be remodeled."

Taking that cue, he said, "I'm proud of you. Cleaning this room couldn't have been easy."

Her smile faded a bit. "It wasn't. But having people here helping me sort helped a lot. I don't know how I'm ever going to repay them for today."

"You know what they're going to say. They don't want to be repaid. They probably don't even want to be thanked."

"I daresay you're right." After a small pause, she said, "Hey, Harley?"

"Hmm?"

"I just want to tell you thanks for being here for me."

"Hey, what happened to us not needing to thank each other?"

"Still . . . I know this job hasn't been what you expected."

She was right—and wrong. Starting this remodel hadn't been what he'd expected at all. But it also hadn't been "just" a job for him.

Oh, it might have started out that way, but then it had become something else entirely.

He shrugged off her comment. "Believe it or not, every remodel has a little bit of drama. I don't think it's possible to take apart and put back someone's home without a couple of skeletons falling out."

"Those are pretty wise words, Harley."

"Stick with me and you'll hear all kinds of catchy sayings," he quipped.

True amusement entered her eyes. "I'll consider myself warned."

Feeling pleased, he couldn't resist grinning at her. "This is nice, Katie. I was beginning to wonder if we'd ever get back to how we were."

"What? Trading quips?"

"*Jah*. Among other things. Actually, the truth is that there aren't a lot of people who I enjoy talking to as much. You're quick, and you never let me get away with too much."

She swallowed. "I've often thought the same thing." Looking away, she added, "You know, sometimes I think that the reason we trade so many barbs is because we are so much alike."

"Do you really think so? I promise, I'm not being snarky. I just never thought about us being similar."

"I don't mean in temperament." She wrinkled her nose. "I would give a pretty penny to have even a fraction of your reserve. But I think underneath your reserve and my impetuousness might be two people who enjoy teasing each other."

"Teasing, and maybe challenging each other, too." Stuffing his hands in his pockets, he added, "I reckon there's got to be a reason we've never shied away from debating or teasing each other, even when we've been mad."

Katie's eyes widened before she chuckled, but it was hollow-sounding. And Harley knew why. The reminder that wasn't really a reminder had brought them both back to his breakup with Melody, the former girlfriend who everyone in their circle made sure to never mention by name.

She shifted. "So, it's still a little early. What would you like to work on next?"

"Actually, I'm going to take off. I need to head over to the building supply store and get the materials we will need to connect that bathroom to this room. Do you still want white tile and stainless hardware?"

She nodded. "I think keeping things simple and clean will be best. I don't want to have to remodel again for at least six years."

"Six years, huh? That's mighty specific."

"It is. I am giving myself six years to pursue my dream. One year to get the business going, another to develop a decent client base, and then four to make money and replenish my savings account." She took a breath. "I figure by then, everything will need to get fixed up again. I read that people would rather stay in places that are up-to-date and new."

He was impressed. Katie had not just a dream but also a business plan. He smiled encouragingly. "And then?"

"And then?" She glanced at him before averting her eyes. "Well, I guess I'll see what else the Lord has in store for me."

Her expression was wistful. It made him wonder what other dreams she was holding close to her heart but was afraid to reach for.

He really needed to get out of there before he said something sappy and embarrassed her. "Well. It was a great day. I . . . well, I'll see ya tomorrow, Katie."

"Indeed you will. Bright and early, too."

Walking back down the stairs, Harley felt a sudden burst of loss. What was that new pang of longing he felt smack in the center of his chest? Was it because he was disappointed to be leaving her, or just concern for Katie?

He knew she had a lot of friends, not just the rest of the Eight, but also other friends from school and church. She'd always been a social thing.

But right now, it felt like he was leaving a very lonely woman who had been so much for other people that she was only now realizing that she hadn't kept a whole lot left over for herself.

Harley was still thinking about Katie and wondering how he could make things better for her when he got to the building supply store. After greeting the manager and placing his order for tile, he wandered around, half-heartedly looking at the stock.

It seemed that almost every item made him think of Katie, though. The intricately carved crown molding made him think of her spartan bedroom. He could see something so pretty would brighten it. Maybe its beauty might remind Katie that she was special, too.

On another aisle, the burnished spindles reminded him of her banister and how Katie always gripped it tightly when she walked down the stairs.

Even the swatches of paint seemed to remind him of her blue eyes or the blush on her cheeks.

When he picked up a light gold color chip, thinking how close the shade was to the highlights in Katie's hair, he groaned. He was acting like a man in love. What was going on with him?

Was it love?

"Harley?" a feminine voice called out.

His insides clenched. He knew that voice. Even

though he hadn't heard it in more than two years, he'd hoped he wouldn't hear it directed at him for at least another year or so. Preferably even longer.

With a sinking feeling, he turned. And, sure enough, there was Melody Miller. Smiling at him like he was her favorite brand of ice cream and she'd been on a diet for two months. Her parents were gazing at him the same way as well.

"Hello, Melody. This is a surprise." It was also an understatement.

"Not as much of a surprise as it is for me to see you." She stepped closer, like she hadn't broken up with him in a torrent of accusations and tears. "How are you?"

He'd finally begun to live again. That's how he was. "I'm *gut*. Working a lot. How about you?"

She looked over at her parents and smiled. "We came in here to look around because my parents are finally going to remodel their kitchen."

He looked over at Axel and Joan Miller. "Hello, Joan. Axel."

Axel strode over and shook his hand. "It's *gut* to see you, Harley. I was just telling Melody how much we missed seeing you."

Huh? One of the things Melody had told him when she'd been blaming him for everything that had gone wrong between them was that her parents had never liked him in the first place. "I hope you both have been well."

"We have," Joan replied, "though things have been fairly chaotic, what with Melody and Samuel breaking things off."

Harley was trapped in his own private hell. There was no other explanation for why he was being forced to not only speak with Melody and her parents, but now also chat about Melody's relationship with Sam Brenneman. He'd never liked Sam all that much, but then he *really* hadn't, since he'd taken up with Melody barely two weeks after she'd dumped him.

"I'm sorry, but I need to go check in with the manager to see if my order is ready. I'm here for work, you know." There, he'd sounded busy. Like he'd moved on.

Which, he suddenly realized, was true.

"How about you come over soon? We need to hire someone to work on the kitchen. It's sadly out-of-date," Axel said. "You do remodeling, don't you?"

"*Jah.*"

Melody snaked a hand around her father's elbow. "Oh, Daed. Harley is so talented. He doesn't just do remodeling, he has his own very successful company. He might not even have time to give us an estimate."

Axel's expression turned even warmer. "All the more reason for you to work on our kitchen. We want the best. How about tomorrow evening? You could come for supper and then we'll discuss our kitchen after."

"I'm sorry, I cannot. I'm in the middle of a big job right now."

Obviously taken aback by his cool tone, Melody frowned. "But couldn't you still meet with us?" Her eyes widened. "I mean, surely you can fit me in somehow?" Her voice was sugary sweet and wheedling.

If he hadn't been standing with her parents he would have told her straight out that he didn't have time for her games. Not at all.

"I still live at home, so I have my own obligations there. You would do better to find someone else."

"But couldn't you do the work, seeing as it's Melody?" Joan asked.

He wanted to avoid their house at all costs, *because* it was Melody.

"We'll pay top dollar," Axel prodded. "At least give us the benefit of your time. Surely you can spare us a few minutes?"

Axel's request made sense. Harley wasn't eager to do anything with them, but he also wasn't eager to lose money. Plus, he couldn't be rude. His parents would run into them from time to time. "You are right, Mr. Miller. I'll stop over tomorrow around seven."

"It's Axel, son."

Son? "Of course. Axel."

"We'll have already finished supper by then," Melody said. "Can't you come over earlier?"

"I'm sorry. That's the best I can do."

"Oh. Well, all right then. I'll see you tomorrow, Harley." Melody smiled. "I'll start looking out the window for you at seven." Pressing her palm on her father's arm again, she lowered her voice. "It will be just like old times, Harley."

Unfortunately, that was what he was afraid of.

NINETEEN

"Don't worry, Katie. All of us were annoyed with you," E.A. said. After a pause, she looked across the campfire. "Except for maybe Logan, who was trying to stop his leg from bleeding."

FRIDAY

*H*is bike needed fresh air in its back tire.

Aggravated with himself for not checking the bike's condition until just now, Harley rolled it out of the barn and situated it in the middle of the parking area right in front. Then he stomped back into the much darker barn and pulled out the air pump. He hoped it still worked. Otherwise, he was going to be late getting over to the Millers' house, which would necessitate a lot of explanations and apologies before he even got around to telling Melody and her parents that he couldn't do any work for them.

Just as he was giving the air pump a few experimental pumps, his father walked over from the garden.

"You know, you don't have to go over there,"

Daed said as he watched Harley fasten the pump to the bicycle's back tire. "You don't owe that girl anything, and it ain't like you need the work."

Harley could hardly stop himself from gaping at his father. They didn't have conversations like this, conversations about how he was feeling about women in his life. Actually, they hadn't had too many conversations ever. Usually his father told him to do something and Harley did it.

Feeling tentative, he said, "Are you talking about Melody or Katie?"

"Melody, of course. You know your mother and I have always liked Katie Steury."

Harley looked up at him in surprise before crouching on one knee to refasten the cap on the tire.

Some might say that his father would think the opposite. Katie's sister had been disruptive and had left as a teenager, and her mother had become something of a recluse. On the other hand, Melody Miller's family seemed like they could have been on an Amish calendar at one of the town's gift shops, their lives seemed so perfect.

"I'm surprised to hear you say that."

"I don't know why. The girl not only broke your heart, but she also never seemed to appreciate you." He grunted. "Or what she had. She always wanted something more." Looking embarrassed to have said so much, he shook his head. "I mean, that was always my impression."

"It was a *gut* impression. The right one," Harley said slowly as he began pumping air into the front tire. "I had thought that her confidence and spirit might complement mine, but now I have to say that I should've known better."

"If you can say that, why are you going over to her house?"

After checking to make sure the tire was properly filled and capping it, Harley got to his feet. "I don't want to make things worse between our families."

"Worse?"

"Melody can hold a grudge. And, she can, at times, be a touch vindictive." More than a touch. "And you know how her parents can be . . . it is hard to tell them no."

Still looking aggrieved, Daed said, "I see."

"I'm not planning to take on a job for them, though. I really can't. You are right, I don't have time or the inclination. But I didn't want to say that in the middle of the hardware store."

Daed folded his arms over his chest. "All right. I *canna* say that I agree, but I do understand."

For most of his life, Harley had always simply nodded when his father said things like that. Explanation hadn't been expected or appreciated. But now, given the way his father had started the conversation—and after his recent conversations with Kyle—Harley felt like he should try to give a little bit more.

"Daed, lately, I've started thinking that Katie and me might have a future together. Do you think that's odd? All we ever used to do was bicker."

His father looked thoughtful. "A couple of years ago, I might have said marriage between you and Katie would be a terrible idea, but now I'm thinking it might be exactly right."

"Really?"

Looking over at the garden on the side of the house that he'd just weeded, Daed murmured, "You and Katie have always kind of been like those raspberry bushes that your mother keeps in pots. They are thorny and often seem more trouble than they're worth. But they also provide the sweetest fruit."

The effort was a little prickly and painful but worthwhile in the end. "I like that analogy."

"Me, too. I reckon some people always want the easy way in life. They want things to go quickly, be painless, simple. They think if there is anything unpleasant involved, it must not be worth going after." He sighed. "But in my experience, it seems that the opposite is true. Anything worth having takes time, patience, and a little bit of struggle."

Thinking of his construction business, Harley said, "I can see that. I've always felt that way about work. I just never thought about applying those same principles when it came to relationships."

"Your mother and I have had a long and *gut* life

together. But I would be lying if I said that it was always easy."

Harley laughed. "Mamm might disagree."

"*Nee*, your mother would say that I've been a source of great fortitude her entire life."

His mother might frown at that descriptor. "I won't tell her you said that."

"I would appreciate it if you didn't." Pulling his hat further down on his forehead, he said, "Well now. I better let you get on your way. But, ah, Harley?"

"*Jah*, Daed?"

"Back to those raspberries. Don't forget that the bushes do yield *wonderful-gut* fruit, but the berries are mighty delicate. They bruise easily and they spoil if not taken care of and left on a hot counter. I have a feeling Katie might be a bit like that, too. Your relationship with her might never be so sturdy that you want to risk bruising her."

Harley swallowed. Even the thought of causing Katie pain made him feel physically ill. "I don't want that."

"*Gut*." He raised a hand good-bye and then turned back to the garden.

Harley was tempted to call out to tell him that he appreciated his advice and that he was glad they'd talked, but he held back.

It was enough that they'd said what they did.

Getting on his bicycle, he rode quickly, hoping

to be headed back toward his house before too much time passed.

All three Millers were waiting for him when he arrived at their older one-story ranch. When he entered their home, slightly sweaty from his four-mile bike ride, Melody and her parents greeted him like a returning long-lost relative.

"You're here!" Joan Miller called out. "We didn't hear your buggy come up the drive."

He doubted that was the truth. He'd seen Melody watching him from their front window when he parked his bike.

"I rode my bicycle here." Realizing that his shirt was a little damp, he said, "That's why I'm a little sweaty."

"We surely don't mind." She gestured to their parlor, which had a plate of sandwiches, cookies, and a pitcher of lemonade and two pretty glasses set out. "Come sit down and Melody will fetch you a nice glass of lemonade."

Feeling more awkward by the minute, he glanced at Melody. She'd never liked him to come over courting straight from work. She used to say if he cared enough to see her, he should care enough to shower before he did so.

Now, though, she was smiling at him very sweetly,

almost as if she was pleased that he'd shown up a little rumpled. It truly made no sense.

"Harley, please do sit down," she said. "You must be ready to relax."

He held his straw hat in his hands and finally did just that. "*Danke.*"

When Melody handed him a full-to-the-brim glass, he sipped carefully. It would be just his luck to spill some all over himself or their furniture. Realizing that Mr. Miller wasn't in sight, he said, "Is your father waiting on me in a different room? I don't want to keep him waiting."

"Daed? Oh, he's not home yet."

He was confused. "Is he running late?" He hoped not too late. He was really ready to get out of there.

"I don't know," Melody replied in a bored tone. "Mamm, do you?"

"He should be home within the hour. Don't worry about Axel, Harley. It will give you and Melody plenty of time to catch up."

He did not want to sit in their parlor for an hour and catch up. "Perhaps you two would care to show me the kitchen and explain what you need done? It's been my experience that the women have a better idea what is needed than the men."

Joan primly folded her hands on her lap. "I couldn't possibly do that, Harley."

"Oh?"

"I promised Axel that we would wait. He knows best, you see."

It took effort not to roll his eyes. He couldn't think of a single woman he knew who would think her husband knew his way around a kitchen better than she did. Especially not his own mother.

He glanced at Melody. She looked almost as uneasy as he felt. "Well. Perhaps—"

"That will give you plenty of time to have some of the delicious sandwiches and cookies Melody made for you," her mother interrupted.

Delicious sandwiches? If Will or Katie were here, he would have grinned. Joan Miller was laying on everything as thick as peanut butter.

Melody popped back onto her feet. "So, would you like one?"

"A sandwich?"

"*Jah,* Harley."

For some reason, he felt like she wasn't actually offering him a sandwich but instead a relationship. There was no way he was going back there. "*Nee, danke.*"

"But I made them for you."

"I appreciate it, but I ain't hungry." Nor was he willing to do anything that she might perceive as encouragement.

Melody glanced over at her mother, who fluttered her hands. "I think I'll leave you two alone," Joan said.

After she rushed out, Harley eyed Melody curiously. "What is going on? Do you even need your kitchen remodeled?"

"Of course we do." Her voice hardened. "Why? Do you think all of us are lying to you?"

"I'm not sure. It's just that . . ." His voice drifted off, because how, exactly, could he tell her that back when he'd been so taken with her, Joan and Axel Miller had barely acted like he was worth a glass of water? Not once had they presented him with such a meal when he arrived. "It's only that I am surprised to see that you went to so much trouble for someone to do a job for you."

"Come now, Harley. You know you are much more than a prospective job to my family."

His former self would have kept quiet. No, his former self would have eaten a sandwich and the cookies no matter what, because he wouldn't have wanted to make waves.

But his father's words still rang in his ears. His heart was making itself known to him as well. It was reminding him that there was another woman in his life now, and that woman never played games.

He was also discovering that he liked speaking his mind, even when it wasn't easy. "*Nee*, Melody, I don't know what I am to either you or your family. I loved you and I was courting you in earnest."

"You also allowed some of your friends to speak badly about me."

"I was never responsible for anyone else's opinions, Melody." He barely refrained from adding that he had almost lost a good friend in Katie because he'd been so determined to keep Melody.

Realizing that he needed to finally hear what happened, he said, "Perhaps you'd like to tell me what happened with you and Samuel."

"There's not a whole lot to share. I thought we were a good match, and I thought Sam did, too. But after a time, things fell apart." She bit her lip and then gazed up at him with big, doe-like eyes. "And Samuel, well, he wasn't all that easy to get along with."

His protective instincts rose up. Concern for her made some of his irritation with the visit fade. Sam Brenneman had always been impatient and easy to anger. "What happened? Did he hurt you?"

"He hurt my feelings, of course!" Running a hand down her apron, she continued. "But I suppose that pain was also a blessing, because his difficulties showed me how poorly I'd treated you."

"I see."

"*Jah.*" She nodded. "It was as if I'd needed to be with Sam in order for me to see just how much you meant to me, Harley. I want you back."

She wanted him back. Now, after she got another man out of her system.

He stood up and picked up his hat from the cushion beside him. "I think it would be best for me to leave. Please tell your father that I am sorry, but I really am too busy for this job."

"But . . ." She jumped to her feet. "You can't do that, Harley."

This time, he didn't even try to hold back a smile. "*Jah*, Melody. I can."

He walked out, ignoring Melody's glare.

Ignoring her mother's cry of dismay as he strode by the living room, where she'd been obviously trying to spy on the two of them.

After he threw open the front door, Harley allowed himself to stand on the porch for a moment and breathe deep. Exhaling, he looked up. And then he noticed the sky was bedazzled in layers of pink, orange, and gold. It was beautiful, transforming the night sky into something worth remembering.

And it had been right there. If he'd stayed inside the Millers' house, he would have missed it. "*Danke, Got*," he whispered.

This spectacular sunset was a good reminder that often something special was just in sight, if one was willing to look around.

Exactly like Katie. She'd been there in his world all along, coloring it with beauty and sparks.

All he'd had to do was allow himself to see her. And when he did?

Everything in his world was better, brighter.

Unique. *Right*.

TWENTY

"He gave us five minutes to get off his land. We had to run like the wind to get off in time."

Will nodded. "It was hard, but to be fair, I *canna* really blame Mr. Schlabach for saying what he did. After all, we had been trespassing."

Marie threw a marshmallow at his chest. "Shut up, Will. He'd been really mean, and you know it."

SATURDAY

"*I* can never decide whether to get roasted chicken, chicken pot pie, or a salad," Elizabeth Anne complained as she scanned the restaurant's lengthy menu for what had to be the third time.

Katie smiled at Kendra before taking a sip of her iced tea. "Oh, we know."

"You say the same thing every time we come to Der Dutchman," Kendra murmured under her breath. "Every. Single. Time."

"Come on, I'm not that bad."

"Yes. You are," Kendra said succinctly before breaking into a smile. "But I don't mind. It's rather comforting to know that some things never change."

E.A. rolled her eyes as she sat back in her chair. "Like you don't always get the soup and salad bar."

"I do, it's true. However, I don't sit and fret about my decision for a full twenty minutes every visit," Kendra pointed out. "That's the difference."

Katie lifted her napkin to her mouth so E.A. wouldn't see her smile.

But Elizabeth Anne must have sensed something because she turned to her with a hopeful expression. "Katie, help me out."

In the past, she would have had no problem speaking her mind. But now? Well, she was learning the benefits of holding her tongue. "Ermm . . . well . . . "

E.A. narrowed her eyes. "Really? That's all you have to say?"

Luckily Katie was saved by the appearance of their server.

"Are you girls ready for me to take your order?" a Mennonite lady old enough to be their mother wearing a light blue dress asked.

Kendra arched a brow. "I've been ready. But what about you, Elizabeth? Would you like time to examine the menu a fourth time?"

"Oh you." Turning to the waitress, E.A. smiled brightly. "I'm ready. I'll have . . . " She paused, bit her bottom lip, then finally uttered, "The roasted chicken, please. With whipped potatoes and vegetables. And water."

The server turned to Kendra. "And for you ladies?"

"The salad bar," Kendra said.

Katie grinned. "I'll have the meat loaf sandwich and an iced tea."

"You get a side. Fries or the salad bar?"

"Can I have both?"

After the server left, Katie blew out a burst of air. "Boy, I'm sure glad that's over with. I'm starving."

Kendra giggled. "I bet. When did you last eat? Two hours ago?"

"I'm sure it's been at least three." It was a standard joke among her girlfriends that she had a difficult time putting on weight. It drove them all crazy when she ordered sandwiches and fries while they had to be far more careful about their diet.

"At least this time you have a good excuse for a *gut* appetite," E.A. said. "You've been working so hard on your house."

"I have, but really it's been Harley who's been working so hard. He and Kyle." Thinking over the last two days, she added, "They arrive at seven on the dot and barely take thirty minutes for breaks."

"You know, I've always just known Harley did remodeling work, but I never really thought too much about it," E.A. said. "It was fun to see him in action the other day."

Katie smiled. "I've found myself thinking that, too. He's mighty talented."

She'd always been so occupied with her family and her mother's problems and the house that she had never dated much. Her social life had been the Eight.

But now that she did have more time for herself, she couldn't help but appreciate the irony that the man she was becoming attracted to had been there by her side all along.

With a wink in Kendra's direction, E.A. said, "So, I've been wondering, just how strong is Harley?"

"What are you talking about?"

"Have you seen his muscles? He is awfully brawny."

"So handsome, too," Kendra added.

"He is that."

E. A. lowered her voice. "So, you must tell us, Katie. Has our Harley ever gotten so hot doing all that construction that he's taken his shirt off?"

"Elizabeth Anne!" Katie covered her face with one hand. "I *canna* believe you!"

"Is that a no?" E.A. was somehow looking disappointed, but her sparkling eyes gave it away.

"*Nee*, it's an 'I don't think about Harley like that' answer." At least she didn't think about him like that very often.

E.A. didn't look perturbed by her outburst in the slightest. "Really?" she asked, just as if they were speaking about the weather. "I would."

Kendra choked on her tea. "You would think about Harley if you were Katie . . . or you already do?"

"It's not a 'do' at all. It's more of an 'I would' . . . if I had a special relationship with Harley the way that Katie here does. If I did, then I imagine I'd be thinking all sorts of things about him."

"E.A., there isn't anything going on between us."

"All right. If that's the way you want to go, so be it. But I hope you realize that you're only fooling yourself, not us."

"Are you ladies hungry?" the server asked as she set down a loaded tray next to their table.

"*Jah*," E.A. said. "It all looks *wunderbaar*."

"I'll be right back," Kendra said. "The salad bar calls."

"I'll go get my salad with you. Start though, E.A. Don't wait for us."

"I'll wait."

By the time they picked up their plates and had joined the line, Kendra smiled at her softly. "Katie, you know E.A. is just funning you."

"I know. I'm used to it, but sometimes I wish she wouldn't go quite so far." Almost as soon as she said those words, she felt her cheeks heat. She'd spoken impetuously most of her life. Wasn't this a case of the pot calling the kettle black?

"There really is something between you two. I know it," Kendra said. "We've all seen the sparks that flare between the two of you."

"I don't know." She paused to pour salad dressing on her plate then stopped and stared. Surely this wasn't who she thought it was?

But Melody Miller was definitely standing right in front of her. "Hi, Katie. Hi, Kendra. I'm sure surprised to see the two of you here."

Kendra recovered first. "No more surprised than me to see you. I thought you moved away."

"I did. But I'm back." She lifted her chin in that full-of-herself way that had always grated on Katie's nerves. "I decided living in Middlefield wasn't such a good fit for me."

"Are you still dating Samuel?" Kendra asked. Her voice was cool.

"Sam? Oh, *nee*. That fell away and I'm so glad it did, too. You never know about someone until you spend hours together. He was certainly someone I am better off without."

"If you are happy, then I am glad," Katie said as she edged away. "Now, I guess—"

"What about you?" Melody asked. "Are you serious with anyone right now? I mean is *anyone* courting you yet?"

The way she asked was so rude. Katie didn't like lying, but boy, was she tempted to do that, just to get that awful look off Melody's face. But, of course, no good would ever come of that. "I'm not seeing anyone right now."

"Ah. Well, it is hard to find the right man who the Lord intends for us to have."

"What about you?" Kendra asked.

"Well, of course, I have Harley again."

"Harley Lambright?" Katie choked out the words.

"Is there another Harley you know?" Melody asked with a chuckle. "I'm sorry. There probably is. I guess in my mind, there's only one. No matter what happens, he and I just can't seem to stop what's between us. I told him as much when he came over last night."

While Katie gaped at her, Kendra said coolly, "We need to go sit down. Elizabeth Anne is waiting on us."

"Oh! To be sure." Melody smiled. "I'm so glad we had this moment to catch up."

Katie turned away before Melody could see just how much that conversation had affected her.

But as they walked back to the table, she knew it was already too late.

TWENTY-ONE

"By the time we got to Andy's car, we were all out of breath and sweating. So we decided to go to Andy's house. I mean, to your house, Tricia."

Tricia wrinkled her nose. "Really? I don't remember that."

$\mathcal{K}$atie had been acting odd all afternoon. Every time Harley attempted to start a conversation or encourage her to linger by his side a little longer, she'd rebuffed him. Honestly, it was almost like she was mad at him.

However, for the life of him, Harley couldn't imagine why.

Eventually, he'd decided that she was simply having a bad day. Everyone woke up on the wrong side of the bed from time to time. Maybe this was her day to do just that. The only problem with his hypothesis was that she was all smiles and jokes with Kyle. Harley had never been jealous of his brother but he was starting to feel that way.

He was also getting tired of the awkward silences that were pulling between them. Real tired of it, and running out of ideas of how to make her smile.

Finally, when it was close to three o'clock and he'd sent Kyle home, he walked outside in an attempt to get some answers.

Katie was weeding in her garden. Well, rather, she was pulling each unwanted plant out of the ground like it had done her an injustice by simply existing.

"Hey," he said, after watching her for a few minutes.

She squinted up at him. "Did you need something, Harley?"

Katie had a smudge of dirt on her cheek. For some reason, that little smudge made her look even fiercer.

And, to him, rather adorable.

"I did," he said as he knelt down on one knee. "I wanted to talk to you."

After meeting his gaze for a moment, she looked back down. "Can it wait? I've got a lot of weeds to pull."

"I know you do, but I think this is too important to wait."

She sighed. "All right. Let me get up and wash my hands."

He was afraid that if he let her leave he wouldn't

get her to look at him for more than thirty seconds at a time again. "Actually, we might as well do this right here. I promise, it won't take long."

"Is something wrong with the *haus*?" Her brow wrinkled. "Do you need another payment?"

Boy, she was in quite the mood! "*Nee*. The *haus* is fine. And you know I wouldn't bother you like this about a payment."

"Harley, what is it?"

He plunged ahead. "I've noticed that you've been really distant today. I think I must have done something to upset you, but I'm not sure what it could be."

"*You* haven't done anything."

She wasn't meeting his eyes. "Katie, please talk to me. Whatever is wrong, I'm hoping we can work it out."

"There's nothing to work out. Don't worry."

Feeling both disappointed and a little irritated that they were back to having stilted conversations, he said, "I thought we got past all this."

She got to her feet. "Got past what?"

"Come on. You know. Got past us not talking. Moved beyond the two of us not sharing our thoughts. Of not being open with each other. I thought . . . well, I thought we were starting to have a relationship."

She folded her arms over her chest. "To be honest, I thought the same thing."

"But not now?"

"I realized that was going to be pretty difficult, given that you are already in a relationship."

"What in the world are you talking about?"

"I am talking about Melody Miller, Harley." Each word she uttered felt like a poke to his chest.

It took some effort, but he kept his voice impassive. "Why are you bringing up Melody now?" Boy, that woman was starting to turn up everywhere like a bad penny.

Her eyes flashed. "Because Kendra and I saw her at the Der Dutchman salad bar today."

"And?" He was still at sea. It wasn't like he'd had anything to do with Melody and Katie being at the popular restaurant at the same time.

"And right as I was putting ranch dressing on my lettuce, the three of us had a nice little chat about you and her." She knelt back down and yanked another weed out of the ground. Tiny dots of dislodged dirt flew out into the air, landing on his feet. "Melody told me all about how you are *hers*, Harley."

This time, he didn't even care that he looked shocked. Because, well, he was. "There is no me and her. I'm certainly not her Harley." How stupid did that even sound?

"Are you certain about that? Because she had no problem telling Kendra and me that things between the two of you were as wonderful as ever." Her voice darkened. "Because you called on her last night."

He was so frustrated, Harley didn't know if he wanted to start yelling or start praying. "Listen to me. I didn't go calling. I went to the Millers' house about a job." When he noticed Katie had stilled and was listening intently, he continued. "Furthermore, I didn't even stay long. I realized as soon as I got there that I shouldn't have gone in the first place. When I got up to leave, Melody and I had words. Now she's not happy with me, and neither are her parents."

"She didn't share any of that."

"Obviously."

"Harley, she really did insinuate that you two were back together." She pointed one gloved finger at him. "And don't even try to say that I was imagining things or that I misunderstood her. Kendra was there and she thought the same exact thing that I did."

"I don't understand what game she's playing, but I'll talk to her about it." Perhaps he could find a way to ask her at church? It would be awkward, but at least she wouldn't make a scene when they were in front of all their friends and family.

"So you really are planning to see her?" Hurt punctuated Katie's every word.

Boy, he was hating this conversation. He should've just left with Kyle. No, he should have made his feelings to Melody so clear that she wouldn't have been tempted to imagine that there was more to their relationship than there was.

Though, how could he have known that her family would not only return to Walnut Creek, but that Melody would also have wanted him back in her life?

And then there was Katie. They were navigating new territory with each other, and he was sadly adrift. He needed to figure out how to gain control of the little ship he was sailing.

He frowned. He really needed to stop with the nautical comparisons. He'd never been on a ship in his life.

Katie sighed. "Harley, are you even listening to me?"

"Sorry. Of course I am. And, to answer your question, *jah*, I am going to talk to Melody again, but not at her house. I'll speak with her after church. I promise, I'm not anxious to see her. All I want to do is tell her to stop pretending that there's more to her and me than there actually is."

"If you are really done with her—"

"I am. We've *been* done."

"Then I'm surprised that you went over to her house in the first place."

He was, too, now that he had time to think on it. "It was for work," he explained, though she knew that he had no need to book another job. "Her parents are interested in me doing a job for them and I didn't know how to refuse. And Melody? Well, she likes to stir things up. I don't know why, but she does.

Melody is a woman who loves drama and to make sparks fly when there was never any thought of a fire in the first place. And her parents . . . well, they've always given her what she wanted, which makes not giving her everything difficult. She don't take no for an answer easily. I don't know what else to say."

"I just wish you would've said something."

"There was nothing to say!" When she winced, he blew out a burst of hot air. "I'm sorry. I don't know what is going on between us. I just want it to get better."

"Truly?"

"Truly. For the last time, Melody and I aren't in a relationship, I don't want to be in a relationship with her, and I have always regretted that I was in one with her in the first place." Frustrated with both the situation and the fact that Katie could argue better than a barky wiener dog, he raised his hands. "I know you're upset, but I'd appreciate it if you would listen to me. Can't you at least give me that?"

Breathing hard, like she'd just gotten done with a run, she gaped at him.

Finally they were getting somewhere! Also, to his surprise, he was discovering that he was now staring at her slightly parted lips.

He wanted to kiss her.

Right there, in the middle of her garden, while they were kneeling on the warm dirt. It seemed that Katie Steury had woken him up. She made him speak more, share more, and yes, want to show her how much he cared.

Honestly, if he thought she wouldn't push him away, he would pull her to him and kiss her, and then kiss her again.

But that would not be the right thing to do. Exhaling deeply and reminding himself that this conversation was what was important, not his fierce attraction to her, he blurted, "Do you believe me?"

"*Jah.*" Swallowing hard, she gazed up at him, her blue eyes wet with tears. "I owe you an apology. I don't know what's gotten into me."

He had a pretty good idea. Jealousy and attraction. Insecurity and hope . . . all nestled together in years of friendship and the promise of love. He reckoned any one of those things was enough to keep them up at night. But all together? It was almost more than they could handle.

Almost.

"At least we talked about it instead of stewing, *jah?*"

Looking amused, she nodded. "At least we did that."

"So, are we better now?"

"We are. I mean, we are . . . if you can forgive me?"

Reaching for her hands, he carefully pulled off her garden gloves and tossed them to the ground. Then, he brought her knuckles to his lips and kissed each hand softly. "There's nothing to forgive, Katie."

TWENTY-TWO

After sharing a look with the others, Harley said, "Tricia, that's because when we got there, nobody was home."

Three hours later, when they were all seated at supper, his father and Jimmy had a long discussion about the prices of some new seed for the north field. While they weighed the pros and cons of paying the price or contacting other sources, Harley focused on his plate of roast pork and mashed potatoes.

And the fiery exchange he'd had with Katie. What would life with her be like? Would they always rub each other the wrong way, say things they shouldn't, speak before thinking?

It was in direct contrast with the usual way things were around this house. Everything was so contained, they might as well be confined to the inside of a Mason jar.

In contrast, he'd had enough meals at Melody's house to know that an even different way of communication reigned there. At the Millers' everything was always wonderful, fantastic, and good. Melody was a champion of smiling even when she wasn't happy and of saying the exact right thing even when it didn't ring quite true.

Was one better than the other? He didn't know. He wasn't even sure if one was supposed to be thinking about things like that. He reckoned everyone had their own way and it did no good to try to analyze it. Maybe one simply had to decide what one could live with.

Or, perhaps, live without.

"What do you think, Harley?" Daed asked. "You've been mighty quiet."

"Hmm? Oh, I have no opinion about the price of alfalfa."

To his surprise, everyone at the table burst out laughing. Even his father.

He felt his ears burn in embarrassment. "Uh-oh. What did I say?"

After dabbing at her lips with her napkin, Mamm said, "Nothing, son. Which is why it's now even more obvious that you haven't been listening to any of the conversation we've been having. What's so important that it's taken all of your attention?"

When he hesitated, Beth learned forward. "Is it Melody?"

Her, again? Before he thought the better of it,

his temper snapped. "Do I have to talk about visiting Melody with you, too?"

He could practically feel the tension in the air get thicker. Ugh. What had he done?

After another couple of seconds passed, Jimmy frowned. "Oh, Harley. Really?"

"What does that mean?"

"Exactly what you'd think it does," he replied.

"Come now, James," Daed admonished. "That ain't no way to speak to your brother."

"Daed, you know I'm right," Jimmy protested. "Melody is no good for Harley—or for the rest of us."

"I'm sorry, but I don't think Harley actually said that his mind was on Melody," Betty murmured. But still, there was a thread of distaste in her voice.

"You didn't like her, either?" Harley asked. How had he been so wrong about her?

"*Nee.*" Betty raised her chin. "I tried to, but it was difficult."

"*Nee, she* was difficult," Jimmy muttered under his breath.

Harley glanced at his mother, half-waiting for her to chide Jimmy for not being more kind. But his mother looked across the table and smiled softly at his father. "Relationships can be difficult, that's true. But only when the two people aren't meant to be together. But it's much different when it's the right person, ain't so?"

Daed looked surprised, then chuckled softly. "Indeed."

Harley could barely stop himself from staring at his parents. "Daed, Mamm, are you talking about the two of you?"

"*Jah*, what happened?" Beth asked. "You two are acting like there's a story there."

Their father leaned back in his chair. "That's because there is, Beth. When we first met, I was courting someone else."

Betty blinked. "Truly?"

"Don't look so surprised. I was once a strapping young man."

Jimmy shared a smile with Harley before speaking. "What happened with the other girl, Daed?"

"Her name was Evelyn," he said softly. "Her parents and my parents were friends and wanted us to be together, but she and I weren't a *gut* match."

"Evelyn didn't like your *daed* being so quiet," Mamm supplied. "She was always nagging him, or saying that he needed to try harder."

"She told you that?" Harley asked. He couldn't imagine anyone daring to criticize his father.

Daed shrugged. "All that really mattered was that she and I thought we were supposed to get married because our parents wanted that to happen. But love don't work that way." Glancing over at their mother again, his eyes warmed. "Everything changed when I met your mother. I took one look at her and knew she was special."

"Where did you first see Mamm, Daed?" Betty asked.

"At the park. She was chasing after a puppy—"

"I had a tiny poodle named Silver," Mamm said. "She never listened."

"*Nee*, she never did," Daed said quietly, still looking at their mother. "But because Silver wouldn't mind, you were chasing her, and I? Well, I fell in love."

Harley had so much emotion churning inside him, he felt like a giant rock was lodged in his throat. He glanced at his siblings. Each looked as affected as he did. "That's . . . that's a *gut* story."

"The best," Betty said.

Mamm chuckled. "That's why it's *gut* that our Harley here didn't settle for the wrong person. When it's right? Well, one knows."

"Now we just have to figure out if Katie is the girl for Harley," Kyle said.

Though he knew Kyle was joking, Harley wasn't in the mood to be teased about his feelings for Katie. "Honestly, Kyle. One would think you had enough to worry about with Gabby. There's no need to be interfering in my love life."

"Or lack thereof," Jimmy murmured under his breath.

If their father hadn't been sitting there, Harley would have said something snide about only dating one woman ever, but their father wouldn't have put up with that.

It wouldn't have been fair to Jimmy and Sarah, either. They were perfect together.

Fortunately for him—and unfortunately for Kyle—his comment had done what it had been designed to do, move the focus off of him.

Their mother was now staring at Kyle with bright eyes, their father far less so. "Gabby, is it?" she asked.

Kyle somehow was looking both pale and flushed at the same time. "*Jah*, Mamm."

Beth glanced over at Harley and shook her head slowly.

Harley knew what she was thinking. It had been a low blow to bring this up in the middle of a family supper. He had known both of their parents would jump on the fact that Gabby wasn't Amish. Kyle was also only eighteen years old. His older brother should be looking out for him, not using him to deflect difficult conversations.

Feeling guilty, he said, "Is everyone done? I can start taking the dishes to the kitchen."

"No one is getting up until I find out more about this girl," Mamm said. "Kyle, tell us something, please."

"I don't know what to say."

With exaggerated patience, she spoke again. "Let's start with something easy. Is she Mennonite?"

"*Nee*. She is English. Gabby goes to the high school. She's a senior there."

"I'll look forward to meeting her one day soon," Mamm said.

"You'll meet her on Sunday afternoon," Kyle mumbled. "I invited her over."

Daed stared at Kyle intently. "Because?"

Kyle squirmed then seemed to straighten his backbone. Looking at their father square in the eye, he said, "Because I like her, Daed."

Betty inhaled sharply. For a good thirty seconds, that was the only sound that was heard.

Harley now felt even worse. Here he'd been telling Kyle that he was nothing like their father and that he wanted a good relationship with him . . . and then what had he done? Practically fed the kid to the wolves.

Sitting so stiff and straight as time ticked by, Kyle wouldn't even glance his way.

"Well, then," their father said slowly. "I will look forward to meeting this Gabby then."

Almost in unison, every one of them stared at their father in shock.

"I believe you may now start clearing the table, Harley," Daed said, his voice much cooler.

Yes, his father wasn't happy with him, either.

At one time, it would have been so easy to have blamed Katie for this debacle. But this time he could blame no one but himself.

He stood up. Then, all by himself, he began carrying the supper dishes into the kitchen. It looked like he had a long night of dishwashing ahead of him.

TWENTY–THREE

"You all should've just gone there in the first place," Kendra said.

"We weren't supposed to be there at all. Andy had promised his parents that he would be staying at Logan's all weekend."

SUNDAY AFTERNOON

$\mathcal{K}$yle felt like an anxious child, standing at the front window of his house and watching for Gabby to arrive.

"What kind of car does she drive?" Betty leaned her elbows on the windowsill.

"I don't know. Why?"

His little sister shrugged. "I don't know. Just curious."

"Well, all you need to know is that it's not a courting buggy."

But instead of looking chastised, Betty frowned. "Are you still angry with Harley or with all of us?"

"I'm not angry with anyone." And to his surprise, he actually wasn't. Though of course he would rather have told his parents about Gabby in a different way, but he had been putting it off for days. Harley's comment had been like ripping off a Band-Aid. The attention had stung for a few minutes, but in the end everything was out in the open and he didn't have to dread what would happen anymore.

Especially since their father had been surprisingly calm about the visit.

Now, he only had to worry about what would happen when Gabby arrived. What would she think of their house? Of, well, how "Amish" it was? Looking around at the light blue walls, simple furniture, and lack of electronics, he started fearing that she might feel completely out of place.

Betty was still staring out the window. "I think Harley thinks you're mad at him."

"I know."

"Do you want me to tell him that you've forgiven him?"

"*Nee.*"

"How come?"

"Because it ain't any of your business," he snapped.

Betty huffed. "I'm only trying to help."

"If you want to help, then stay out of it."

"Sometimes I really hate being the youngest around here. Everyone tells me that their business isn't any of my business, but the minute I do anything everyone wants to hear all about it."

Kyle knew she was right. Until recently, their older siblings had treated him like he was forever twelve years old. "Don't let anyone else hear you say that. Beth, especially, will point out how many more chores she has than you."

She sighed. "I suppose you're right." Practically placing her nose on the glass, she murmured. "I wish Gabby would get here already. I can't wait to see what she looks like."

"She's pretty."

"What do you think she's going to be wearing?"

"I don't know." Betty was being so weird. What did it even matter what Gabby had on?

Suddenly looking scared, she blurted, "What if Gabby shows up here in shorts?" She pointed to the top of her leg. "Like, a pair of those really short ones?"

He hadn't thought about Gabby showing up in something so revealing. If she did, Daed would no doubt have something to say about that. Turning to Betty, he glared. "If she is wearing short shorts, you'd better not say anything."

She rolled her eyes. "Like I would. It's not like I haven't seen a girl in shorts before."

"Then that makes two of us."

"Really? Is that what she has on when you go calling?"

"Betty, stop."

"But—"

"Betty, come into the kitchen, please," Mamm called.

His sister looked ready to argue for a moment but started walking. "I'll see ya later."

"Yeah." He hoped much later.

After he heard their mother tell her to arrange cookies on a plate, Mamm came into the front room and stood beside him. "She should be here any time now, *jah*?"

He nodded. Actually, he was starting to think Gabby was more than a little late. Maybe she'd changed her mind? For about the hundredth time, he wished he had a cell phone. Then he could text her or call to see if she was lost.

Or if she didn't want to hang out with him anymore.

"I'm having Betty arrange some cookies on a plate," Mamm said, just like it was the best idea in the world. "We have lemonade, too."

"*Danke*, Mamm." He was far too old to be serving girls cookies and lemonade. But he was so grateful that his parents hadn't forbid him to have Gabby over that Kyle simply nodded.

"Do you think she'll want anything else? I could make her a sandwich."

"Cookies are plenty. I told her how you always

make a good Sunday supper, Mamm. She knows you will be busy making that."

Her eyes widened. "Is she staying for supper?"

"*Nee*." Not that he didn't want her around . . . but there was no way he was going to make Gabby suffer through a whole meal with his nosy family. She'd never want to see him again.

Since they were still standing there, no car was in sight, and he didn't want to simply stew on all his doubts, he said, "Hey, Mamm?"

"Hmm?"

"How come you and Daed didn't get mad about Gabby coming over?"

She sat down on the arm of the couch. "That's a funny question. Why are you asking? Did you want us to get mad?"

"Of course not. But I was afraid you might make it hard for me to have her here." It had been more than that, of course. He'd been afraid they'd try to talk him out of seeing her. Make it seem like there was no way he and Gabby would ever have anything in common.

"Well, I *canna* speak for your father, but I, for one, wasn't all that shocked you like an English girl. You've never been too interested in any of the Amish girls you were in school with." She shrugged. "Then, too, it meant a lot to both your father and me that you invited her here. You didn't have to do that." Still looking reflective, she murmured, "If you really do like her, I wouldn't have been surprised if you'd rebelled a bit."

"Rebelled how?"

"Like started acting like John Byler and only wearing *Englischer* clothes." She bit her lip. "Deciding to only see Gabrielle at her house. You know."

"Doing all that *rumspringa* stuff."

She smiled sheepishly. "*Jah.*"

Other kids in other families might have permission to do all kinds of shenanigans during their run-around time, but that had never been the norm in his family. He couldn't recall any of his three older siblings ever acting like they wanted to be anything other than Amish. As far as he knew, they'd never drunk alcohol, tried smoking, got a driver's license, or even gone to the movies.

He'd never had an urge to drive or drink, either.

Sure, it probably had a lot to do with their strict father. But it also had much to do with the fact that he was happy the way he was. He liked their traditions, liked his family, liked their way of life.

That feeling of satisfaction had only started to waver recently, when he'd developed a terrible crush on Gabby Ferrara.

Treading carefully, he said, "Mamm, I don't know if my liking Gabby is a matter of rebelling. I like her because she's Gabby, not because she's English."

Though her expression was grave, she said, "Then I hope we will like her, too."

Just as he was about to assure her that Gabby was sweet and kind, his mother pointed out the window. "Ah. Here she is."

His heart jumped. For a moment Kyle was tempted to ask if she thought he should wait for her to come to the door, then he shook himself. He wasn't a shy, naive boy, he was a grown man, and he needed to start acting like it. Gabby was probably nervous and worried about how she would be received.

"I'm going to go outside to get her," he said as he walked to the door. Maybe he heard his mother chuckle behind him, he wasn't sure.

Because once he started walking down his front porch steps, he only had eyes for the prettiest brown-haired girl he'd ever seen in his life.

She had just gotten out of her old-looking gray sedan. It was a Toyota Camry. He made note of that for Betty.

And, to his relief, she was wearing a pair of jeans and a loose pale green cotton blouse. The sleeves ended just after her elbows and the neckline was curved and modest. She'd left her hair down, and it curled around her shoulders. There was nothing about her clothes that his parents would find objectionable.

But then, the last of his silly worries vanished into thin air. Because the moment she looked his way, Gabby smiled.

And it lit up his day.

TWENTY-FOUR

Tricia frowned. "All this time, Andy never told me about you all being there without Mom and Dad. Was there even a reason?"

Logan sighed. "Unfortunately, yes."

*K*yle smiled right back as he walked to her side. "Hiya, Gabby. You made it."

She beamed. "I did. Am I late?"

"It doesn't matter. I'm just glad you didn't change your mind."

Moving a lock of hair behind her ear, she said, "I have to be honest with you, there was a moment this morning when I actually considered doing that."

"But you still drove over here."

"I did." But she still looked a little worried. She pulled on the fabric of her blouse. "Is . . . is what I have on okay?"

"It's perfect."

"I don't have any dresses. I mean, I do, but they're all pretty short." She ran her hands down her thighs.

Probably to wipe the moisture from her palms. He'd done that a lot today as well.

But all he seemed to want to do was watch her hands slide down her legs. Which, of course, made his cheeks heat in embarrassment. Boy, he had it bad for her.

"Come on in. Or, would you like to go to the barn first? We could go see the goats I told you about."

She looked down the hall. "Are your parents home?"

"Yes . . . is that okay?"

"Yes. But what I meant was I don't want to smell like a barn the first time I meet your mother."

She currently smelled like flowers and vanilla. Even if she walked around the barn for an hour, he didn't think it would change that.

"Let's go meet my mother then and get that over with." As they started walking, he said, "I better warn you. She made us cookies and lemonade." He slowed down. Waiting for her to snicker.

But instead, she looked shocked. "She did all that because I was coming over?"

"My mom likes to bake." And get in her children's business.

"That's the nicest thing."

They walked up the steps. Just before he opened the door, he said, "Have you been in an Amish house before?"

"No."

"Well, um, we don't have electricity, you know. So it's going to be a little dark. And maybe a little warm for you? We don't have air-conditioning."

"I don't have air-conditioning at my house, either, Kyle. I promise, I'll be fine."

"Okay. But, um, if you are worried or confused by something, just ask."

Some of the worry that he'd spied in her eyes evaporated. "I'll do that. But if I do something you don't think I should, just tell me, okay?"

"All right." At last he opened the door and walked her inside. Of course, part of him figured half his family was going to be standing in the foyer staring at them. But it was empty and silent.

He closed the door behind him, just as he noticed that there were two glasses of the lemonade, napkins, and a tray of cookies on the coffee table.

"Where is everyone?" she whispered.

"I think they're doing their best to give us some privacy." When she raised her brows, he grinned sheepishly. "I might have told everyone not to make you uncomfortable. Come on, let's go to the kitchen and we'll say hi."

Looking around as they walked, Gabby didn't say a word.

They passed the living room where the cookies were set out. The library, the dining room, and another big room with a large fireplace.

"This place is huge," Gabby said.

"It's been added on a lot," he said just as they walked through a little room his mother called a pantry and finally entered the kitchen.

Sitting around a big island was his mother, Betty, Beth, and Jimmy. All four of them looked at them when they entered. Kyle could practically feel their curious stares settle on Gabby and hang on tight.

Gabby stiffened but gave a tentative smile. "Hi. I'm Gabby Ferrara."

Those four words put his mother in motion. She slid off her stool and rushed over to Gabby's side. "I'm Emma Lambright. And these here are Kyle's sisters, Betty and Beth, and his brother Jimmy."

Gabby smiled shyly at all of them. "Hi."

Realizing that Betty was wearing her "earnest" look, the one that signified she was about to start asking a million questions, Kyle gave all of them a warning look. "I was about to introduce everyone, Mamm."

"Well, now you don't have to." She smiled at Gabby like she was her long-lost daughter. "Are you hungry?" she asked eagerly. "Would you like a sandwich?"

Gabby glanced at Kyle before replying. "Um, no. Thank you. I already had a sandwich today."

"I made you some cookies."

"She saw them, Mamm," Kyle said, trying to take

control of the conversation. "Gabby just wanted to say hello."

"Thank you for having me over. And thank you for the cookies, too. I noticed them as soon as we got inside. They look really good."

"We made them yesterday afternoon," Betty announced. "Mamm wanted to make sure they were perfect so they took three hours."

Gabby looked taken aback. "That was really nice of you."

Since he was standing a little behind Gabby, Kyle glared at Betty. Really, she was a walking social disaster. "Like I said, we only came in here to say hello. Let's go into the living room, Gabby," he said, ushering her out of the kitchen.

She looked a little startled by his abrupt motion but followed.

When they got into the living room, Kyle sat down on the couch with a sigh. "I'm sorry about that."

She sat down on the couch, too, looking like she was careful to leave a full two feet of space between them. "What are you sorry about?"

"My *mamm* offering you a sandwich. She gets a little excited when it comes to food."

She smiled. "That's spoken like a guy who's used to someone fussing over him."

He supposed it did. "I guess I sound ungrateful."

"Only a little bit." But the way she was holding

out her hand, with a wide gap in between her thumb and her index finger, told a different story.

Now he was embarrassed. She was probably thinking that he was spoiled. She might be right, too. He took an awful lot for granted. "I'm sorry. I'm not usually like this."

"Like how?"

"So awkward." Figuring he had nothing to lose by being completely honest, he added, "I figured our house might be different from what you're used to and I was wanting to help. I think I've only made things worse."

"This is a lot different from my house, but that's in a good way, Kyle. I've been nervous, too. I didn't want everyone to hate me."

"No one could do that."

"Your mother and your siblings seem really nice."

"Thanks." He noticed then that her eyes drifted to the cookies and lemonade. "Would you like cookies and lemonade?"

"I sure would." Leaning forward, she picked up the pitcher and filled both their glasses. Then she picked up a napkin and placed two cookies on it. "Are you going to have any cookies, too?"

"Not right now. But you eat all you want. My *mamm* bakes all the time."

Not wanting her to be too self-conscious, he started telling her about how chaotic the house had been that morning when they were all getting ready for church.

It really had been crazy. Beth had woken up late and stayed too long in the bathroom showering, which made Jimmy start knocking on the door every five minutes. Those two things set off a strange chain reaction that had all of them doing things out of the ordinary. Harley had spilled a whole glass of milk, he'd stuck a foot in a puddle, and splashed dirty water over his pants. Even their father had gotten pecked when he'd tried to help out and gather eggs.

Gabby laughed. "You know, I always wished I had more siblings than just my brother but now I'm kind of glad I don't."

"It ain't always like this, but believe me, I would've rather had your morning. I'm sure it was a lot quieter."

For some reason, that had been the wrong thing to say, because some of the light that had been shining in her eyes faded. "It was quieter, but I don't know if it was better."

"Gabby, I wanted you to meet Kyle's father," his mother's voice rang out.

Eyes wide, Gabby got to her feet.

Kyle stood up also. "Daed, this is my friend Gabby. Gabby, this is my father, William Lambright."

"It's nice to meet you, Mr. Lambright," she whispered.

"Welcome to our *haus*," he said quietly. Turning to Kyle, he said, "I trust you are behaving yourself?"

"*Jah*, Daed," he said, just as he noticed a gleam in his father's eyes. Kyle would've never thought it, but his father was teasing him.

Just as he was about to turn back to Gabby, his father sat down in one of the chairs across from the couch. "Kyle told us that you are a senior in high school."

"Have a seat, Gabby," Kyle whispered.

When she sat, Kyle sat down, too. But this time a little closer to her. If Gabby was going to have to answer questions from his father, he was going to make sure she knew she wasn't alone.

After setting the cookies carefully on the table, she smiled. "I am. I can't wait to graduate."

His father nodded. "And then what will you do? College?"

"Oh, no. College isn't in my plans. We can't afford that."

"What will you do, then?"

If it had been anyone else asking those questions Kyle would have put a stop to it. But correcting his father wasn't something he'd ever considered doing. The idea was as foreign as planning a trip to Russia.

Because of that, Kyle was forced to sit helplessly as Gabby fumbled for an answer.

"Well, I just got a job working over at Walnut Creek Cheese Shop, and I help watch Mr. Anderson's mother one night a week. I think I'm going to do more of that for now."

"Why do you have to watch his mother?" As usual, his father's voice was gruff and his expression was intent. Kyle knew he wasn't trying to be scary, it was just his way.

But from the way Gabby was gripping the edge of the couch, it was obvious she didn't know that.

Finally gathering his courage, Kyle cleared his throat. "Maybe—"

"No, I don't mind talking about it, Kyle." She took a breath. "Mr. Anderson's mother has gotten kind of absentminded and she lives in a garage apartment. She gets lonely. I go over and clean up her kitchen a little, do some laundry, and we watch TV together. That's all."

"That's mighty nice of you," his mother said.

"I like Mrs. Anderson, but I can't say that I'm only doing it to be nice. Like I said, I get paid to go over there. The money helps with gas and food and stuff . . ." Her voice drifted off.

Daed stared at Gabby for a moment before standing up. "We should leave you two alone. I hope you will come again, Gabby."

"Thank you." Looking over at Kyle, her brown eyes warmed. "We were just talking about how we were both nervous for me to come over, but you all have made it so nice."

"You come over again, soon, dear," his mother said. "We want to see you."

After they walked out, Kyle sat back down with a sigh. "I'm really sorry," he began, then realized that she had tears in her eyes.

Before he could stop himself, he moved to kneel down in front of her. Reached out to grasp her hands. "Gabby, I'm so sorry. My family is large and constantly in my business. I didn't expect they'd be quite so much into yours."

"Oh, Kyle." Her lip trembled and one of those teardrops he'd spotted drifted down a cheek.

Seeing that lone drop made him feel even worse. He gently squeezed her hands for a second. Realizing that this was a sorry way to comfort her, he finally pulled her into his arms. Right there in the middle of his living room.

Gabby tensed, then wrapped her arms around his neck and hugged him back. She didn't make any noise, but he could feel the dampness on his neck.

She was crying.

It was only natural for him to gently rub her back and whisper nonsensical words into her neck. "It's okay, Gabby. Shh, now. I'll make it better."

She shook her head, then, to his amazement, relaxed against him.

Kyle had no reference about what to do. Try as he might, he couldn't recall Jimmy ever holding his

Sarah like this. He couldn't even imagine his parents in such an embrace.

But at the moment, he didn't care whether he was doing the right thing. All that mattered was that Gabby seemed to find comfort and he liked being the one giving her comfort.

Her body felt good next to him. Right. He stopped patting her and ran a hand up and down her spine instead. Noticed that her hair felt soft and smooth against his cheek and smelled like flowers and mint.

"I'm sorry. I'll . . . "

"Hush, now, Gabby. There's no need to cry. I've got you," he murmured. "I promise, whatever is wrong, I'll help you make it okay."

Then he looked up and saw his mother standing in the doorway. Gaping at him. At them.

He swallowed hard. Met her eyes, and knew. Knew.

Everything in his life had just changed.

TWENTY-FIVE

"What would it have mattered?" Tricia asked. "What exactly was so bad that happened?"

"Oh, we decided to go swimming in his pool," Harley said.

*S*he'd ruined everything. Self-loathing coursed through Gabby as she realized that she'd dissolved into tears from just a few kind words from Kyle's parents.

And now?

Now, sweet, amazing Kyle was kneeling on his own floor attempting to comfort her and apologizing for things he hadn't done. If his arms around her didn't feel so good, Gabby knew she would always regret this moment. But Kyle's comfort felt too sweet to ignore, definitely too special to ever regret.

So even though he was probably going to usher her out of his house as soon as possible and then probably go out of his way to never see her again, Gabby let herself relax in his strong arms for a few more minutes.

At the very least, she'd always have this memory. The memory of being held close and cared for. The feel of a really good boy's arms around her like she was something special.

She was going to memorize every little bit of this moment, the way his skin smelled like fresh soap, how his hands felt strong and calloused but he rubbed her arms and back carefully—just as if she were so fragile she might bruise. It was sweet, and in spite of her turbulent emotions, she found herself committing to memory the way his voice sounded as he attempted to get her to calm down. It was raw and scratchy and strained. Caring.

Yep, she was going to put this episode firmly into her heart and lock it up tight before everything between them changed.

Before Kyle realized that she was way too much trouble and completely undeserving of such care.

Huh. It seemed that was all it took to bring her back to reality. Well that, and the realization that his parents or one of his siblings could walk in any second and catch them.

Hating the idea that he would get in trouble for something that was all her fault, Gabby straightened and pulled away. "Thanks. I'm better now."

But Kyle hardly budged. "Hey," he said, swiping

a thumb along her cheek, wiping away the wetness. "Are you sure you're all right?"

"Yeah." Releasing a ragged sigh, she got to her feet. "I . . . I really am sorry for acting like this. I'll get out of here and leave you alone."

"*Nee.* Halt."

"Huh?"

Scrambling to his feet, he shook his head, as if to clear it. "Sorry. I mean, wait a minute. What are you doing? You can't leave right now. You just got here."

"I know." She stopped herself before she started trying to explain. Because she was pretty sure if she started talking and telling him about why she cried? Well, she was going to tell him too much.

He stepped closer. "Gabrielle, I'm serious. We need to talk about what's wrong."

How could she ever attempt to put all that she was feeling into words well enough for it to mean something to him? "We don't need to talk about me, uh, losing it. Actually, it's probably best if we both try to forget about this. I promise, if we happen to see each other around town I won't make a big deal about it."

"You won't, huh?" His blue eyes turned icy. "That ain't gonna happen, Gabrielle," using her full name yet again. "You're going to sit down and talk to me."

"Because you're ordering me to?" She raised her chin, just like she had every right to get in a snit after the way she'd behaved.

"*Nee*, because I care about you. Now sit. Please?"

Please. How could she refuse that?

She sat on his comfy couch. It was massive and light gray and looked like it could sit his whole family on it at the same time. Maybe even a goat or two. Curling her feet under her, she tried to sit primly.

But then he went and sat down right next to her, far closer than when his parents were in the room. To her surprise, he linked her fingers in his. Maybe it was to keep her there, she didn't know. But it sure felt good. Before she realized what she was doing, Gabby turned her hand so it was encompassed in his more fully.

Looking oh-so-serious, he said, "Now, first, I'm real sorry about my parents. I promise that I'll talk to them and warn them to give us more space the next time you come over." Looking annoyed, he said, "I'll say something to my siblings, too. They . . . well, since I'm one of the youngest, they sometimes forget that I deserve the same respect." He took a breath. "Except for Betty, I mean. But Betty is sixteen and full of herself. I don't know what's going to help her."

He sounded so matter-of-fact, she had to try not to giggle. "Kyle, no one in your family did or said anything wrong."

He frowned. "Actually—"

She cut him off. "No, I promise. This was on me."

"Gabby, I don't understand."

She knew he didn't. And actually, she loved

that about him. Kyle Lambright didn't know her as the poor girl with the single mother and the popular brother who was counting on a football scholarship to take him far, far away from here.

No, Kyle actually thought she was a lot like him.

"I don't have a father, Kyle."

He blinked, obviously startled by the statement. Then he gathered himself and spoke. "I'm sorry, Gabby. Did . . . did he die recently?"

Ugh. This was so awful. "He's not dead. I mean, I don't think he is."

"Then?"

"Kyle, what I'm trying to tell you is that I never knew him at all. He was never around. My mother never married him." She waved a hand, frustrated with herself. "Or maybe they weren't ever in a relationship in the first place. I don't know." Keeping her eyes away from his, she continued. "My brother, Lane, is actually only a *half* brother. He's from another of my mom's failed relationships." She hated talking about Lane like he wasn't everything to her. Hated talking about her mother like there weren't many good things about her, but she needed Kyle to know the whole truth about who he was holding hands with.

Because if, for some reason, he still wanted to know her, she didn't want to wonder if it was just a temporary thing. That it might end as soon as he discovered all her secrets.

"Okay . . ."

Even though she knew the rest of her story wasn't pretty, she forced herself to continue. "Now, she's okay. I mean, Mom has a pretty good job. She works as a hairdresser and has a lot of clients." Thinking about how different she seemed at the salon, she added, "I've seen my mother at work. There, she looks happy and put together and easygoing. I'm pretty sure most of the people she sees at work wouldn't ever think that she doesn't have it all together. But back at home? Well, everything there is a mess. Sometimes I think everything about our house is dysfunctional."

"I don't understand."

Of course he wouldn't. Because Amish people didn't do things like her family did. "My mother works a lot, and she's always paid for everything we need. Lane and I have never gone without a meal or shoes that fit or anything like that. But she's not at home much. It's almost like as soon as she takes care of her obligations—Lane and me—she'd rather go off and do her own thing."

"Does she, though?"

Feeling self-conscious, she nodded.

"So that is why you are always trying to do so much," Kyle stated.

She nodded slowly. "Even though I'm just two years older than Lane, in a lot of ways I feel like I raised him."

"I'm sorry about all of that, Gabby, but I don't understand why being here made you so upset."

"When your father looked at me and said I was welcome back . . . it was like he thought I was good enough to be here with you. With all of you."

"But of course you are."

"No, he said that even though I'm not Amish." She gazed up at him, suddenly feeling uncertain. "Even though I'm not close to being good enough for you to spend time with."

"He knew you weren't Amish, Gabby. And of course you're good enough to be here. Just because my parents are married and we're Amish doesn't mean our lives ain't without problems. We certainly aren't perfect."

"Do you really mean that?" It was kind of sad how much she wanted his family to be imperfect, too. She needed them to be on more even ground, or at least close to that.

"Of course. And, what's more? There's nothing wrong with you. Not one thing."

Kyle looked so sincere, his words so sure, she almost believed him. "I'm afraid that one day soon you are going to decide I'm not worth it."

"Gabby, of course you are. We're all worth it, don't you see?"

"I know you think so, but . . ."

"*Nee*, I *know* so. The Lord doesn't make mistakes,

Gabby. He might have given you challenges, but He's given all of us challenges."

"Kyle." But even as she said his name, Gabby knew her voice sounded pained. Why in the world had she decided to bring all of this up?

Looking at Gabby intently, Kyle paused to take a breath. "No, listen to me. I'm not just telling you this to make you feel better." He'd never been one to share his faith so openly. Never had he actually tried to make another person see his point of view. But this felt right and it felt important.

And because of that, he pressed on. "Gabby, what I'm trying to say is that I believe that you and me were meant to know each other and meant to be friends."

"Even though so much about me is so different from you?"

Looking at her, seeing how earnest she looked, he wanted to smile. The fact was, she was different from him in most every way. She was a pretty English girl who had a messed-up family and needed him. He liked that. No, he loved that.

"Maybe I like you because you are so different, *jah*?"

Her eyes opened in surprise, she looked a little sheepish . . . and then she smiled. "*Jah*," she repeated.

He smiled. She sounded so cute even trying to say one word in Deutsch. "*Gut*." He stood up and, holding out his hand, said, "Now, come see the goats.

They're ornery and silly, but mighty cute. I know you're gonna love them."

"I bet I am, too," she murmured as she slipped her hand in his.

Kyle couldn't remember a time when he'd ever felt more alive.

TWENTY-SIX

Kendra wrinkled her nose. "Wait, did you all just happen to have bathing suits with you?"

Harley rolled his eyes. "Of course we didn't. We decided to go swimming in our underwear."

"Careful now, Kyle. There're nails sticking out of most every piece of that cabinet," Harley warned.

"I got it," Kyle grunted as he carried the kitchen cabinet toward the back door.

Unable to help himself, Harley watched his brother carefully angle himself sideways to get through the doorway. When Kyle stepped out of sight, he breathed a sigh of relief. The old cabinets in the kitchen were of solid oak and heavier than they looked. The wood was also dry and brittle. Because of that, it was splintering under their leather gloves and breaking in odd places. When he'd first begun the renovation, he'd contemplated selling the old cabinets to help Katie allay the costs. Maybe even donate them to a shelter or charity so they could be used again. Now it was obvious that they would be going directly to the dump.

"Is it safe to come in yet?" Katie asked from the doorway.

He heard the teasing note in her voice, which made him smile. When they'd first started tearing out the laminate countertops and original cabinets, she'd looked like she might cry. He was glad she had now put away the memories and was looking ahead to the improvements.

"It is, but step carefully. There are nails every-where," he warned, taking a moment to gaze at her in appreciation. Today she had on a blue dress and apron, almost an exact match to her eyes. She had on black stockings and thick, serviceable-looking shoes. She looked like a bright blue jay in the middle of the dusty, dirty room.

Entering the kitchen, Katie stepped carefully, looking a bit like she was playing hopscotch over the nails and chunks of wood he hadn't swept away yet. When she stopped beside him, she looked about with wonder. "Wow, Harley. It looks so much bigger."

"I think it's going to continue to feel that way after we put in the new cabinets and countertops, too," he said with a nod. "They're much sleeker."

"I'm glad we chose to do everything in white."

"Me, too, but you did most of the choosing."

"You advised me though." She continued to walk around, even running a hand along the torn-up walls. "What's next?"

"I need to patch up the walls and bring in the plumber to put in that extra sink."

"How long is that going to take?"

"Darren told me he could get here in a day or two. Once he gets here, it shouldn't take more than another day or two to do his part."

"And then the new cabinets can be delivered?"

"*Jah.*" He'd just checked the status of them early that morning. Right now they were supposed to be delivered on time, and he was grateful for that. He didn't want to make everything harder than it already was. "Once your shiny new cabinets come in, Kyle and I can get them installed in just a day or two."

Her eyes widened. "There're a lot of cabinets. You really think you two can put them in that quickly?"

"We're manly men," Kyle joked as he walked back inside. Making a muscle with his left arm, he bragged, "Cabinets are no match for us."

"Oh, brother." She grinned at Harley. "Remind me not to give you too many compliments, Kyle. If I do, your head will swell up."

"You mean it will swell up even bigger," Harley quipped, grinning, too.

"Ha-ha," Kyle retorted before turning to Harley. "What now?"

"I think this is it for the day. How is everything around the Dumpster?"

"It's *gut*. Clean."

"You checked for nails?" He really didn't want Katie—or her horse—to step on one.

"I did." He held up a hand. "And *jah*, after I took a good look around, I did it again."

"*Danke*. I'm proud of you."

Kyle's posture eased. "So?"

"So, you can head on home. Ask Betty to save a plate for me if I'm not home by supper."

Kyle raised his eyebrows, but after darting a look at Katie, nodded. "Will do. See you later. Bye, Katie."

"Bye, Kyle. Have a *gut* night."

"You, too," he said before walking back out the door.

After the door shut behind Kyle, Harley waited for the vague feeling of tension that plagued him and Katie whenever they were alone together. Of course it wasn't there to the same degree as it once had been, but it was usually there to some extent.

Except now, all he felt was a sense of peace. With some surprise, he realized that he was glad they were alone. He felt relaxed around her.

"You seem deep in thought," Katie murmured, breaking the silence. "Is there something wrong with the kitchen that you are afraid to tell me?"

"Hmm? Oh, *nee*. Actually, I was just thinking how different things are between us now."

"They're better, aren't they?"

"I think so." He smiled. "What do you think?"

"I think . . ." She paused. "You know what? I was about to say that I think that things between us are now like they used to be, but that's not quite true. It's better."

"Maybe we're better, too."

She smiled. "That would be nice, wouldn't it? I'd like to think of myself improving by the day."

Harley almost corrected her, to explain that he hadn't meant that each of them was better, but that their relationship had finally healed.

But Katie's observation was probably more correct than his was. This renovation wasn't just revamping her house, it was restoring each of them to a certain degree, too.

TWENTY-SEVEN

"Not just in our underwear. The girls put on Andy's T-shirts, too," Marie added primly.

ONE WEEK LATER

*C*hurch was at Miriam Schrock's house that morning. Though she knew it wasn't nice, Katie heaved a sigh and half-contemplated not going. No matter what time of the year it was, something always, *always* went wrong when Miriam hosted. Either her field was so muddy people's buggies got stuck, or she ran out of food, or something broke. Once, the bishop's table had wobbled so much that his bowl of vegetable soup splashed all over him.

Miriam had been apologetic, of course. And the bishop? Well, he'd just laughed and said that a little bit of spilled soup never hurt anyone. But the rest of them? They'd inwardly groaned.

After all, serving vegetable soup had been a silly idea in the first place. The *kinner* didn't like it, people had to carry around hot bowls, and it was a mess to clean up. No one wanted to stand around and wash forty or fifty bowls after a three-hour church service and another two-hour lunch. But that is what they'd all done . . . all while Miriam had wrung her hands and apologized.

There was no telling what minor catastrophe was going to happen today. She just hoped whatever did occur didn't happen to her.

Just as she finished the thought, Katie felt ashamed. That wasn't fair to Miriam, to any of the people in her church district, or to the Lord. After all, this was His day. Why, she could practically feel Him shake His head in dismay. Closing her eyes, she whispered, "Please forgive me, Lord. I know I have many faults and I will try to be better." After a pause, she added, "Um, also, please look out for Miriam today. I'm sure she could use your prayers and guidance."

Feeling better, she slipped on black tennis shoes over her black tights, put a black bonnet over her white *kapp*, and got out her bicycle. Two years ago, she'd bought herself a sporty blue bike with a lovely handwoven wicker basket. After popping her purse in the basket, she headed out to Miriam's. Though clouds were forming, the sun was still peeking through. She had much to be grateful for. It was going to be a brilliant day.

But then the clouds got darker. An hour later, it started raining. Eventually, the light drizzle turned into a downpour. And then, because it was at Miriam's house, half of the food and all of the serving dishes that had been neatly set outside on tables became soaked.

All this was before Libby Wengard's youngest slipped and fell and likely broke his wrist.

Soon, even the kindest and most patient members of their church district began to wear a glazed look. Even Bishop Thomas looked pained. And who could blame him? Their day of worship and rest had become one of stress and cleaning.

After Libby and her husband got small Anson into their buggy and headed to the hospital, Katie joined the other men and women her age and started the cleanup. Feeling guilty about her continued uncharitable thoughts, she took one of the worst jobs, cleaning out the now-muddy and soaked serving bowl of potato salad. Who knew that mayonnaise would make such a terrible mess?

Soon after she deposited the soggy remains into the trash and squirted a liberal amount of dish soap in the sink, Harley walked to her side.

"Hey, do you need a hand?"

"Harley." This was the first time all day they'd had the chance to visit. She was so happy to see him, Katie couldn't resist teasing him. "Hello to you, too. I am doing well, *danke*."

He smiled sheepishly. "Hiya. I was going to talk

to you as soon as the service was over . . ." He paused, then continued. "But I wanted to clear things up with Melody."

She'd noticed from the way Melody was reacting earlier that she wasn't very pleased with what Harley had had to say. "I saw the two of you speaking."

Looking wary, he raised a brow. "And?"

"And, I hope it went all right?"

"It went as well as could be expected. I told her that I wasn't pleased with her insinuating that we were back together." He shook his head. "At first, she tried to deny it, but then she kind of tossed her head and walked away."

"Oh, my."

"It wasn't easy, but it needed to be done. That's all that counts, I think."

"Thank you for talking to her." Unable to help herself, she reached out and pressed her hand on his bare forearm. "It means a lot."

He placed one hand over hers. "Don't thank me for that. I'm sorry she caused you any worry." After smiling at her softly, he dropped his hand. "Anyway, I was planning to come right over to see you but—"

After making sure poor Miriam wasn't nearby, Katie said, "But the rain came."

His eyes lit up. "Exactly. So, would you like me to help you clean up anything?"

"*Nee.* I'm sure there are other things you could be doing."

"Katie, that wasn't what I asked. I asked if you would like my help. Would you?"

His voice was warm. Until recently, she didn't imagine that Harley was capable of speaking that way. At least, to her. Now that he was different, she wasn't sure how to respond. "If you would like to stand here and talk to me while I finish, I would like that."

He chuckled. "That's you, ain't so? Always so intent on being independent."

No, that wasn't how she was. If she was independent, it was because she'd had to be. She'd learned not to depend on other people. If she did, they often let her down.

But Harley didn't need to hear all that, so she kept her voice light. "Washing a bowl is hardly anything to worry about."

"Did you enjoy the service?"

"I did." Preacher Josiah had talked about forgiveness and turning the other cheek. Both were noble pursuits. She'd often found that they were always far easier to talk about than to practice. But, of course, she was imperfect. "Did you?"

"Hmm? Oh, *jah.* I did." He watched her again.

At last, the bowl was clean enough to rinse and dry off. Seeing a dish towel on the counter, she handed it to him. "You may dry."

He took both the towel and the giant bowl and dried it. "What are you doing the rest of the day?"

"I am planning to read a new mystery I got from the library and maybe bake some banana bread. What about you?"

"I was planning to take a walk. But since it is raining I won't be doing that."

"Where were you headed?"

"Nowhere special. Just walking to clear my mind."

"Ah."

He rolled his eyes. "What does that mean?"

"It means we've known each other most of our lives, Harley Lambright. You are a man who walks with a purpose. Not one who wanders fields and thinks about nothing."

"You don't know everything about me. Maybe I am."

"I would agree that I don't know everything about you. But I *canna* believe that you have taken up a new hobby like that without my knowledge."

He gazed at her. Seemed to come to a conclusion. "Would you like to go for a drive with me instead?"

"I rode here on my bicycle."

"I could drop you off here later to pick it up. What do you say?"

She wanted to say yes. But still, she hedged. Riding off with him in front of their friends and his family felt like a big step. "Well . . ."

He snapped his fingers. "I know. We could drive over to Sugarcreek."

"Where?"

"I don't know. Wherever you want to go." He grinned slowly. "We could head over to Schlabach's farm."

"Harley, I can't believe you brought that up!" She hadn't been anywhere near Mr. Schlabach's farm since they'd gotten run off on Andy and Marie's graduation day.

His eyes lit up. "What do you say?"

If she said yes, she risked bringing up so many memories there were almost too many to name. Sweet, almost painful memories of Andy and the way they'd all been years ago. But if she said no, she would always regret it and wonder what would have happened if she'd been brave enough to say yes.

She was a lot of things, but she had never been one to shy away from something because she was afraid. "I say yes to the drive, no to the farm."

"Fair enough. We'll leave as soon as you are ready."

She agreed and told him that would most likely be in fifteen minutes or so. But as she watched him walk away, she wondered if she would ever be completely ready for where they were heading.

TWENTY-EIGHT

Tricia gasped. "I cannot believe you all did that."

"It wasn't our finest hour," Marie mumbled. "Or even our finest couple of hours."

Harley nodded. "Especially when Andy's friends got word that he was having a party and brought beer."

"*M*amm, I'm gonna be going soon."

His mother was sitting on Miriam's back porch holding a baby and talking with Will Kurtz's *mamm*.

They both looked at Harley curiously.

"Where are you going off to?" Mamm asked. Looking just beyond him, she frowned. "It's still raining."

"It's already lessened, I think it's about to stop."

"All right . . ."

"So I'm going to take Katie for a drive."

"Say again?" Mamm asked.

"You heard me, Mamm. I just offered to take Katie out for a drive and she said yes."

Mrs. Kurtz smiled. "So it's like that, is it?"

It felt nice to have everything out in the open. "Hope so."

But his mother, on the other hand, was still looking at him in confusion. "You like Katie Steury, so you're going to take her for a buggy ride in the rain?"

Put that way, he had to admit that it didn't sound like the best idea, but he was committed now. "Mamm, I'm letting you know because you'll have to go home with Jimmy and Beth. Betty is staying late with her friends."

"Do they know about this change?"

"*Jah.*" He was definitely not going to share all the teasing jibes they'd cast his way.

"I can take you home later, or Will can," Mrs. Kurtz offered.

"*Danke,* Mary." Mamm smiled at her before shifting her attention back to him. "I'm mighty happy about you and Katie, Harley. I'm glad you've come to an agreement."

"Mamm, it's a buggy ride. That's all."

"But—"

"I'm not talking about this now."

"Not that it is any of my business, but people are going to talk whether you want them to know or not," Mrs. Kurtz said practically.

"I don't mind anyone talking about me and Katie." As far as he was concerned, the more they got things settled between them, the better they would be. "However, I only came over here to tell you so you could find a ride."

She chuckled. "I see. Well, you have put me in my place, haven't ya? Enjoy your outing, dear. And please take care with Peanut. She don't care for rain much."

"I will."

After glancing toward the front yard and not seeing Katie, he walked over to the covered carport, where Will was standing with Logan and a few of their other longtime buddies. They all stopped talking when he approached, a sure sign that he'd been the topic of conversation. He decided to nip the gossip in the bud. "Okay, let me have it. What's on your minds?"

"Nothing other than the fact that you have finally made your move toward our Katie," Logan said.

"How did you discover that?"

"Tricia told me."

"I didn't even see Tricia over near us."

"She wasn't," Logan said. "But Betty was."

"I should've known she wouldn't have waited a moment to share her news." His little sister could relay information faster than most.

"Oh, don't be upset with her for talking. It's natural to want to share that."

Though it was on the tip of his tongue to point out that just because something was easy, it didn't mean it was a good idea, he fought the urge. Comments like that were his father's forte. "I guess so."

Benjamin Weaver folded his arms over his chest. "You'll be glad to know that I don't care who you are seeing."

"Thank you for that."

"Anytime. Hey, at least the rain stopped."

Surprised, he looked out beyond the covered area. "I'm glad of that."

"Perhaps you should run home and get your courting buggy," Will teased.

"Stop. And listen, don't tease Katie about this none."

"I won't." Will's expression turned serious. "Of course I wouldn't do anything to embarrass her. I may not want to court Katie but I still care about her."

"Sorry. You're right. I knew that." As usual, he considered telling Will that he was feeling a little unsure, and so because of that, he was handling things wrong. But he didn't.

"I hope so. You know, unlike Logan, I never thought of the two of you together."

Feeling a little stung, he said, "Why not?"

"Probably because she's so vulnerable. I always thought she needed someone who wouldn't mind her needing an extra dose of care and affection."

"And you didn't think that could be me?"

Will raised his hands like he was fending off an

attack. "I'm not saying you're an ogre or anything. Only that I didn't think you were a good match. I'm glad I was mistaken."

"I don't know what is going to happen between us but I'm well aware of the type of person Katie is. Of course I'm kind to her."

"That has been noted. Settle down."

Just as he was about to reflect on his cold reputation yet again, he caught Katie gazing at them curiously. It was time to step away quickly. No way did he want her to discover that she'd been the topic of their conversation. "I'll see you later, Will. Looks like Katie's ready now."

He didn't wait for Will's response, but he still heard it. The man was chuckling behind his back.

Harley felt like rolling his eyes. He knew he had flaws, but this courtship thing was hard. He couldn't wait for Will to get a taste of his own medicine when he found the right woman.

Thinking of how much he hadn't been exactly a fan of John B. and Marie getting together, Harley realized *he* was getting a taste of his own medicine.

It looked like the Lord was always watching out for him, even taking the time to remind Harley of areas where he needed to grow.

"Is everything all right?" Katie asked. "You and Will were having quite a conversation."

She sounded stressed, and he hated that. "Everything is *gut*," he replied lightly. "And don't you worry about me and Will none. I don't think old friends can ever not share their opinions. Even when it wasn't asked for."

"We both know that I've been guilty of that from time to time."

He grinned, because she didn't lie. "You aren't the only one."

"What was Will giving his opinion about?"

"Nothing. Like I said, it weren't anything important."

She frowned. "I hope you're telling me the truth. Because if it concerned me, I would want to know."

"You've got enough on your mind without worrying about stupid conversations. Ain't so?"

"I can't argue with you there." They were at the side of the buggy now. "I'm so glad it stopped raining."

"Me, too, especially since the rain brought in some cooler air. What do you think about rolling the windows up so we can get some of the fresh breeze?"

"I think that sounds almost as good as sitting in a courting buggy."

Her comment hit him squarely in the center of his chest, reminding him of his friends' teasing and how confused he was about their changing relationship. "*Jah*. I agree." He reached in and started detaching the side plastic windows and rolling them up. Katie stood and silently watched him.

He was glad she didn't offer to help, but maybe

it was because she knew as well as he did that it was often easier to simply do some tasks oneself than to delegate.

Finally, he walked to the passenger side and held out a hand. "Here, let me help you."

Her cheeks pinkened as she placed her hand in his, gripped his palm, and pulled herself into the carriage.

After he made sure she was settled, he walked around to the other side and caught his whole family watching him with knowing grins.

Even his father.

What was it about his relationship with Katie that drew so many amused looks? He didn't remember Melody ever inciting such reactions.

When they started down the lane, Katie looked back at the crowd on the front lawn and groaned. "Harley, your whole family is staring at us."

"I know."

"Why? Is it me?"

Motioning Peanut into a canter down the empty lane, he shook his head. "Of course not, Katie. They like you a lot."

"I hope you're right."

"I am. I promise, my siblings enjoy teasing me about as many things as possible, as often as possible."

"Because?"

"Because I'm the oldest . . . and I might have tried to boss them around a bit too much over the years." No, the truth was that he *had* bossed them around too much. Why, he didn't know. Their father had no trouble ordering them around at all. Taking a deep breath, he added, "Kyle accused me of acting just like our father."

"Your father is a well-respected man," she pointed out quietly. "What's wrong with that?"

"Nothing. However, *mei faddah* also has a tendency to be too silent and somber. I promise, being told that I was like him wasn't exactly a compliment." Eager to get the focus off himself, he said, "I'm sure you, Caleb, and June have teased and chided one another from time to time."

"Oh, we did when we were small and my father was still alive." She leaned back against the bench. "But as June and Caleb got older, they started to argue more. Then, as my mother got more reclusive and started to gather things and hide them away . . . it was stressful. No one teased each other anymore."

"I remember when your father went to Heaven, but I don't recall your age." He directed Peanut toward a sleepy side road that ran behind the brick factory. He'd always thought the wildflowers that bloomed on either side of the road were pretty.

"I was eleven. June and Caleb were in their late teens."

He remembered the funeral well. Samuel Steury had been well liked by many. Practically the whole village had come to his funeral. Sitting in between his parents, Harley had realized that it was the first time that he'd really felt as if death had touched him directly. He'd worried about Katie and couldn't help but keep wondering about how he would be holding up if his father had passed away suddenly. During the service, Katie had been holding June's hand and looking like she was about to shatter in a hundred pieces.

Glancing over at her again, he noticed that her expression was tight. She was troubled.

His reminder had put that there. "I'm sorry for bringing up your father. I didn't mean to upset you."

"You didn't. It's, well, it's nice to remember him. I don't mind."

"We can talk about him anytime you want, Katie." Looking into her blue eyes, he murmured, "Actually, we can talk about anything at all."

"Are you sure?"

"Of course."

"Even about what's been happening between us?"

Needing to concentrate fully on this, he pulled up on the horse's reins. "Katie, I know I ain't much for talking, but surely you know my intentions are true."

"I do. And . . . I feel the same. But if I can be completely honest—"

"There's no other way I want you to be."

"Then, well, I sometimes am having a hard time keeping up. I mean, just a few weeks ago we were barely talking. And now . . ."

"Now?"

"Now you've become the person I find it easiest to talk to. The person I first search for in a crowd."

Her words were perfect. So honest and true. So Katie. "Katie, when I look at you, I see something new. Something that I haven't seen before in any other girl. You make me think harder, question myself, yearn to be better. It makes me yearn for something more than I ever had before."

She smiled softly. "It seems we have stumbled upon something special, Harley."

He clasped her hand. "I think so, too." And now he was sure of it, too. Funny, here he'd been convincing her, but what he'd also been doing was convincing himself. Looking at their hands intertwined, her small hand fitting so snug in his own, he felt all the things he'd always assumed were simply talk. Something tender and almost possessive. Something sure and steadfast.

He wanted to hold her close. To kiss her, to show her how much she meant to him.

"If we've waited this long to consider a future together, you can be sure that I won't push you. We can take our time, if you want."

Looking down at their hands, Katie ran one of her fingers along his knuckles. "I've known you all my life, Harley. I trust you more than anyone in the world." She swallowed. "I don't think time is what I need right now."

He almost smiled. This was a typical Katie

maneuver. Over and over, his heart slammed in his chest as he realized what she was telling him.

He leaned closer, brushed his lips against her cheek. "Are you ready for something more, Katie?"

Her gaze flickered to his lips. She didn't say a word, only smiled.

Leaning in, he placed his free hand around the back of her neck, glancing at her to make sure she wasn't unsure.

Her eyes were bright. Her lips were slightly parted.

He needed no more encouragement. Very gently and carefully, he brushed lips against hers. She yielded against him and fluttered her eyes closed.

And then she kissed him back.

When he at last pulled away, Katie was wearing a stunned look. Her lips were a little swollen—like she'd just been thoroughly kissed.

Seconds later, when she leaned back against the bench with a sigh, Harley realized that at the very least, he'd learned something new.

All it took to render Katie Steury quiet was to give her a kiss.

As he moved the buggy forward once again, he grinned to himself. Kissing Katie often? Yes, he could absolutely do that.

TWENTY-NINE

Harley folded his hands behind his back. "Well, after all of Andy's friends from school showed up, things got fairly awkward."

"I refused to get out of the water until they left," E.A. said. "At least it was dark out."

Logan continued. "So Andy being Andy suggested that his buddies go inside his house until everyone got dressed."

"But by the time that happened, there was a party in the Warners' living room," Will said. "Music was blaring, everyone was sipping beer, and next thing we knew? Well, it turned out that we all started getting along just fine."

*E*very couple of weeks, a few of the Eight visited Andy Warner's parents. Oh, they didn't have a schedule or anything, they'd just realized that visiting Mr. and Mrs. Warner helped each of them as much as the visits seemed to help his parents.

Though the visits made some of them

uncomfortable—Elizabeth Anne had confided that she never knew the right thing to say—Katie enjoyed them. Simply being around Mrs. Warner, with her polished English manners and eager smile, reminded her of Andy.

Not that he'd been all mannerly, but he had been in a perpetually good mood when they were growing up. And though she reckoned that had changed in recent years, it was also how she wanted to remember Andy. In her mind, Andy would always be the leader of their little group, the handsome boy with the grand schemes, the bright laugh, and the ability to make everyone in his circle feel like they were glad to be around him.

Today, Katie was visiting Mrs. Warner with Marie and John B. She'd confided to Harley that she used to wonder if being around the couple would feel a little bit like being a third wheel on a bicycle, but she'd soon realized that while Marie and John's relationship had changed, the way they interacted with the rest of them had not.

What was taking a bit more getting used to was John's transformation into an *Englischer*. His hair was now shorter, he wore a watch on his wrist and had a cell phone in his pocket, and he seemed intent on studying all kinds of things in an effort to expand his education.

Marie looked so smitten with him, Katie knew she didn't care how much John changed. But Katie could sympathize with John. Their Amish world was rich in tradition and a beautiful one, but at times it made her long to expand her boundaries.

"What did Mrs. Warner say when you called and asked if we could stop by, John?" Katie asked.

"Only that she was happy to hear from me and that all of us are always welcome."

"That's what she always says," Marie mused.

John clasped her hand. "She means it, Marie."

Marie glanced at Katie and smiled. "I think Mrs. Warner enjoys hearing about John and me as much as talking about Andy."

"I bet. She's known us all our lives," Katie said. "It's wonderful that the two of you have found love."

The two of them shared a smile. "It really is," Marie murmured.

They reached the Warners' front porch before Katie had time to ask Marie what was going on.

Just before he rang the doorbell, John winked at Katie. "Mrs. Warner always makes something tasty for us. Maybe she'll have something chocolatey for you, Marie."

Marie looked down at the little bag she'd been carrying. "I hope she didn't go to any trouble. I brought some blondies that I baked last night. I hope she'll like them."

"Of course she will," John said.

"I know I will," Katie said as they waited. "Since

my kitchen is currently torn up, I'll be thankful for anything."

"We need to hear about your kitchen and the rest of the house," John said just as Mrs. Warner opened the door.

"Hi, John," she said with a smile. "And Marie and Katie, too." Her smile widened. "It's my lucky day. Come on in."

As soon as she closed the door behind her, she hugged each of them. Hugging her back, Katie was engulfed in Mrs. Warner's familiar fragrance.

"Thank you for letting us come over," Katie said.

"Don't be silly. You know this is my pleasure." Looking more solemn, she added, "I know all of you visit because of Andy, but I have to admit that I enjoy seeing each of you simply because of who you are. I would miss you all terribly if you moved away for good."

"My parents say the same thing," Marie said. She held up the brown gift bag. "We brought you some blondies."

"Oh, thank you, honey. My goodness! We'll certainly be eating well today. I happened to be in Mount Hope this morning and picked up a chocolate and coconut cake for you all."

Katie knew there was no "happened" about it. Everyone knew Marie loved Mount Hope Bakery and their chocolate coconut cake especially. She also knew that the cake had to be special ordered in person as well.

Marie beamed. "Mrs. Warner, that is so kind of you. And so much trouble."

"It wasn't any trouble at all," she said as she ushered them inside. "Besides, we needed to do something to celebrate being together."

They walked through the marble-floored entryway, past a dining room with a table big enough to sit fourteen or sixteen people, and an office that looked like no one ever stepped a foot inside except to dust. Finally, they got to the living room, which featured two couches and an easy chair facing a large stone fireplace. A sizable flat-screen television was mounted above the fireplace. It was all warm and cozy and completely familiar. Katie figured she'd sat in this very room dozens of times over the years.

After they got settled, John smiled at Marie. "Mrs. Warner, as a matter of fact, we do have something special to celebrate."

Mrs. Warner's eyes lit up. "That sounds prophetic. What happened?"

"John proposed yesterday," Marie said.

"She said yes, too," John said, grinning ear to ear.

"Obviously!" Katie said as she rushed over and gave them hugs. "Congratulations! I can't believe you didn't tell me earlier."

"We were going to get the Eight together tonight and tell you all at the same time," John explained. "But Will has to work and E.A. already had plans."

Looking back at Andy's mom, he finished, "We decided to simply tell friends and family one at a time. You two are the first."

"Oh! Oh, my!" Mrs. Warner jumped to her feet. "That is such wonderful news. Simply the best!"

Marie sighed. "It really is." Looking fondly at John, she said, "I'll have you know that he did a really good job asking me, too."

Sitting back down, Mrs. Warner clasped her hands in front of her. "Well, don't delay. I want to hear every bit of what happened." With a wink at Katie, she chuckled. "Within reason, of course."

"First, John came over to my parents' house while I was over for dinner, which was odd. But my parents didn't act like it was at all."

"Because they knew I was coming over already," John supplied. "I talked to Marie's father a month ago about my plans."

"Good for you. Logan did the same thing with Dave when he and Tricia got engaged."

"My father was so happy that John had asked his blessing, but I really think he was just as excited as my mom about planning this secret dinner." Marie shook her head. "I had come over around four o'clock to help my mom cook and work on a craft project. But they both were so happy, I couldn't figure out why."

"And then you discovered the real reason."

"Yes." Marie sighed. "Anyway, after John came over, my mom acted like he had to stay for hot fudge sundaes, just like it was our normal dessert. It wasn't normal at all."

"But it's my favorite dessert," John said.

Sharing a look with Mrs. Warner, Katie shook her head. Marie truly had stars in her eyes, and never had she seen John B. act so animated. It was both surprising and cute.

"So we made these monster sundaes, even my mom and dad," Marie continued. "And then, just when I said I couldn't eat another bite, John walked over to my side, knelt on the floor, and told me he loved me and asked if I would become his wife."

"Right in front of your parents?" Katie asked.

"Yep." Marie smiled again, as if that was the most beautiful idea in the world.

Katie turned to John. "Wow."

"I'm glad we did it that way. Marie is close to her parents, and they have been good to me."

Marie reached out and grasped his hand. "Then, my mother shooed us out to the backyard and said they'd do the dishes. And guess what?"

Mrs. Warner leaned forward, obviously eating up every word. "What?"

"My father had strung little white lights around the back patio. It looked magical. We sat out there, under the lights, just the two of us."

270   *Shelley Shepard Gray*

Katie sighed. Their engagement sounded like every girl's dream. Romantic and happy.

Mrs. Warner wiped a tear from her eye. "Oh, you two. I couldn't be happier. I can't wait to call both of your parents. I can't imagine a pair better suited to each other than the two of you."

Looking at Marie and John, and the way they were so comfortable with each other, Katie couldn't disagree. But it still surprised her. They'd been brought up so differently yet were still able to come together. So easily. It was practically the opposite of how things had gone with her and Harley.

She and Harley were Amish and had known each other all their lives. One would have thought that everything between them would be perfect and easy, but it wasn't.

So, did that mean that everything wasn't meant to be . . . or that they still had more work to do in the relationship department?

When Mrs. Warner dabbed at her eyes again, Marie knelt by her side. "Mrs. Warner, I didn't mean to make you cry."

"Believe you me, these are happy tears." She sighed. "I'm sure you already know this, but I can't help but think that Andy is smiling from up in Heaven."

John laughed. "He might be smiling, but I know if he thought I could hear him, he'd be telling me one thing."

"Oh? And what is that?"

"That it was about time."

Mrs. Warner's eyes got big, then she burst into laughter. "I'm afraid you're right. That boy never could keep his opinions to himself."

An hour later, when they were walking home, John said, "That was a good visit."

Katie nodded. "I thought so, too. Before I go over, I'm always a little worried about how the visit it going to go, but it's always so nice. Mrs. Warner is really a special lady."

"I was thinking the same thing," Marie mused. Holding up the box that contained the remains of the cake, she added, "Here we were coming over, hoping to do something for her, when she turned the tables and did something really special for us."

Continuing the walk, Katie stuffed her hands in the pockets of her coat. "Your engagement really is wonderful news. The rest of the Eight are going to be so excited."

"Thanks," Marie said. "You looked shocked when we shared our news. I'm sorry I didn't tell you earlier."

"It's your engagement," Katie replied. "I think you should do whatever you want." She realized then that she'd just given some advice that she, herself, needed to take. There was no "perfect" way to start a relationship or get engaged. It was up to the people involved and the Lord's timing. She needed to stop worrying so much about her and Harley and simply start appreciating the change in their relationship.

As they continued to walk, Katie said, "Tell me what your wedding is going to be like."

"Oh, boy," John murmured. "You might need to sit down for this."

"Why? Is everything okay?" Katie asked, already thinking of the worst. "Is someone upset?"

"Oh, it's nothing like that. Instead, it's a strange combination of my mother intent on planning the wedding of her dreams and John's family determined to invite every person they know."

"That ain't quite true," John said. "I think it's only about half."

"It's a lot of people. Not that I have any reason to talk. At least your mother isn't going to insist on chair covers and engagement photos."

"Erm, probably not. That ain't the Amish way," John said.

Katie burst out laughing. "So you two are telling me that it's going to be the wedding of the year."

"I wouldn't go that far," Marie murmured. "It's just going to be a three-ring circus. I'm hoping we'll all survive it."

"You will, because you have each other," Katie said.

"Don't forget, we'll have Tricia and Logan's ceremony first," John said.

"It's going to be an Amish wedding though, and small, on account of Andy," Katie pointed out. "Tricia told me that she's really happy about that."

"I bet," Marie said. After they walked a couple more yards, Marie broke the silence. "What about you and Harley?"

Katie wasn't sure she was ready to share too much yet. Especially not with John standing there. "Oh, you know."

"I know he took you out for a buggy ride on Sunday," John said. "And that neither of you seemed to care that it was raining."

"The rain had stopped," she pointed out, not that it really mattered.

Marie chuckled. "Katie, what happened? Did you have fun? Was it romantic?"

"It was *gut*."

John stopped. "*Gut*? That's it?"

Thinking of that kiss, of their many kisses, she smiled. "Fine. It was *wonderful-gut*."

Marie leaned toward her. "Will you share more when it's just girls?"

Katie laughed. "Maybe." Who knew? Maybe by the time she got together with all her girlfriends, she would have even more news to share.

She certainly hoped so.

THIRTY

"Oh, calm down," Harley said. "It wasn't like it was an episode of Amish kids gone wild. We all got dressed in a hurry. And nobody had any beer."

Logan chuckled. "Well, nobody had any beer after it was all gone."

SATURDAY

"*D*on't forget to do at least three loads of laundry," Gabby's mother called out as she continued to toss a couple of sodas and a bag of pretzels in the canvas tote bag she always carried to work.

"I won't." Gabby hated going to the Laundromat, but she would do it.

"And watch out for your brother."

Like he needed watching. He was sixteen and at least twice her size. "I will."

"And no boys in the house." Her voice hardened. "Do you hear me?"

"I hear you, but I don't know what you think I'm going to do even if I did."

"You're eighteen years old. Don't act like a child."

"I wouldn't do anything. Besides, Lane is here."

Her mother picked up her keys. "I don't have time to talk about this, but we both know why I brought it up."

"No. I really don't." She was irritated by the warning, too. "The only time I've ever had anyone over was when Kyle stopped by, and we told you what happened. He just happened to be in the neighborhood."

"I'm not sure if you really believe that or if you think I'm that stupid." Once again, her mother shot a knowing look her way.

"Mom, what have you been hearing?"

"All right. Fine. More than one person has told me that you've been seen around town with an Amish boy. Like you have any business hanging out with one of them."

One of them? Sometimes she really disliked her mother. "I've been spending time with Kyle, but you knew that."

Her mother popped a hand on a hip. She was wearing tight black pants and black strappy heels that always made her feet hurt, but she wore them anyway. "I knew Kyle was your friend," she said sarcastically, "but that don't mean I understood it. I still don't."

"All right."

"No, not all right. What I'm saying is that I really don't like it when one of my customers at the shop takes the time to tell me that they saw you turn into his driveway. You shouldn't have gone over there."

Gabby didn't even want to know how one of her mother's clients knew where the Lambrights lived.

Pushing that thought away, she said, "Kyle lives at home with his family. I went over there last Sunday afternoon."

"And?"

"And nothing. It was nice. They were nice." What did her mother care, anyway? She was never around on her day off, and Lane was usually hanging out with one of his friends on the team.

"They were nice, huh?" She shook her head, like Gabby had disappointed her. Which, she probably had. "I guess you've already made up your mind about spending time with those people."

Gabby ached to finally tell her mother exactly what she thought about her being so narrow minded and prejudiced. But it wouldn't make a bit of difference. Her mother was who she was, and Gabby needed to keep living at home until she finished high school, at the very least. "I'll watch Lane."

"Good. Don't forget to fix him dinner while you're at it. I left you thirty dollars on the kitchen counter." While those words rang in the air, she turned and walked out the door.

Staring at the closed door, Gabby tried hard to

fight the sting of tears that were threatening. But still one slid down her cheek.

Swiping it angrily away, she told herself that it was useless to get so upset. Her mother was a bitter woman who'd been hardened by a difficult life.

She'd also had a fling with some teenaged Amish boy in the middle of his *rumspringa* who had gotten her pregnant, and then had gotten baptized and pretended not to know her. Because of that, her mother's parents had called her a liar and had pretty much thrown her out when she was sixteen.

Even though she'd later been briefly married to Rick, who was Lane's dad, the experience, Gabby reckoned, had already changed her.

Or maybe it was just she didn't like seeing Gabby, because she was a reminder of all that had happened.

Did it really even matter?

"Boy, she's in a bad mood today," Lane said as he came out of his room. "Do you think it's worse than usual?"

Looking over at her tall, handsome brother who was wearing an old pair of black gym shorts and a tight T-shirt, she shrugged. "I don't know. Maybe?"

"Wonder what happened? Do you think she broke up with that Trent guy?" Lane yawned as he stared out the window. "He's not much of a prize, but he could be worse."

Lane was right. Trent was their mother's latest boyfriend. He worked at a car dealership, made pretty good money, and best of all, never looked at her and Lane with anything besides surprise that their thirty-something mother could have two teenagers. Some of her mother's men over the years had been total losers.

"I don't think so, but I'm not sure. You know she doesn't tell me much." Not much, besides what chores needed to get done, she thought bitterly. "You could've asked Mom yourself if you would've ever come out of your room, you know."

Lane smirked. "No way. She already gave me a list of chores to do and told me to get my homework done. Besides, you know I had a game last night."

"I know. You looked great making those two tackles. I bet your coach was happy."

"I guess," he replied, though his tone told her he was pleased.

That was Lane. He loved to play football and was good at it. But he also knew that the sports fees and equipment cost a lot and that getting a college scholarship wasn't a foregone conclusion. Scouts could always change their minds or they could only pay him a percentage of his tuition. He'd also told Gabby more than once that he felt bad because he knew that she had to bear the brunt of the chores until the season was over.

"Hey, do you really have homework?" Her

brother was the king of procrastination, which meant he was constantly in a nighttime panic, trying to get all of his assignments done. "Please don't tell me that you have a project due on Monday morning."

"Nah. Just a test in world history."

"Well, you can bring the textbook along when we go to the Laundromat."

For a minute, she thought he would refuse to go, but he nodded. "Yeah. All right. Want to get it over with?" Looking at the clock on the microwave, he said, "It's still early."

Which meant that they might have a chance of missing most of the creepy men who hung around in the parking lot. "That sounds good. Go get your backpack together. I'll grab the laundry bag."

Fifteen minutes later, both had backpacks on their backs, she was holding a big bottle of Tide, and Lane was holding a really big bag of laundry, which was mostly filled with his uniforms and sweaty gym clothes. "Ready?"

Lane nodded. "Let's get it done."

She was proud of him. Oh, he wasn't a child anymore, and she knew she shouldn't expect him to fuss or whine, but she was still grateful that he never tried to get out of doing chores like this. If he'd been mean, it would've made everything they had to do ten times harder. And sometimes she thought . . . well, sometimes, that if that happened, she might not have been able to survive the way that she did.

Pulling out her keys, she locked the front door and then handed them to Lane so he could pop open the trunk.

Just as they started down the steps, a guy riding a black bicycle stopped in front of their place.

Lane grinned. "Look who's here."

"Don't say anything to Mom."

"I won't."

Kyle walked over and looked up at them. "Oh no. Were you two about to leave?"

"Yep," Lane said. "We've got a date with the Laundromat."

"How come?"

"Uh, because we like wearing clean clothes?" Gabby asked.

Realizing how rude she'd just sounded, she said, "Sorry. Going to the Laundromat is just about my least favorite thing to do. It always puts me in a bad mood." After taking a breath, she gestured to her brother. "Kyle, this is my little brother, Lane. Lane, this is my friend Kyle."

Kyle smiled at Lane. "You ain't so little."

Lane grinned. "I keep telling Gabby that, but I think she introduces me that way to make herself feel bigger."

Kyle was still smiling when he stared at her

directly. "You know . . . we have a washing machine at my house and it's a sunny, warm day. You could hang your clothes on the line."

"Um, I'm glad for you."

"What I'm trying to tell you is that I think you should bring everything over to my house. You can do it there."

Just as Lane was about to take him up on it, Gabby shook her head. "I couldn't do that."

"Why not?"

"Well, first of all, that's rude."

"Not really, because I asked you over. So, I'm thinking if I ask you politely and you say no to that, then *that's* rude."

Lane grinned at her. "He has you there, Gabby."

Still unsure, she blurted, "But what would your mother say if I show up to do laundry?" Remembering that Kyle had once told her that his sisters help a lot around the house, she said, "Or your sisters? What are they going to say?"

Instead of making a stupid comment, Kyle considered it. "I don't know. Maybe that they're sorry you don't have a washing machine at home?"

"He has you there again, Gab," Lane said.

"But—"

"Look. If you want to go to the Laundromat and spend a bunch of money and sit there and watch it get clean, I'll go with you. But if you'd rather be at my house while it's going to save your money, it might be a good idea."

"Are you sure no one will care that I come, too?" Lane asked.

"Not at all. Plus, we have some baby chicks. You can hold one."

Gabby glanced warily at her brother. But instead of looking like he'd rather eat chicken than hold a baby one, Lane stared at Kyle. "Your parents would let me?"

"Of course, Lane. My parents are going to be happy to have you. They'll probably let you do most anything you want."

And that did it. Now she knew that she'd do just about anything with Kyle if he could make that innocent look of happiness appear on her brother's face. "I guess it's settled, then."

Kyle's blue eyes lit up. "So, that's a yes? You'll come over?"

She nodded. "Everything you said made a lot of sense. Thanks."

"Anytime." Looking back at his bicycle, he said, "I'll ride home and meet you there."

"We'll head out in a half hour." She wasn't sure how long it would take to ride a bike from her house to his, but she was pretty sure it wouldn't take any longer than that.

"Sounds good," Kyle said before taking off.

After Kyle disappeared from sight, Gabby looked at Lane hesitantly. What was he going to say?

But all he did was open up the back door and toss the bag of laundry on the floor of the car. "Awesome. Now I can get something to eat. I'm starving. Want some eggs, Gab?"

Laughing in relief, she said, "Yeah, sure. I'll make the toast."

THIRTY-ONE

"I can't believe you did that," Tricia uttered, sounding shocked.

Looking completely the opposite, Kendra sighed. "I can't believe I missed it."

"*W*hat is all that?" Betty asked the minute Kyle walked Gabby and Lane into their kitchen.

Gabby was right by his side. Lane was holding the laundry bag and obviously trying hard not to stare at Betty, who was dressed in a dark pink dress and flip-flops. She looked like she was on vacation in Pine Craft instead of standing in front of the stove and stirring a pot of chili.

As usual, she was also sorely lacking in social niceties.

After shooting her a warning look, Kyle said, "Betty, you remember Gabby, *jah?*" After Betty nodded, he continued. "This is Gabby's brother, Lane, and their laundry bag."

Gabby smiled. "Hey, Betty."

Betty kind of half-smiled at Gabby before turning back to Kyle. "Why are they here?"

"Because we have laundry to do," Lane replied. "Is that okay with you?" He was kind of smirking at Betty. It seemed her rudeness wasn't phasing him in the slightest.

Kyle shook his head as Betty stared at Gabby's brother like she'd never seen an *Englisch* boy before. "Lane, this here is my little sister, Betty. Sometimes I think my parents found her in the woods."

Lane tossed the bag on the ground as he stepped forward. "Hi."

Betty blinked. "Hi, back."

While Gabby turned to Kyle and raised her eyebrows, Lane kept talking. "It's really nice of you to let us use your washing machine. Are you sure your mom won't mind?"

"Mind about bringing over your laundry?" Betty asked, rather stupidly, Kyle thought.

"Well, yeah." Lane smiled softly.

"*Nee*. She won't care. I'm the one who does most of the laundry, anyway."

"We still appreciate it," Gabby said quietly. "Thanks."

Betty turned to Gabby. "Oh, it's no problem. You two just caught me off guard. Kyle didn't tell me that we were having company over today."

"It was kind of a sudden thing," Kyle interjected.

"I'll go tell Mamm that we're here. Can you help them get started?"

"*Jah.* Sure."

Realizing that usually their mother would have rushed in as soon as she heard new voices, he frowned. "Where is Mamm, anyway?"

"Upstairs sorting sheets." Betty wrinkled her nose. "While you've been seeing friends, I've spent most of the day inspecting and matching twenty sets of sheets and making chili."

"It smells good," Kyle said.

"*Danke*," Betty said.

Gabby was still gaping at his sister. "You really have twenty sets of sheets?"

"That's a lot," Lane added.

Turning to look at Gabby's brother again, Betty blushed. "There's a lot of us here. Seven, you know."

"Oh." Gabby smiled at Kyle. "I guess I never thought about all those beds."

Lane frowned. "If there's only seven of you, how come you have so many sheets?"

"Don't you have more than one set per bed?" Betty asked.

Lane shook his head. "No."

"It don't matter," Kyle said gruffly. How come they were even talking about beds and sheets anyway? "I was working all morning with Harley, and you know it, Betty. You should stop complaining."

She rolled her eyes. "Whatever."

"I promise, she's nicer than she seems," he joked to Gabby and Lane.

Even though Betty was acting like it had never occurred to her that English teenagers had laundry to do, too, he knew she wouldn't deliberately make them feel out of place. "I promise, I'll be right back," he said quietly to Gabby before tearing up the stairs to the second floor.

He found their mother in the extra bedroom right off the landing, doing exactly what Betty had said she was doing—sorting and matching old sheets. "Hiya, Mamm."

"Hi, Kyle." She smiled. "It's *gut* to see you home so early. I thought you had plans for the day."

"I did. I had planned to stop by and see Gabby."

After a pause, she smiled again. "I see. Well, how is she?"

That pause made him a little worried. He might want to pretend that his parents were willing to accept Gabby in his life, but he was pretty sure that it was more of a case of them loving him enough to put up with what they thought was a passing attraction.

He really should have thought things through before inviting her over.

But, well, there wasn't anything he could do now. "Actually, she's here again and her brother is, too."

She slowly got to her feet. "They both came over?

Are they here for supper?" Before he could answer, she said hurriedly, "Kyle, you know we like Gabby, but you must at least give me some warning before you invite people over for meals. How old is her brother?"

"Lane is sixteen."

She frowned, obviously already making mental lists. "So, he'll be hungry. I suppose I could make another side dish. Do you think they like pasta salad? Does that even go with chili?"

Pasta salad? He wasn't even sure if *he* liked that. "I don't have any idea."

"That's all right. I'll ask them. I can always make a broccoli cheese casserole if they'd rather have something hot."

"Mamm, they didn't come over to eat," he blurted impatiently. "Lane and Gabby need to do laundry so I told them they could use our washing machine."

Slowly, she blinked as this new bit of information sank in. "You invited them over here to wash their clothes?"

Her voice had risen. "Shh, Mamm! They're still in the kitchen. They'll hear you!" He held up a hand when her eyes narrowed. "And, I know I shouldn't tell you what to do, but I've got to get back downstairs."

"Right this second?"

"Mamm, they're alone with Betty. I just wanted to let you know what was going on."

Just as he turned to leave, she grabbed his shirt-sleeve. "Oh, no you don't. First you tell me why they need to do laundry here."

"Because they have a ton of it and Gabby was going to have to take it down to the Laundromat. She was going to have to sit there for hours, paying the machines. That didn't seem right. Plus, her brother was with her because all the clothes are heavy and I don't think he wanted her to be alone there. There's no telling who would be hanging around."

"No telling who," she repeated, looking worried now.

Imagining Gabby already regretting the visit, Kyle edged toward the door. "Mamm, I've really got to get downstairs now. Betty was acting like she was in charge of the washing machine. You know how she can get."

She pressed a hand to her face with a laugh. "Oh, boy. *Jah*, you had better go check. I'll be right there in a moment, too."

"There's no need. We'll be fine."

"Oh, nonsense. Maybe I want to just say hello, dear. Don't worry."

He smiled weakly before descending the stairs again. But with every step he took, he had an even bigger feeling that his mother was going to do something far more than "just say hello."

Every time she told them "don't worry," it always

meant she had something in mind—and that was never a good thing.

Gabby thought it was pretty obvious that Betty didn't know what to think about her being there. It was also extremely clear that she only had eyes for Lane.

He was smiling at Betty like he'd never been alone with a girl before, or maybe he'd never seen a girl so pretty as she was.

If that was the case, Gabby wouldn't blame her brother. Betty really was beautiful. If she were English and at their high school, she'd have more dates than she could count. And though she was kind of mouthy, Gabby liked her spunk. It was so normal, like just about every teenaged girl she knew. And it seemed to catch Lane off guard, which was kind of cute.

Though there was a part of her that was pretty worried about what their mom would say if Lane ever told her about Betty, Gabby quickly pushed the worry away. Lane wouldn't tell her that they were over here.

And if Mom found out?

Well, Lane wouldn't pay much attention to what she said, anyway. Unlike Gabby, he had a dad and they spent time together every couple of weeks. Rick sent their mom a check once a month, too.

All that seemed to give Lane more confidence

than Gabby had ever had. He'd told Gabby more than once not to worry about him when she graduated.

"Sorry it took me so long," Kyle said as he strode into the kitchen. "Let's go start that laundry."

"I'll go down to the basement, too," Betty said. "I don't remember the last time you worked the washer."

Altogether, the four of them went downstairs. Betty leading, Kyle right behind, then Lane, lugging their laundry bag. Gabby brought up the rear.

There were three large windows in the basement, which allowed plenty of sunlight in. It was also mostly finished, though there was still a small unfinished section. That was where a large white washing machine stood. Surrounding it were white cabinets and shelves, and hanging from the ceiling were three or four lines of cords, which were obviously used to hang laundry.

The clotheslines reminded her of something. "If you don't use electricity, how come you have a washing machine?"

"We run it on a gas generator," Betty said.

Just as Kyle bent down to help Lane pull out clothes, Gabby rushed forward. The last thing she wanted him to see was a bunch of her underwear. "We've got this, Kyle. Thanks."

"Uniforms first?" Lane asked.

"Yeah. Let's get those over with." While Betty and Kyle stood by, Lane started pulling out jerseys and his uniform pants and passed them to her. She popped them in the machine.

When it was full, Betty started it. "Are you a football player, Lane?" she asked.

"Yeah."

"I've never met a football player before. What do you do?"

Gabby could have sworn Betty batted her eyes. Not that Lane noticed. His chest was all puffed up and he was talking about tackles and the defensive line like Betty was trying to learn the game.

"Gabby, come on," Kyle said under his breath. "They're going to be here for a while."

Sure he was right, Gabby followed him back upstairs. She wasn't sure what was going to happen between their siblings, but chances were looking good that neither of them was going to be complaining about doing laundry.

"Want to get something to drink and go sit outside on the back patio?"

Really glad to have a few minutes alone with him, she nodded. "Sure. That sounds great."

THIRTY-TWO

"We ended up sleeping there in the Warners' living room after Andy got everyone else to leave and we cleaned the whole place up," Harley said. "But before we went to sleep, we all made a couple of promises."

$\mathcal{K}$atie was fairly sure that her house had never been so noisy. Plumbers, electricians, and carpenters occupied almost every room. All day they worked, sawing, hammering, tiling, and painting, moving up and down the steps like dutiful ants. They also were a chatty bunch. From morning until night they talked to one another, called out answers and questions to Harley, and continually joked or ordered things on their phones.

It had taken some getting used to, but Katie had learned to decipher most of the conversations. Now she knew when there were problems, when everyone was simply shooting the breeze, and when projects were done and they were ready to leave for the day.

It wasn't like she had all that much extra time to worry about the workers, anyway. She had a house to transform into a bed-and-breakfast. That meant that every room needed to be reorganized with guests in mind. Quilts needed to be inspected and mended, digital clocks, lamps, and throw pillows bought, and lots of fresh towels and linens ordered.

It was surely a blessing to have her girlfriends. Marie, Tricia, E.A., and Kendra often stopped by and lent a hand. Each was so helpful in her own way. Marie had an eye for what *Englischers* wanted when they went on vacation and how to arrange things in a pleasing manner.

Tricia put her big brain to good use and was reading books for prospective inn owners and shared with Katie some of the best things she learned. Tricia also helped Katie set up her own business plan. E.A. was wonderful at getting Katie organized and developing lists and task sheets . . . and keeping all of them on track. She also had the distinction of being able to sweet-talk the workers into doing all sorts of little things, such as hanging towel bars and hooks in each of the bathrooms.

Finally, Kendra was the hardest worker of them all. No job was too dirty, aggravating, or even boring. She simply got to work and didn't stop until the task was finished.

Katie's only problem with their help was that she usually didn't know when any of her girlfriends would stop by. They all had their own lives, jobs, and obligations. Because she was worried about inadvertently taking advantage of them, she never asked them to come over, only said their help would be welcome when they could spare the time.

All that is why when Katie heard the front door open at four o'clock one afternoon, she didn't think anything of it. She continued to sort through her grandmother's and great-grandmother's recipe cards. She'd had an idea to display them in frames and hang them on the walls in the breakfast area.

"Hello?" the voice called out.

"I'm in the kitchen," she murmured, only paying half attention to the voice.

She was attempting to decipher her great-grandmother's handwriting when footsteps approached.

"Mamm, what is going on?"

Stunned, she looked up into her sister's face, and dropped all the cards in a flustered gasp. "June?"

June looked just as surprised as Katie felt. Still staring at her like she was a ghost, June shook her head. "Katie. Boy, for a moment, I thought you were Mamm. You look just like the way I remembered her."

"Truly?" Katie stood up, thinking as she did that June looked hardly anything like she used to. Her blond hair was cut short, almost as short as a boy's.

It was also a lighter shade than it used to be. She was wearing faded jeans, leather flip-flops, and a white collared shirt, much like a man's. She was slim and had her ears pierced. And, she had on a gold toe ring. It was simply the strangest thing to see and Katie couldn't help but stare at it. How did one get a toe ring on? And why would they want such a thing?

"I might look like Mamm, but you look so different."

"I know." Fingering a fold in her jeans, June murmured, "I guess it's hard to see me dressed like this. It's been so long, I didn't even think about how I might look to you."

June had left two years after their father had died. Though it had been a long time ago, Katie did remember that June had been restless and unhappy for years. Caleb had once told Katie that he thought June had only stayed with them so long because their father had gotten sick and then they'd all been mourning.

But even though she'd never seen June dressed English, June's blue eyes were just as piercing and her high cheekbones were just as prominent.

"*Nee*. Not hard." No, instead of the dark shadows under her eyes—which had one time matched the thick dark eyeliner around them—she had on very little makeup, and her skin looked rosy and pretty. "You look happy. Are you?"

Visibly relaxing, her sister nodded. "*Jah*." She

shook her head impatiently. "I mean, yes. I haven't spoken Pennsylvania Dutch in ages."

"Luckily, I still understand both."

June gave her a startled glance, then grinned. "Some things never change. You still say exactly what's on your mind."

"And you still wait to see how you will be received," Katie replied softly.

"Does this mean you're now ready to give me a hug?"

"I've always been ready, June." Katie walked right into her sister's arms and breathed in deep. They were older and practically strangers, but some things couldn't be denied. June still felt comfortable and soft, just like the big sister she remembered. Her hair even still smelled faintly of vanilla.

"You are still so tiny."

"I can't help it. I prayed to grow, but I guess the Lord didn't care to listen."

June chuckled. "That's because He knew you were already perfect." She squeezed her tight once more before stepping away, though they kept their hands on each other's arms. "I've missed you."

"I've missed you, too, sister." It was almost impossible to choke out the words, so many tears were threatening to fall.

June's eyes were filled with unshed tears as well. Smiling softly, she whispered, "Goodness. Look at us."

"It's hard to believe I'm holding on to you. I think

part of me fears that if I let you go, you'll disappear from my life again."

"I shouldn't have stayed away so long."

No, she shouldn't have. Katie wanted to ask her why she had. No, she wanted to yell at her, make June feel guilty, make her ask for forgiveness . . .

And then she remembered that she was the one who could forgive without needing anything in return. Releasing an exhale, she murmured, "I'm glad you are here now. Will you be staying long?"

"Only a couple of days."

Katie silently looked at her, trying to be patient and hear what she had to say. But as each second passed, she realized that wasn't going to happen. At least not right then.

"Katie?" Harley called out as he walked down the corner. "Are you okay? Craig thought he saw a strange woman . . ." His voice drifted off. "Ah. You found her."

"Harley, this is my sister, June."

He blinked as a reluctant smile formed. "June. Look at you."

June was eyeing him, too. "I'm trying to place you but I can't remember. Are you one of the Eight?"

"*Jah.*" He looked toward Katie and smiled. "Your sister can't seem to get rid of me."

And, like it always seemed to now, that smile filled Katie with a happy warmth.

June noticed. Looking from Katie to Harley, her eyes widened. "Oh my word. Are you two married now?"

"*Nee!*" Katie blurted as she darted a look at Harley. His cheeks were red. "He's my friend, but . . . well, we've also become close."

"Close?"

Harley nodded. "Very close."

"I see," June said.

Beyond embarrassed, Katie inhaled. "Harley is here working on the house. I'm remodeling it."

June looked around. "It looks like you're doing a lot. Why?"

"I'm going to turn it into a bed-and-breakfast."

"But what about Mamm? And Caleb and his family?"

"Caleb wanted to farm and bought some land in Kentucky. He and Vanessa have two *kinner* now and another on the way, so he convinced Mamm to go."

"And she did?"

"*Jah.* It wasn't easy, but I think Caleb's needing her helped Mamm be willing to leave everything." She shrugged. "She hasn't said this, but sometimes I think it must have been a relief for her to leave all her stacks and debris."

June still looked to be trying to put all the pieces together. "How did you get the house?"

"Mamm gave it to me with Caleb's blessing."

June blinked as she stiffened. "Well. That's good to know."

Katie felt like sinking into the ground. It was obvious that June felt forgotten. "I don't know what else to say."

"I do," Harley said as he lightly pressed one hand on her shoulder. "It's going to be the prettiest B and B in Walnut Creek, Ohio." Turning to June, he said, "Will you be staying here? If so, I can tell the workers to cut out early."

"Here? Oh, no. I got a room at the Wallhouse Hotel."

"Definitely not. You can stay here, June." When June's expression tightened and it was obvious she was about to refuse, Katie rushed to explain. "You can have my room. I promise, it's clean and orderly."

"It's not the accommodations, Katie. It's the memories. Daed dying, Mamm gathering odds and ends like they would fill his void . . ." She shook her head. "I'm sorry, but I can't deal with them."

Katie could feel Harley's gaze on her, could practically feel the questions in his eyes. She swallowed. "I understand. But could you stay awhile? Maybe stay for supper? I was going to make some chicken and rice. Do you want some?"

"Of course. That sounds great. Now, why don't you take me on a tour of this soon-to-be fancy bed-and-breakfast?"

"All right."

June's phone chimed. "Oops. I'm sorry. This is

work. I've got to take this." She lifted the phone to her ear and walked outside.

"Are you really okay?" Harley asked when they were alone.

"I think so. I'm surprised and confused about why June showed up now, after all this time. But I'm still really glad that she came back." Thinking about it, she murmured, "No matter the reason, she's still here, right?"

"For sure, Katie."

"Um, *danke* for coming in and checking on me. That meant a lot."

"I want to do that. I hate that you're alone so much, Katie."

"One day, thanks to you, I'll always have a houseful of people."

He ran a finger along her cheekbone. "Maybe one day you'll have more than that." Looking over at the door, he edged away. "I'll get back to work now. Don't forget to mind your feet when you come upstairs."

"I won't forget. Thanks."

He smiled at her again before turning away. She realized then that his care for her gave her strength. Strength she'd never realized that she'd needed or had been lacking.

But now that she had been gifted with his support, she knew she would never willingly let it go.

THIRTY-THREE

"The first thing we promised to one another was that we'd do our best never to
bring up that day and night again," Harley
said. "Andy said the more we talked about
something the more real it got."

Tricia leaned forward. "And the second?"

This time it was John B. who answered. "We
all agreed that we'd tell our parents that we
were over at a barbecue at the Warners'
haus. Andy told his parents that he was
over at Logan's eating pizza all night."

*T*hree days after she'd met Kyle's whole family and
done three loads of laundry in their basement, Gabby
ran into his older brother, Harley, and Mrs. Lambright
at Walnut Creek Cheese. She and Lane hadn't seen
Harley when they were over on Saturday, and she had
been secretly relieved about that. Her first impression
of Kyle's eldest brother was that he was extremely serious and maybe even a little mean.

Kyle had once told her that of all his siblings, Harley was the one he could depend on the most though, so she knew he wasn't all bad.

Mrs. Lambright, on the other hand, had instantly grabbed hold of her heart. She was so kind and loving and accepting. If it wasn't so wrong, Gabby knew she would want to continue seeing Kyle just so she could be around his mother.

With all of this in mind, she walked right over to the pair when she spied them in the middle of the produce section. "Hi, Mrs. Lambright and Harley."

"Gabby! How nice to see you here." She smiled. "Are you shopping for your mother?"

"Kind of." She was shopping for all three of them. Like she usually did. She also had just finished her first three-hour training session, but she wasn't quite ready to share that.

"You don't have much in there," Harley said.

What did that mean? Harley hadn't sounded rude but not very happy, either. Feeling a little more flustered she tried to laugh. "You're right. My basket is pretty empty. I promised Lane I'd get him some fried pies. This place has his favorites. I'll head to Walmart after this." She'd drive over to the super center in Millersburg to get the majority of their staples.

While Harley only nodded, Mrs. Lambright smiled even more brightly. "I often do the same thing."

"You do?"

"I've got five *kinner* and a hungry husband, Gabby. I shop for bargains just like you do."

"How do you get over there?" She didn't know a lot about the ins and outs of being Amish, but she did know it was too long a distance to take a horse and buggy.

"Mamm hires an *Englisch* driver," Harley answered.

That sounded like a lot of trouble. "If you ever would like me to take you, I'd be happy to."

"Truly?" Mrs. Lambright looked delighted.

"Of course. It's no trouble."

"I just might take you up on it then," Mrs. Lambright said. "Maybe even Kyle would want to go with us."

Gabby couldn't imagine Kyle getting too excited about going to Walmart, but it probably would be good if he was there, too. "If he'd ever want to go, that would be awesome."

"Oh, I think he would," Harley murmured, looking just over her shoulder. "Ain't that right?"

Mrs. Lambright chuckled. "Harley, don't you be teasing him."

"I can take care of myself, Mamm."

Knowing that voice, she turned and found herself looking directly into Kyle's blue eyes. "Kyle."

"Hiya, Gabby." His smile was sweet and true,

almost like he didn't care that they were standing right in front of his mother and older brother.

"We were just discussing all going to Walmart together," Mrs. Lambright said. Her voice was merry. Almost like they were planning a trip to Disney World.

Gabby found herself trying not to giggle as Kyle visibly tried to smooth his expression into one of interest. Taking a chance, she smiled at Harley. "I just said that I go to Walmart for basics and could take your mother if she ever wanted to go with me. Your mother thought you might enjoy going with us."

"Well . . . *jah*. I mean sure. Going to Walmart sounds fun."

Gabby thought he could have been talking about getting his teeth pulled, he sounded so unexcited.

"*Gut*, Kyle," his mother said. "Now, Harley and I need to pick up the meat I ordered. You visit with Gabby and then meet as at checkout."

"I will."

"Enjoy your day, dear," Mrs. Lambright said.

"Yes. You, too." She smiled again when Harley nodded in her direction.

When they were alone, Kyle looked around, then pulled her cart over to the side, out of the middle of the fruits and vegetables. Then, to her surprise, he left it and started walking down the back aisle. "Leave the cart a sec, Gabby. It'll be okay."

Following him down the aisle, she was vaguely

aware of a selection of bulk nuts and dried fruits. Unlike the other parts of the store, it was relatively empty. When he stopped, he reached out and smoothed a hand down her hair. His hand lingered on her shoulder blades.

The touch, though completely innocent, surprised her. "What? Was it a mess?"

"*Nee.* I simply like it. Your *hoah* is *shay*, Gabby."

"What does that mean?"

"That your hair is pretty. It is, you know. I love how it's thick and the ends curl around your shoulder blades." His gaze was sweet. Warm and intimate.

Standing there in her jeans and T-shirt and Kyle in his blue shirt, pants, and straw hat, Gabby knew if she hadn't been halfway gone for him already, she would've fallen hard right then and there. "You always say the sweetest things."

"Maybe I only speak the truth, *jah?*"

She rolled her eyes. "I don't know about that, Kyle. But thank you."

"I need to go in a minute, but what are you doing later?"

"Nothing much. Lane is getting a ride home from football practice, so I guess just the usual. Homework for a while, then I'm going over to sit with a neighbor lady tonight."

He shoved his hands in his back pockets. "Maybe I could come over tomorrow night?"

Wouldn't that be so perfect? But just thinking about how her mother would react made her shut that idea down fast. "You can't come over. My mom doesn't want me to have any boys over when she's not home."

"When will she be home? I'd like to see her again."

She should have told him about her mother's past before now. She might be civil to Kyle, but she was never going to be very nice to him. "How about I come see you instead? I could even bring Lane."

"Do you not want me to talk to your *mamm?*"

"It's not that. I mean, not exactly."

"I know we got off on the wrong foot, but I *canna* say I blame her. I mean, I was at your house without her being there. I'm sure when she gets to know me she'll realize how much I respect you."

He respected her. Sometimes Gabby felt like she was dating a boy from the 1950s. Until Kyle, she hadn't thought that a boy her age could be so polite and kind.

Which was another reason she didn't want him around her mother. Her mom would only reinforce what an unlikely couple Gabby and Kyle would be. There was a really good chance that he'd decide she wasn't worth his time.

"It's not that I don't want you to get to know her, it's . . . well, it's a long story. Can we talk about it another time, like when we're not in the middle of the grocery store?"

"We can, if that's what you want." He took a small step backward.

Kyle looked hurt, and she didn't blame him. Deciding to tell him something instead of leaving him hanging, she lowered her voice. "Kyle, I really like you. I like your whole family, and my brother feels the same way. But . . . well, my mother has some problems with the Amish. She not only doesn't want me to see any boys right now, she really doesn't want me to be friends with any Amish boys."

"Truly?"

What could she do? Feeling miserable, she nodded. "I haven't been lying to her though. I have told her that we are friends. And if she ever asks how I got all the laundry done, I'll tell her that I did it at your house. But I'm not going to bring you to meet her."

"Because she would be upset?"

"No. Because she would upset you."

"You really care that much about me?"

Looking into his eyes, she smiled softly, hoping he would be able to tell how much he meant to her, even though she wasn't ready to say the words. "I really do."

His expression eased. "Come over in two days, then."

"I'll be there. Now, go before your brother comes looking for you."

He smiled again, and without another word, he turned and walked quickly toward the front of the store.

Gabby waited a couple of seconds, then walked to her cart and wheeled it toward the back of the market. She hadn't planned to get anything else, but she wanted to be sure Kyle and his brother and mom were gone before she checked out.

And, if she was honest, Gabby realized that she needed a minute to process what had just happened.

Without so much as even kissing Kyle Lambright once, she'd made her choice. She was willing to go against her mother's wishes and threats in order to be near him. She had no idea what was going to happen, but she was pretty sure her mother was going to be furious.

At least she was just a few weeks away from graduating high school. Then, if she had to make a choice, she was going to do what she wanted.

Waiting eighteen years was long enough.

THIRTY-FOUR

"So you all agreed to tell a bunch of lies," Kendra said.

Harley paused, then finally said slowly, "I'm not saying that was the right thing to do . . . but sometimes? Well, I think it's better to let the past go and move on. Ain't so?"

FRIDAY

"*I*'m really glad you rounded all of us up, Harley," John B. said as he grabbed a plate and started piling on chicken wings, chips and dip, and one of the tasty sliders that E.A. had made. "It's been too long since we got together."

"I'm glad it worked out," Harley replied. "We've all had so much going on, I thought it was surely time for all of us to be in the same room."

Looking around Marie's living room, where all seven of the remaining Eight were, along with Tricia and Kendra, Harley had to admit that he was pretty proud of himself for arranging the evening. With all of their busy work and social schedules, it was always a minor miracle when a get-together worked out. Which was probably what happened! They'd all dropped their plans in order to be here—thanks to a promise they'd all made at Andy's funeral and no doubt a bit of divine intervention.

After everyone had committed, the rest of the plans were quickly made. Marie offered to host, and E.A. organized all the food and drinks. Now, here they all were, eating a regular smorgasbord of snacks, catching up, and enjoying every minute of it.

Well, everyone looked especially happy except for Katie. She was still wearing the same strained expression that had first appeared when her sister showed up out of the blue. His heart had been breaking for her.

He'd also been trying to get her to talk about her feelings but hadn't had much luck. Last night, when he'd tried to convince her to go on a short walk with him before he went home for the night, she'd refused, saying she had plans with June.

He hadn't doubted that was true, but he also knew that she was having a tough time reconnecting with the woman June was now . . . and with the fact that when she left, she might not see her again for another few years.

He was still learning a lot about communication,

but even he knew that Katie needed a safe place to talk about things. He figured that was in the company of their best friends.

"Hey, Harley," Logan called out from the couch where he was sitting next to Tricia on one side and Will on the other. "Care to tell us why you really gathered us all together?"

He was disconcerted to realize that while he'd been standing next to the buffet reminiscing, the rest of them had gotten settled.

"Well, um . . . first, I thought it was about time we all toasted our newest happy couple, John and Marie."

Laughter rang out as John and Marie looked a little stunned but also very pleased.

"You don't want us to make a speech or anything, do you?" John asked.

"Of course we do," Will said. "Stand up, John, and thank us for coming over here to help you celebrate."

Leaning down, John took hold of Marie's hand. "Come on, Marie. I'm not going to do this without you."

Blushing slightly, she stood up by her fiancé's side. "Thank you all for helping John and me celebrate. It really means a lot."

John wrapped a hand around her waist. "And we owe our thanks to Harley here, too." Grinning wider, he added, "No offense, but I never knew you had party planning in you. I'm mighty impressed."

Harley bowed slightly. "Thank you, thank you very much." While they all clapped, and some of the guys teased him under their breaths, Harley took a seat on the floor next to Katie.

E.A. shook her head. "I don't think we are thanking the real person who is responsible for this get-together—Katie."

Katie, who'd been sitting quietly next to Kendra, shook her head. "What? *Nee.* This was all Harley's doing."

"But you've certainly gotten him to come out of his shell," Kendra said.

As Marie sat down she said, "Maybe John, Logan, Tricia, and I aren't the only ones who are falling in love."

Hating that Katie was now looking like a deer in headlights, Harley said, "Hey now. There ain't no call to go embarrassing Katie like that."

"I didn't mean to embarrass her. I just noticed how the two of you have been getting along. And that our usual chatty Katie is being extremely quiet tonight."

Marie hadn't exaggerated. Realizing that this had no doubt been a bad idea, Harley felt his stomach tighten into knots. Here he'd been hoping to help her, but all he'd done was make her embarrassed. "This ain't the night to talk about—"

"My sister, June, came back," Katie blurted. "She's English now."

"I always liked her," Will said. "Remember how she used to always make huge bowls of popcorn when we all came over to your house?"

"*Jah.* Popcorn and Hershey bars."

Elizabeth Anne smiled. "I thought she was amazing. She was so pretty and liked junk food."

Katie giggled. "She was good to me in a lot of ways." She'd forgotten all about that. Back when she was nine or ten, the Eight would still come by her house sometimes to play. June somehow always had a bag of candy for them to eat along with the popcorn.

"How is she doing?" Will asked.

"I think she's happy, but I don't know for sure. Maybe I don't know her anymore at all."

"You will," E.A. said. "Before you realize it, all those years she was gone won't even be an issue."

"I'm afraid they will. See, she ain't staying." Taking a shaky breath, she continued. "She's already planning to leave on Sunday morning."

Marie frowned. "I'm sorry. That's really tough."

"That's why I haven't been myself. I don't know what to do."

Harley shifted so he could see her better, so she could see him and remember that he was there for her, that he would always be there for her now.

But she seemed to have retreated into herself again, folding her arms around her middle and holding on tight. Helplessly, he looked at the others.

Of course, their happy expressions were replaced by concern. Harley wanted to stand up and apologize to them all. He'd known that she was hurting, but he shouldn't have arranged this party under the guise of celebrating Marie and John's engagement. It wasn't fair to either them or Katie.

But what to do? Maybe he should take Katie home? It wouldn't be ideal, but at least she'd have some privacy . . . and maybe she'd even be ready to talk to him?

"Why did June come back?" John said.

"I'm not exactly sure. At first I thought it was to see the house, but she doesn't even want to sleep there—says it has too many bad memories."

"Maybe she wanted to see you?" Tricia asked. "Or your mother?"

Katie shrugged. "Maybe, I don't know. She was surprised that Mamm wasn't there and even more surprised that she moved to Kentucky to be with Caleb and Vanessa. But . . . I wouldn't exactly say that she looked sad not to see them."

"I remember one of my older sisters being pretty good friends with her right before they both graduated eighth grade," Kendra murmured. "Elizabeth always said June was close to you, Katie."

"Maybe she was, maybe she wasn't. As much as I had wanted to be close to her, we really weren't. We were too different, I guess." She sighed. "Anyway, June keeps acting like she came back for a reason, like she needs to tell me something important. But every time I try to press her for information, she backs off."

"She'll tell you in her own time," John said.

"I know. But until then . . . we're walking in circles around each other, and we don't have much time left."

And here was yet another reason to feel terrible about this gathering. "Katie, you should have told me that you couldn't do this tonight because June was in town."

"No, she um . . . well, she said she wanted to see some friends tonight." Looking crushed, she added, "Honestly, I didn't think she knew anyone here anymore."

"Maybe she doesn't," Kendra said quietly. "Maybe she wanted a little break."

"Do you really think so?"

"*Jah*. Sometimes the memories—when they aren't all sweet—aren't that easy to remember. That's how it's been with me, anyway."

John spoke again. "Katie, I forgot. Did June leave because she got in a fight with your *mamm* or had she simply had enough?"

"June left . . ." Her voice drifted off. "You know, I had always thought that she'd gotten into a fight with my mother, but I couldn't recall a fight. And every time I used to ask Caleb about it, he would tell me not to worry so much."

John frowned. "This is only my opinion, but I'm not sure how you could not worry. She is your sister and you missed her."

Slowly, her expression cleared. "You're right. I have missed her. And I didn't know what to say whenever Caleb told me to settle down. What I was feeling was normal."

"What about your mother? Did you ever ask her about June leaving?" E.A. asked.

"Oh, *jah*. But she would just cry every time I mentioned June. So I stopped asking." She pressed a hand to her face. "I can't believe I'm sharing all of this with you now. I'm so sorry I ruined the party, Harley."

Harley realized it was time to fess up. "Well, to be completely honest, I was kind of hoping all of us together would get you to talk. I've been worried about you."

"I'm glad you're sharing, Katie," Will said. "That's why we have each other, true?"

Harley knew every person in the room was also thinking about Andy. He'd been hurting but had kept his worries inside. Never again did they want one of their members to ever imagine that they were alone.

"I agree," Marie said. "Being an only child, I don't know what it's like to have siblings, of course, but I do know what it's like to have all of you. All my life

I've relied on the Eight. You all are the reason I moved back."

Katie stood up. "Thanks for listening, everyone. You all helped me. More than I can say."

Throwing an arm around her shoulders, Logan looked down at her. "That's what we're here for, Katie. For good times and bad."

Will nodded as he picked up another paper plate and headed to the buffet. "*Jah.* As long as there's food involved, I'm in."

"Good to know we can always count on you, brother," Harley said. He was joking, of course, but he meant every word.

"Anytime," Will replied. Letting Harley know that he felt exactly the same way.

THIRTY-FIVE

"I've never regretted keeping all those secrets," Harley said. "I always figured that's
what friends do. They stay loyal to each
other, especially when it's something important."

Will grinned. "*Jah*, when it's something important, for sure. But the thing about us?
We keep secrets, even when it's just about
goats, shotguns, pool parties, and a long
line of bad decisions."

FRIDAY NIGHT

*I*t was late, almost eleven o'clock. Elizabeth Anne had
offered to drive both her and Harley home, and Katie
had known that the right thing to do was to accept. But
just a few minutes before, Harley had asked if he could
walk her home, and she'd wanted that very much.

She needed some quiet time with him before
returning to her house. Though the house was now
free of clutter and was looking very much like a bed-
and-breakfast, it was still in disarray.

It was also filled with too many memories.

After saying good night to everyone, Harley had taken her hand and pulled her to an empty field. Cutting across it would shorten the journey to her house by half. She reckoned it was also a little safer to walk in the field instead of on the dark road.

The grass was already a little damp, and all sorts of crickets and other creatures were chirping as she and Harley disturbed their evening. That fanciful thought amused her. For some reason, she liked to think that humans weren't the only ones to like order and peace in their lives.

"Will you ever be able to forgive me?" Harley asked, breaking the silence.

She looked up at him but could only see his profile in shadows. There weren't a lot of stars out, and the moon was taking a break behind the clouds. "For what? Encouraging me to speak about June?"

"*Jah.*" His voice was strained, pulled taut.

"I'm not angry, Harley. There's nothing to forgive."

"You sure?"

"Of course I'm sure." After a couple more steps, she said, "If you were so worried about me, why didn't you just tell me that you wanted me to talk about it?"

"I didn't think you would talk just to me. I thought . . . well, I thought that maybe you needed all of us."

The comment surprised her, but she couldn't disagree. While some members of their group might have hated talking about something so personal to everyone, she wasn't one of them. To her mind, each one of the Eight were all cogs in a wheel. Each of them offered something different to the group, and only when they were all together did she feel whole.

Ironically, she'd even started to feel closer to Andy, now that he was in Heaven. When they were all in a group like that, she was sure he was lurking just in the background, offering his support.

"Harley, after my father's death, things at home got off-kilter. We were all grieving for Daed, but un-like how we are about Andy, no one in my little family ever brought him up." She released a sigh. "Because of that, it always felt as if a hole had been ripped in our family's fabric and left there to fray."

"Could it have been mended?"

"Maybe not well, but even if any of us had been able to put a patch on it, or even clumsily bind the rip shut, I think it would've been better. But we didn't."

"I don't know if you can take that responsibility on, Katie. You were young."

"I was. But, like I said, even if I had tried to fix things, it would have been better than nothing."

They'd reached the end of the field. Carefully Harley helped her over the worn fence and then clasped her hand when they were on the road.

"Anyway, there we all were. Mamm had taken to her room, Caleb had started spending more and more time with Vanessa's family, and me? Well, I started depending on the Eight more and more."

Remembering that time, she shook her head. "I know you always thought I was being pushy, always wanting to be with one of you, but I needed that so much. I was afraid to be alone."

"I never realized, Katie. I . . . well, I don't know what to say."

Even though he couldn't see her, she smiled. "It doesn't matter now. I did what I thought I had to do, and we all survived. But June? Well, she didn't have someone special like Caleb had Vanessa."

"And she didn't have her own Eight, did she?"

"*Nee*. June was alone."

There, in the dark, where she could hardly see more than a few feet in front of her, it was all becoming clear. "Harley, I think maybe June really just had had enough. She'd had enough of not fitting in. Had enough of feeling left out. Maybe she'd had enough of trying to be Amish when she really wanted to be English. Harley, June wanted a change. She was running *toward* something—not away from us."

Harley stopped and faced her, pressing both of his hands on her shoulders. "Katie, if that was the case, then June's leaving wasn't your fault or Caleb's or your mother's. Maybe not even your father's death.

It was like you just said—June needed to find her own path."

"And God had intended for her path to be very different." She was half-whispering now. Really, she could hardly believe that she was only now putting this all together.

But maybe, like all things, the time was only right when the Lord decided it was right.

A weight slowly lifted from her shoulders. "Tonight helped so much, Harley. You helped so much. *Danke*."

"You're welcome, but I don't think it's a matter of me helping as much as of you simply giving yourself permission to truly think about it."

"Maybe so. I wonder why it was so hard to see a different point of view all this time? Why couldn't I have let go enough of my hurt to even write to June about it? I might not have seen her, but I knew her address."

"You're a mighty loyal person, Katie. I reckon it's as hard for you to change your loyalties about an idea as it is for you to give up on a friend."

They were close to the house now. To her surprise, June's car was in the drive and a single light shone from the living room window. She had to smile. It was as if June had known that Katie wanted her nearby. "It looks like June is here after all."

"I'm glad. I'm glad you won't be walking into an empty house tonight."

They stopped at the foot of the driveway. "It's really late now. Probably close to midnight. Would you like to sleep on the couch?"

"*Nee*." Standing to face her, he reached for her hands, folding them in his. With him tugging her closer, she had to tilt her chin up to see his face. "I knew I would be walking home late tonight. I don't mind."

He had done so much for her tonight. Brought all their friends around because he knew she needed support. Stayed by her side when she dared to tell everyone about her hurts. Walked her home in the dark, tried to alleviate her guilt about June leaving. "How did I get so blessed?" she murmured, half to herself.

"Blessed how?"

"To have you." Seeing his expression, so intent, so caring, she felt a new wave of emotion flow through her. "Harley, what did I ever do to deserve you?"

He smiled softly. "You didn't need to do anything to deserve me, Katie. I love you."

She blinked, because he was right. It all made sense. One didn't need to earn someone's love, it just was. "I love you, too, Harley." And then, because she didn't think there was anything more to say, she wrapped her arms around his neck, pulled up on her tiptoes, and kissed him.

THIRTY-SIX

"But, boy was that a great day," Katie said with a wistful sounding sigh.

"It was better than that," Logan said. "Epic."

$\mathcal{F}$ive minutes later, after waving good-bye to Harley, Katie walked inside. "June?"

"I'm in here. In the kitchen."

Walking through the dark rooms, she found her sister sitting at the kitchen table. She was dressed in a big T-shirt, sweatpants, and thick fleece socks, and was looking through the same pile of recipe cards that Katie had been organizing for picture frames when June had first arrived.

She had the battery-operated floor lamp on as well as two candles burning. The three bands of light created a soft glow in the room, making June look even younger. Almost carefree.

She smiled at Katie when she pulled out a chair next to her. "I hope you don't mind that I came on inside when I got here."

"I guess you found the spare key?"

"Under the second rock to the left, just like it used to be."

Katie shook her head. "I had forgotten it was there. Half the time I forget to lock the house."

"I was glad that at least that part of the house stayed the same," June joked. "Especially since I got done with my dinner early."

"You don't ever have to ask to come here. As far as I'm concerned, this is your house, too."

Pointing to the cards on the table, June said, "I finally sat down to see what you've been arranging. I can't believe they're Mamm's recipe cards."

"I couldn't believe my eyes when I found them, either. They were hidden in the back of one of the cabinets." Katie fingered the intricate floral design that had been hand drawn around the edges of the faded pink paper. "They're really lovely though, aren't they? Our grandmother or great-grandmother was a talented artist."

June nodded. "I've been taking pictures of them on my cell phone so I'll always have them."

The idea of June only having digital pictures of something so special made her sad. "You can keep them, June. I already have so much."

For a split second, June looked like she might agree, but then she shook her head. "I couldn't. It wouldn't be right."

Again Katie wondered what was really going on in her sister's mind. "Knowing that you have the cards would make me happy, and Mamm won't miss them, either. They were stuck in a box in the back of a cabinet for years. Will you at least think about it?"

After a pause, she nodded. "I'll do that. So, did you have a good night? I was surprised that you were out so late." June smiled. "And no, I'm not judging."

"I'm not usually out so late, but Harley got all of the Eight together. Marie and John B. got engaged."

"Wait, I didn't think Marie was Amish."

"She's not. But John works in a factory among the English and was okay with jumping the fence. They're really happy together." Thinking about how they always seem to bring out the best in each other, Katie added, "It was so great to all be in the same room, we lost track of time."

June's expression warmed. "I'm glad." Looking down at the recipe cards, she murmured, "You know, I was always jealous of your group of friends. No matter how hard I tried, I could never find friends who were so steadfast or loyal."

"We talk a lot about how God brought us together. I'm glad He did."

"Me, too. Hey, if you don't mind, I thought I'd spend the night here. I'll sleep on the couch. Is that okay?"

"You know it is, but you can have my room."

"Thanks, but I think I'll sleep better down here." Her voice brightening, she said, "It will be fun to have breakfast together."

"Now that I have a working stove again, we can make pancakes like we used to."

June chuckled. "Okay, but I'll make them. You always used to burn the centers."

"Although I'm pretty sure I don't do that anymore, you are welcome to make them. It will be just like old times."

"Almost."

When she noticed that June looked a little wistful, Katie said, "Who did you have dinner with tonight? I didn't think you'd kept in touch with any of your friends."

"I haven't, not really." She leaned back in her chair. "But there was a woman here who . . . well, she helped me leave Walnut Creek. I wanted to see her again."

Katie swallowed. "You know, I never thought about how you left or what happened. I mean, I worried about you, but I didn't think about the logistics of it."

June frowned. "There isn't really that much to tell. One night I went over to Cindy's house and told her I was ready. She helped me find a job down in Columbus and a room in a couple's home who help teens leave the Amish."

It all sounded very dark and secretive. And, Katie

realized, almost unnecessary. "Do you really think Mamm would've kicked you out if you'd told her that you didn't want to be baptized?"

"*Nee.*" June frowned again. "To be honest, I don't think I ever really thought about anything but feeling better. I wanted to be English. I wanted to stop grieving for Daed. I wanted to stop arguing with Caleb and worrying about Mamm." After a moment, she added, "I even was tired of always having to look after you because Mamm didn't feel like it." She heaved a sigh. "But, Katie, I promise, it wasn't really any of you. Especially not you. I've always loved you, do you hear me?"

Katie's throat was so tight, she simply nodded.

June continued. "I was in a fog, in a bad place." She started fussing with the recipe cards again. "Anyway, Cindy drove me down, gave me fifty dollars and some jeans and stuff, and dropped me off. I started working at a grocery store the next day."

"Did you make friends with the other kids who left?"

"Not really. A lot of them?" She pulled in her lip. "Well, I can only say that they had it bad where they were living. They were so angry, too. I wasn't as much angry as just plain sad and determined to find my own way." She smiled. "And eventually, I did."

Katie returned the smile. But she knew it was time to finally ask the question that she'd been dwelling on since June had returned. "Now I know why you left. But . . . June?"

"Hmm?"

"Why did you come back?"

Her sister gave her a quizzical look. "Because I missed you, silly."

"That's it?" She didn't even try to hide how shocked she was.

"Well, yeah. Isn't it enough?"

That June missed her was enough. Of course it was. But that explanation didn't feel like enough— until she realized that nothing else really mattered. If they still loved each other, then they still had a bond. "*Jah*," she finally answered. "It's more than enough."

"Katie, you might not believe me, but I really missed my baby sister. I may not have acted like it or told you the words enough, but I still love you, you know."

Tears formed in her eyes as she realized that she didn't need to know anything else. "I still love you, too, June. I never stopped."

Standing up, her sister gave her a hug. Katie hugged her back, feeling a sense of hope and warm happiness in the air. Boy, did it feel good. Stepping away, she said, "I'll help you fix up the couch now."

"I can do it."

"I don't mind. After all, I'm going to be an inn-keeper. I might as well get some practice," she joked as she walked upstairs to the closet in her bedroom. There were plenty of extra towels, sheets, and blankets in there.

June followed her. "Hey, Katie? You know, I just realized that I never asked what you're going to call this place."

Pulling out a set of sheets and a thick thermal blanket, she shrugged. "I haven't even thought about names. Do you have any ideas?"

As they walked back downstairs, June said, "Maybe, but it's kind of odd."

Katie set the linens on the couch. "I'd like to hear it anyway."

"How about The Loyal One?"

"What? The Loyal Bed and Breakfast?"

"I was thinking The Loyal Inn," June said. "I really like it."

"Why?" It sounded awfully strange to her.

June picked up a sheet, shook it out, and then started tucking it into the cushions. "Because it reminds me of you, Katie. All your life, you've been loyal to this family, to your friends, to our mother, even to our religion. And now you're even loyal to this house. You're making it have new life but still honoring our family, like putting Mamm's recipe cards on the walls."

Feeling flustered, Katie grabbed the other sheet and smoothed it on top of the one June put down.

"You're giving me too much credit. All I've been doing is trying to get through every day."

June smiled softly. "That may be true, but guess what happened?"

"What?"

"You still remained true. That, I think, is something pretty special, Katie. Something just like you."

June's words rang in her head as Katie climbed the stairs again a few minutes later—her words about the house and being loyal, their words about still loving each other even though they'd been far apart.

Later, as she fell asleep, she allowed herself to remember Harley's sweet declaration and the way she'd melted into his arms when they'd kissed.

That's when she realized that she wasn't the only one being loyal. Her friends were, too. And so was God. After everything that had happened, He was still there, by her side. Making her world better.

Maybe He was the real "loyal one." And if so, then June was right, there was no better name for her B and B. It was perfect.

THIRTY-SEVEN

"Andy . . . well, Andy had been right. Sometimes it don't matter what happens when you go on an adventure. What matters is that you do it at all."

Looking up at the sky, Harley whispered, "Thanks, Andy. I needed to remember that."

OCTOBER

"Watch the steps, now. They can be a little steep at times," Katie Lambright called out as she led the way up to the second floor.

"They'd have to be steeper than this to be a problem, dear," Mrs. Jackson said with a laugh. "But honestly, the iron banister is so pretty, I have to keep reminding myself to concentrate on the steps."

"Don't worry, Katie," Mr. Jackson said with a chortle. "I've got her elbow. She's safe."

When Katie got to the upstairs landing, she smiled down at them. Sure enough, the elderly couple didn't look like the flight of stairs was bothering them in the slightest. She was glad of that. Sometimes her guests said they didn't mind stairs, but they did.

When Mr. and Mrs. Jackson reached her side, she led them to the April room, formerly known as June's bedroom. "Now, I'll just let you in, show you a few things, and then leave you in peace." And with that, she pulled out the old-fashioned key that she and Harley had once argued about and unlocked the door.

"Oh!" Mrs. Jackson said in a near whisper. "Katie, this . . . this room is absolutely breathtaking."

"I'm glad you like it. I hope you will find it comfortable." As she liked to do, she stood to one side and simply watched her new guests admire the room's pale periwinkle walls, the intricately designed and stitched wedding ring quilt in pale yellow, the cozy love seat upholstered in a cheerful floral pattern, and even the gleaming white woodwork around the twin windows that faced the front of the house.

Pointing to the door on the right, she said, "In there is your private bathroom. There are soaps, lotions, and a few other items to make your stay more pleasant." Opening up the small cabinet situated in between the windows, she showed them the bottles of water, bucket of ice, and door hanger. "We deliver coffee to your room in the mornings. If you care for any, just leave the filled-out form on your door by eight o'clock at night."

Mr. Jackson nodded. "Everything looks good.

Perfect, actually. We've been looking forward to staying here at The Loyal One from the moment we first heard about this B and B. As soon as we read the article highlighting it in *Ohio Magazine*, we got right online and made the reservation."

"Having the magazine write such a nice review about this place has been a blessing."

"It was also accurate," he replied. "So far, you've surpassed our expectations."

"That makes me happy. I'll do my best to continue to make you feel that way."

"I'm sure you will, dear. We're glad you opened this place."

"Me, too." Smiling at Mrs. Jackson, who was now seated on the love seat, she said, "If you need anything, call down to the front. Otherwise, I wish you a good afternoon."

Just as she was walking out, he said, "I'm curious. How did you come across such a beautiful old house? We've often talked about opening something like this one day, but places like this are hard to find."

"Oh, locating this place wasn't difficult at all. It was my home, you see."

"Really?" Mrs. Jackson said. "Was this your old room?"

"Oh, *nee*. My room was down the hall. This . . . this was my sister's." Edging to the door, she waved a hand. "I'll be on my way now," she murmured.

She doubted either of them heard her, however. Mr. Jackson had his arm around his wife's shoulders and was whispering something into her ear. After closing the door quietly behind her, Katie headed back down the stairs.

Harley was standing in the foyer, looking up at her. "How did it go?"

"Oh, fine, I think. They liked the room."

He walked to her side. "Then why don't you look happier?"

"It's nothing. They asked whose room in my family it used to be and it brought back a lot of memories."

Looking solemn, Harley stared up at the empty stairs, then reached for her hand. "Let's go sit outside on the stoop."

"Harley, I should be around in case they have any questions. And you know how guests can be."

"Oh, *jah*, I know. They are always full of questions. Still, I reckon they'll be able to survive without you for a few minutes. Come spend a few minutes with your husband."

Her husband! They'd been married all of two months now, and to her embarrassment, she was still the definition of a blushing bride. She now hated to be apart from him for more than a few hours at a time.

The rest of the Eight were mighty amused.

Giggling, she reached for the door. "You know I can never say no to that."

"I was counting on it." Just as she was about to sit in one of the white wicker rocking chairs, he shook his head. "*Nee*. Let's sit on the steps."

She did as he bid, but she was confused. "Harley, why do you want to sit here?"

"Because this is where you were sitting when I realized that we weren't just friends, we were meant to be more than that."

A lump formed in her throat. "Harley, I know I told you that I'm glad you're sharing your feelings more, but during moments like this, I hardly know how to respond."

He stared at her in surprise, then slowly smiled. "Now isn't that something, Katie? Here, I thought I knew everything about you, but I'm still discovering new things."

"Such as?"

"Well, now I know two ways to make you speechless."

"Oh?" Her lips twitched.

He leaned closer. "Oh, for sure. I know now that if I need you to be quiet, I can either tell you pretty words . . ."

"Or?"

His sweet smile broadened into a grin. "Or I could kiss you, of course. That's my favorite way."

She shook her head. "You're incorrigible."

"*Nee*, Katie. I'm yours," he said, just as he kissed

her right there on the steps of their very own bed-and-breakfast, maybe even being observed by their new guests from their window.

However, Harley had been right. She didn't care in the slightest.

Really, not at all.

Don't miss the next heartwarming installment
in The Walnut Creek Series

THE

PROTECTIVE
ONE

Available now from Gallery Books!

ONE

*T*here were more fireflies dotting the fields around her house than Elizabeth Anne could count. But still she tried.

She'd once read that people used to believe wishing on them, like the stars, might make dreams come true. She'd always thought such a notion was foolish.

After all, everyone knew nothing of worth ever happened by lazing about or daydreaming. The only way to accomplish goals was to adopt a hard work ethic and use the brains that the good Lord gave you.

But lately?

Lately, Elizabeth Anne was beginning to think she'd been going through life a little too *resolutely*. Perhaps she would be happier if she took more time to daydream and count fireflies instead of only check off tasks that she'd accomplished.

Sure, she'd had goals and had reached them and loved her to-do lists as well. But she was beginning to realize that completing tasks didn't make her feel all that satisfied.

Shouldn't there be more to life than satisfaction?

She was starting to think so.

She was a twenty-three-year-old Mennonite woman, had a job at the fabric store that was rather boring, and was anticipating a proposal any day from a man who had never made her pulse race or her heart sing.

None of this made her feel good.

But maybe, just maybe, she wasn't that kind of woman? Were some women simply more romantic and apt to blush and fuss more than others?

"Elizabeth Anne, you've sure been quiet for a while," David blurted. "Is everything all right? Are you ill?"

"Ill? Oh, *nee*."

Folding his hands over his chest, he sighed. "Well, then . . . what have you been thinking about? You know it's only proper for you and me to sit on the porch swing together for thirty minutes. We should make the most of our time."

She almost rolled her eyes. Because *that*, she feared, was the problem. Here they were, a courting couple sitting alone on a porch swing on an early summer evening. The air was warm and comfortable, fireflies were twinkling in the distance, and the faint scent of honeysuckle floated in the breeze.

No one else was around, and even if someone were, no one in her family would so much as blink if

David had his arm around her shoulders. Or if they were kissing.

But they were not. More important, they never did cuddle or kiss or whisper sweet nothings in each other's ears. Not ever.

"Oh, David." Looking at handsome, wholesome David, with his brown hair, brown eyes, full cheeks, and rather thin lips, E.A. wished yet again that there was some kind of spark between them. "I was just looking at the fireflies."

"What about them?" He turned his head to stare out at the soybean field that seemed to go for miles on either side of them. Hundreds of fireflies were dancing and sparking among the rows. The sight was beautiful. Mesmerizing.

"I read once that people used to make wishes on them," she said softly, hoping that would spark a bit of whimsy in their conversation.

He wrinkled his nose. "Wishes?"

"*Jah.* You know, like stars." When he still gaped at her, she cleared her throat. "Do you think that's true?"

Looking back at the field again, he shrugged. "I have no idea. Honestly, Elizabeth Anne, I've given up trying to understand why other people do the things they do."

Elizabeth Anne. David always called her by her full name. Never E.A. like her best friends, who were better known as the Eight. Even her family called her E.A. on occasion.

But David never did.

Thinking about that, about how he didn't see anything in the distance but a bunch of bugs, she pressed her lips together. "Hmm."

His voice sharpened. "Come now. You know I'm right. Why, lots of folks do strange things, things that people like you and me couldn't begin to contemplate."

"I guess that's true," she replied, though she wasn't sure if his statement actually *was* true. Especially since she was currently contemplating all sorts of interesting things right at that moment!

Looking at the fields again, E.A. ventured, "You know what? Maybe we should play a game."

"Out here in the dark?"

She giggled, though he wasn't so much as smiling. "David, how about the two of us make some wishes right now?"

"Um . . ."

"Come on, it will be fun. I mean, look at all those twinkling lights! Why, it looks like Christmas in July. Don't you think that tonight is the perfect night to make a wish or two?"

"*Nee.*"

"No?" That was it?

"Elizabeth Anne, you and I both know that no good ever comes from making wishes that can never happen. It's best to concentrate on what is possible." Before she could comment on that, he continued, just as if he was full of bright and interesting ideas. "That's what I've always admired about you. You don't waste your time dreaming about things that could never happen for a girl like you."

"Like me?" Why did that not sound very flattering?

"*Jah.*" He waved a hand. "Or, you know, give into your weaknesses." While she gaped at him, he nodded. "Or contemplate selfish acts."

"Selfish acts?" That sounded awfully confusing and old-fashioned. "David, what in the world are you talking about?"

"You know who I'm thinking of."

His voice and his look were pointed. She shifted uncomfortably. "No, I'm sorry, but I don't think I do."

David pushed off the swing and stood in front of her. "Come now, Elizabeth Anne. You know that I'm talking about that man."

"Which man?" She was becoming exasperated.

"That man you used to know," he said impatiently. "Andy Warner."

He was speaking of Andy? A chill ran through her. Wrapping her arms around her middle, E.A. took a deep, fortifying breath. Anything to stop the sudden rush of tears that had just filled her eyes. "David, Andy was my friend, not just some man I used to know." Actually, he was so much more than that. The Eight's leader . . . their instigator. At times, her very own protector. Andy had been loud and handsome and caustic and so very kind, too. He'd been a jumble of emotions.

And he'd also killed himself last summer. And though it had happened almost a full year ago, Andy's loss still hurt.

Propping his hands on his hips, David looked at her directly. "Well, Andy Warner might have been your friend—"

"No, he was. Andy was a great friend."

He grunted. "All I'm trying to say is that he must not have felt the same way about you."

Elizabeth Anne gaped at him, shocked. "Why would you say that?"

"Come now. He killed himself. That's the most selfish act a person can do."

"You don't know that." One, two tears slid down her cheeks. "Don't say that."

"All I'm saying is that no man who cares about his friends, who *really* cares about his friends, would take his own life."

His words stung, as did the implication that David could summarize everything about Andy in one or two careless statements. "You need to stop. You didn't know Andy. You don't know what you're talking about."

He stood up straighter, almost as if he were a parent delivering a lecture and she were the recalcitrant child. "I'm sorry if my words made you upset, but you know I'm right, Elizabeth Anne. I'm just pointing out the truth."

"No, you're spouting off your wrong opinion, David." Getting to her feet, she said, "I think it's time for you to go."

But he didn't budge an inch. "Are you really going to get upset with me about this?"

Yes. Yes, she was. In addition, she was going to get upset with him about a lot of things. About the way he timed his visits. And only called her by her full name. And never tried to get to know her other friends. Or held her hand.

But most of all, she was going to make him leave because he always acted like she never deserved anything better.

"*Jah*," she said finally. "I am going to get upset with you."

"I see. Well, then, I guess I should be going." He walked down the front steps. "I certainly hope you will be in better spirits when I come calling on Saturday night."

A quick vision entered her head—a vision of the two of them sitting on this blasted front porch swing again and again. Never doing anything but talking about the weather and their jobs. Never noticing the fireflies. Never being anything more.

She couldn't do it.

"David, don't come back on Saturday night. In fact, I think it would be best if you didn't come back anytime soon."

"You're going to stay mad at me for that long?"

"No. I'm going to finally move on. Good night,"

she called out over her shoulder. "Good night and good-bye." Still fuming, she strode inside.

"Has it been thirty minutes already?" Daed asked as Elizabeth closed the door firmly behind her.

"Yes."

"Ah." Her father, who everyone said looked a bit like Santa Claus, smiled. After folding the latest issue of the *Budget* on his lap, he looked at her over the rims of his reading glasses. "Well, how was your beau tonight?"

For a moment, E.A. contemplated sharing what had happened with her father. Thought about explaining her feelings and how she knew there had to be someone better suited for her than David.

But if she did that, Daed would call for her mother, Mamm would rush in, try to make her eat some cookies, and then the three of them would have a "cozy discussion" that would last for at least an hour. There was no way she was up for that.

"He was the same," she finally said as she started up the stairs.

Yes, David had been the same, but she'd been very different.

Or, maybe, just maybe, she'd finally been her real self. The person she'd meant to be all along.

READER QUESTIONS

1. What were your first impressions of Katie and Harley? How did your perception of them change during the novel?

2. Do you have any close friends who you've had for a long time? What do you think is the secret for sustaining a close friendship?

3. I loved reflecting on the theme of loyalty while writing this novel. Who in your life have you been loyal to? Do you think loyalty needs to be reciprocated? Why or why not?

4. Both Katie and Harley experienced some challenges with their family members. How do you think those challenges prepared them for their future?

5. What do you think will happen with Kyle and Gabby in the future?

6. I enjoyed writing about characters cleaning out a home and remodeling it into something new. Have you ever remodeled a home, or, perhaps, cleaned out a lot of your belongings to start fresh? What was difficult? What did you learn, if anything?

7. I used the following scripture verse to guide me

while writing this novel: "Teach us to realize the brevity of life, so that we may grow in wisdom."—Psalm 90:12. What does it mean to you?

8.   I enjoyed the following Amish proverb and thought it fit Harley and Katie's story well: "Things turn out the best for those who make the best of the way things turn out." Is there anything in your life that you feel it could be applied to?

9.   *The Loyal One* marks the midway point in the Walnut Creek series. What are you liking about the series so far? Who have been some of your favorite characters?